Bullet in the Night

Judith Rolfs

Copyright © 2014 Judith Rolfs
ALL RIGHTS RESERVED
Cover Art by Joan Alley
Editing by Paula Mowery

This book is a work of fiction and any resemblance to persons, living or dead, or places, events or locales is purely coincidental. The characters are the product of the author's imagination and used fictitiously.

Warning: The unauthorized reproduction or distribution of this copyrighted work is illegal. No part of this book may be scanned, uploaded, or distributed via the Internet or any other means without the permission of Prism Book Group. Please purchase only authorized editions and do not participate in the electronic piracy of copyrighted material. Thank you for respecting the hard work of this author.

Published by Prism Book Group

ISBN-10:1940099587 ISBN-13:978-1-940099-58-3

Published in the United States of America

Contact info: contact@prismbookgroup.com

http://www.prismbookgroup.com

CHAPTER ONE

TUCKER LAWRENCE BARGED into my office and collapsed onto a chair. His lower lip trembled as he blurted out, "Lenora's been shot."

Instantly my world turned cold and dark despite sunbeams streaming through the window. My heart began to pound. Usually no one gets past my office manager, Ellen, not even a six-foot-six man with the intimidating posture of a redwood tree. Good thing my next client hadn't arrived yet.

Dressed in khakis, dark blue silk shirt, and dry-cleaner-perfect linen jacket, Tucker could have been mistaken for a GQ model. His face, framed by a silver-gray beard, had held its handsomeness well for sixty years. He sat inert as if saying the words sucked the strength from his body.

"What? It can't be." I covered my gaping mouth with my hand. Stupid response. Like words could change this unthinkable horror.

"One bullet, only one, and it penetrated her right lung as she sat at her desk. She's alive, but comatose." Tucker's breathing came in bursts. "The ER doctor says the oxygen level to her brain was impaired. Lenora lapsed into shock before the paramedics arrived. Even if she survives, her prognosis for recovering normal functioning is poor." Tucker clenched his fists.

I blinked away tears but couldn't control the sick feeling in my stomach. I pictured my vivacious, compassionate friend. When Lenora walked into a room, it lit up like Christmas.

How could she be near death? I shivered and reached for my suit jacket on the back of my chair.

Numb, I stared at the furrow in Tucker's forehead. "Counseling people isn't law enforcement. It shouldn't be dangerous. When Lenora and I became psychotherapists, we didn't expect the job would involve physical risk."

"Exactly."

"May I see her?"

"Sorry. No visitors except family, and I'm all she has." Tucker dragged a handkerchief from his pocket. "I've been at the hospital all night." He blew his nose. "Not that she knew."

"Who would do this?" I rifled through papers on my desk nervously. "A disturbed client? Why shoot such a sweet champion of goodness?"

"My feelings too."

"Was it a robbery?"

Tucker shook his head. "As far as I can tell nothing's missing."

He eyed my coffee pot in the corner.

"Would you like—?"

He was already moving toward it.

The brown liquid dribbling into the paper cup seemed surreal in this moment. I considered Tucker as he drank. Fragile, fearful? Why had he come here in person to tell me?

As if reading my thoughts, he answered. "It happened last night, too late to make the morning news. I knew Lenora would want you to know and pray."

"Of course."

Strange request coming from Tucker. Had this crisis suddenly changed his beliefs? Doubtful. More likely he was anticipating what would be Lenora's wishes.

"And I came to ask a favor," he added.

"Anything I can do to help."

"Lenora has several counseling clients she sees at her office in our home. They'll need to be notified. Hearing about this on the news could upset them even more. Then can you follow up with them if they wish?"

"Absolutely. I'll make time. What about her clients through the foundation?" My eyes smarted thinking of the rehab work Lenora did with prisoners. "Do you need me to make those calls also?"

"The Second Chance board is on top of everything."

"Okay." It seemed such an impotent word. Nothing in Tucker's world could seem okay. "It's all so mystifying, to say the least," I murmured, shaking my head.

Tucker took another gulp of coffee.

I pressed him for more details. Part of me didn't want to hear, yet I had to know.

"Lenora was at her desk in the den. The bullet whizzed through the screen. She probably had no warning."

My stomach tightened. "Who found her?"

"Kirk Corsini called the police."

"The man she hired?"

"The *ex-con* she hired." His tone made it clear he hadn't agreed with Lenora's decision. "If only I'd been there…"

"Were you still at your job in the city?"

"Monday through Thursday, as usual." Tucker's voice edged with sadness. "Kirk would know my routine, catching the last train Thursday night." His voice trailed off. "The police suspect he shot her."

"What would be his motive?"

"Kirk had his job review last night. It may have been what set him off. The police found Lenora's notes on her desk, indicating areas where he needed improvement."

"Hardly a reason for attempted murder." Hearing the word, I squirmed in my chair. How could I know this ex-convict's thought process?

"He could have had a rifle in his car, left upset, then doubled back, hiked into the woods, and shot her. Then hid the gun before he came back to the house to call for medical help."

My eyes widened. "Why call an ambulance if he intended to kill her?"

Tucker shrugged. "Remorse after the act? Or to throw off suspicion? I've warned Lenora about being too trusting with these felons."

"Still...why shoot your benefactor? A confrontation about work skills didn't mean she intended to fire him. Or did she?"

"I don't know." He ran a shaking hand through his hair. "Maybe it was just a warning but it scared him. Who knows the workings of a criminal mind?"

"Did the police find the weapon?"

"Not yet."

Lenora had a strong passion to help ex-convicts. How horrible for her attacker to be someone she'd rehabilitated. She'd bragged to me about Kirk being her first success story when she'd hired him as the Second Chance rehab counselor. How many people would be dissuaded from helping ex-cons if they read about consequences such as this? "Tucker, I'd give Kirk every benefit of the doubt at this point. That's what Lenora would want."

Tucker pressed his palms together. "She had to be wrong about this man."

"She's usually an excellent judge of character. I find it hard to believe she'd make such a mistake."

Tucker raised his voice. "No one's judgment is infallible."

"Perhaps I can assist with the investigation. Maybe one of her clients will know something. Lenora may have told you I've helped with a criminal case before."

"Thanks, but your sleuthing isn't necessary. The police are quite competent, and there's no doubt in my mind Kirk shot her. I'm not surprised. I've never shared my wife's enthusiasm for social engineering."

I stared at him. "But you helped establish the Second Chance Foundation?"

"Because I love my wife." He lifted his chin and gritted his teeth. "Rescuing people was my wife's love."

"An awesome undertaking."

He seemed not to hear me. "Kirk will be punished." He studied his hand then pounded his right fist into his left palm. "I'm going to personally see to it." Tucker stood.

I said nothing. He might be right about Kirk, but the fact Kirk called for an ambulance made me skeptical. I decided to do a little checking on my own. If Kirk carried a ton of repressed anger, Lenora should have glimpsed it with her skills of perception and stayed clear. Sometimes I disliked being a psychotherapist, always questioning. Might someone else have reason to harm Lenora?

"Lenora must have a file on Kirk. May I stop by tonight when you're back from the hospital to collect it and get the names and numbers for those clients you want me to contact?"

"Fine. Come after nine."

I followed him to the door and patted his shoulder. "Nick and I will pray for Lenora's complete healing and for your strength through this."

Tucker straightened his jacket. "Thanks for caring. Lenora is all I have…" He dragged himself through the doorway.

I stared at my hands, needing something tangible to assure myself this visit had been real.

If Lenora's attacker wasn't Kirk, her shooter was still out there, and she wasn't safe even in the hospital.

I taught clients to guard themselves emotionally and keep their personal lives separate from their work through appropriate boundaries, vital for a healthy life. Truth was, I often abandoned my own rules.

As I walked back to my desk, I froze. Might this person be someone else Lenora and I both counseled at one of our joint workshops? I shuddered.

CHAPTER TWO

AT SIX TWENTY P.M. I dragged myself through the front door of our two-story colonial, normally my safe and happy place of respite. Cedar, brick, and locks are no protection against the specter of violence. My heels click-clacked across the ceramic-tiled kitchen floor as Nick strolled into the kitchen, his head halfway through the neck of a gray sweatshirt.

He pulled me gently toward him. I nuzzled my face against his neck then lifted my lips for a kiss. I took advantage of the moment to hang limp in the arms that have held me for eighteen years.

He released me quickly. "Something's happened. It's all over you." Nick read me better than a trained counselor. Discernment was his gift, and I was his life study.

"Lenora ..." I dropped onto one of the caned-back stools at our island counter and related what I knew, ending with "she's in a coma in ICU."

I had just begun to collect myself when our teens, Collin and Tara, bounded through the kitchen door. "Just two of you? Where's

Jenny?" I frowned. "You know you're in charge of your sister until I get home."

"Mom...duh. Her friend, Katlin's, eight-year-old birthday. Remember?" Tara popped her fist on her hip and rolled her eyes.

My all-too-familiar canopy of guilt descended. Moms should remember these things.

"What's for dinner?" Collin charged toward the refrigerator like a starvation victim.

"Fried chicken, KFC, as soon as Dad gets it." I looked imploringly at Nick.

"Okay, guys. We'll eat in a little while. First, Mom and I need to talk. Grab an apple and go shoot some hoops." Nick's tone made it clear this wasn't a suggestion.

When they left, my pent-up tears gushed for the first time since hearing the news about Lenora. Tears have their own agenda. Mine were noisy.

"Honey, don't take it so hard. She's alive; hopefully she'll survive this shooting." He put his arms around my shoulders.

I leaned into him and continued babbling. "She's close as a sister. I'm crying for you, me, the mortality of everyone I love." I reached around him for a napkin to blow my nose. "I just need to get it out."

"Okay. I'll go for carry-out and phone the church to put her on the prayer chain on my way."

"Thanks. I'd like some time alone."

He squeezed my shoulders and released me.

I walked into our bedroom, closed the blinds, and plopped onto our bed. *Lord, don't let her die. Please, please heal her.* Lenora and I had shared so much over the years. My shoulders shook with sobs.

Thirty, maybe forty minutes passed. A hesitant knock on the door caught my attention. I turned to find Collin creeping toward me. He settled his lanky body on the rumpled bedspread next to my mounds of tissue.

"Dad told us, Mom. What a stupid thing. Mrs. Lawrence's a nice lady. I'm sorry for her." He clumsily put his hand on top of mine. "It scares me to think that could have been you, Mom. Sometimes I know I'm a jerk and get mad and wish I didn't have to listen to you, but I'd ... you know."

I sat up and looked into Collin's wet eyes before I lifted my hand to stroke his cheek. Such sensitivity from my usually sports-and-self-absorbed young man. A lump formed in my throat. "I know, son." Behind him, pictures of both sets of grandparents hung on the wall. The death of a close relative hadn't yet touched his life.

Collin stood. "Dad wanted me to tell you he's back."

"Thanks." I dried my eyes and followed Collin to the kitchen where Nick was opening round containers of fried chicken, beans, and coleslaw. My stomach growled.

Tara put plates and silverware for four on the table in the dining room. We might eat carryout often, but we always used regular dishes. Collin grabbed a gallon of milk from the refrigerator. We all settled around the table in our usual chairs.

"Who wants to pray?" Nick asked.

Tara bowed her head. "I think you'd better, Dad."

Nick praised God for the gift of the day and asked God to heal Lenora, comfort her husband, and guard and guide our friends and family members wherever they were. He added thanks for the food before we ended with a group "Amen."

All eyes turned to me and stared. No one made a sound. In answer to their concerned faces, I urged them to go ahead and eat.

Pull me together, Lord. May I respond to this situation in a way that honors You.

Tara munched a baking powder biscuit and with her free hand patted a pile of coleslaw with a paper napkin to absorb the excess mayonnaise, having begun a recent hate affair with fat. "Mom, Dad said you worked with Lenora and she was your friend, too. What was she like?" Tara's pretty fourteen-year-old hazel eyes sparkled above her tiny mouth. Friends were huge priority to her.

"What Lenora 'is' like, honey, not 'was.' We're praying for Mrs. Lawrence's healing," Nick corrected.

How to describe Lenora? I found a smile as I studied the Colonel's picture on the bucket. "Well, even when she walked, she seemed to be running. You know I always urge you to try your hardest. Lenora was the first hundred-percenter I'd ever met. She poured herself into people and any issue that absorbed her."

"Where'd you meet, Mom?" Collin didn't pause from dredging his French fries with catsup.

"In Theories of Personality class almost a decade ago. She was fifty-two at the time. I was thirty-five. But age doesn't matter when you find somebody you click with." I paused to pick the breading off an extra crispy chicken breast. "A few years later, she moved here. We taught several workshops together before she started her foundation and cut back on her general counseling."

"What's Lenora's foundation?" Tara asked. "Who does it help?"

"Ex-convicts. She calls them lost souls in need of resurrection." I explained the basics of how it operated.

"So people nobody but God cares about because of bad things they've done?" Tara wiped her mouth with her napkin.

"Sadly, yes, but they can be reformed and start a new life." *I hoped that's what her protégé Kirk did.* I chose not to add that, unfortunately, the police suspected one of them may have shot her.

"Okay, clear your places. Time for homework. Mom and I will clean-up tonight," Nick instructed.

I went to the sink and filled it with rinse water while Nick stacked dishes. The billowing soapsuds in the warm water took away some of my numbness. Routine household chores had a way of soothing me.

While I loaded the dishwasher, Nick wiped the table. When he finished, he sat down to peruse the newspaper. Close enough to listen if I needed to talk. I touched his arm as I reached for a glass, letting him know I appreciated his nearness.

He looked up from the paper. "What does Tucker do at the foundation?"

"Main paper shuffler. Lenora has him do state and local reports, things like that. She dislikes anything to do with numbers."

"What's his full-time job?"

"Researcher at a small Illinois college. He spends four days a week there and comes home on weekends." I added soap to the dishwasher dispenser, shut the door, and pressed wash cycle. "Nick, I'm wondering how to approach this investigation about Kirk. Any ideas?"

He jumped up and strode over to me. Putting his hands on my shoulders, he turned me toward him, locking his eyes on mine. "If you mean interviewing suspects, you'd be hunting a murderer again. Remember what happened with the Albert Windemere situation?"

I trembled. It had been a year since I'd almost been shot myself. "I'll be careful."

"I'd rather you not get involved, but I'll help any way I can."

"You're a good man, Mr. Trevor." I wrapped my arms around his neck. "Come with me to Tucker's to pick up Kirk's file. The kids will be okay for forty-five minutes."

Nick's eyebrows lifted. Normally, I was very independent.

"I know, but tonight I don't feel like driving alone to the scene of a crime. Humor me, please."

"Sure."

We left at eight forty-five with the kids settled doing homework. A lump formed in my throat as I realized I was about to see the shooting scene.

CHAPTER THREE

EVENING SHADOWS STREAKED the forest with a blackish hue as Nick steered around sharp curves on Old Bend Road. Tucker's driveway, a half mile straight up and carved through wooded terrain, came into view. "How appropriate Lenora named this place Wooded Hill, don't you agree, Nick? No houses on either side or directly behind their house and must be a hundred trees on the property, most of them huge."

Nick whistled softly. "Impressive. It seems remote, yet it's only ten minutes from downtown Lake Geneva."

"What a find. Lenora loved—*loves*—this place."

"I can see why."

My limbs went numb. "The rustic beauty of Lenora's hilltop home with its quaint small wings seems to mock her absence. I've never been here without her." My heart fluttered in my chest. "It isn't right."

A few raindrops seeped through the clouds and spattered our windshield. "That's a warning of more to come." Nick frowned. "Did you bring an umbrella?"

"I usually keep one in my car." I groped behind me. "Sorry, must have taken it in. At least it's only a light patter."

Nick parked in front of the house. "Ready to make a dash for it?"

We hurried up the flagstone path leading from the parking area to the main house. My toe caught in the gravel filling the space between the stones. I staggered and almost lost my balance.

Nick grabbed my elbow. "Careful, honey."

"Right." *Remember, Jennifer, rushing gets you into trouble.*

Nick surveyed the house. "How long have the Lawrences lived here?"

"Since they married, seven, maybe eight years. There he is now," I mumbled.

Tucker's huge figure filled the open door frame. He must have seen our car lights approaching. He'd changed into a denim shirt and jeans and still managed to look suave.

"Hurry before you get wet. This shower seems to come out of nowhere." He motioned us onto the porch.

A few seconds of silence followed. Were we both thinking about the shot coming out of nowhere to penetrate Lenora and change everything?

Tucker's hulking form reminded me of Gulliver entering the land of giants. He remembered his manners, bent over and stretched out his huge hand to shake mine.

"Sorry I'm not more presentable." Tucker threaded his fingers through his near-perfect hair, moving aside to let us enter the foyer. I might have laughed if I wasn't still traumatized.

"Please accept my sympathy over your wife's tragic shooting." Nick offered condolences with his usual graciousness. "We're praying she'll recover fully."

Tucker nodded. His eyes narrowed as he answered quickly, "Her condition's the same."

Unchanged. Lord, I'd been hoping for an instant miracle. I hunted for words of comfort counselors provide and only came up with platitudes I bit back.

"I'm going back to the hospital to spend the night."

"I hope you didn't come here just for me?"

"I needed a change of clothes." That's right, he had said that earlier. Where was my memory? Floating about somewhere in the tragic event threatening Lenora's life.

We followed Tucker down a quarry-tiled hall. A sense of heaviness overpowered me. *What if Lenora never returns here?* I'd last seen my colleague in her living room in a tailored black pants outfit looking elegant, her chestnut hair swept off her forehead, except for a few strands that had escaped the barrette.

Two teardrops slid down my cheeks. I pushed them away with the back of my hand and focused on the pattern of the Berber carpet in the great room, the array of natural wicker and painted baskets strewn extravagantly on shelves, tables, on the floor next to furniture and in corner nooks.

Not simply showy, her accessories held audiotapes, CD's, tea, and napkins. This open, cozy setting reflected Lenora's sense of beauty and practicality, making me even sadder.

Tucker dropped into a chair at an oak dining table with carved legs massive enough to support a grand piano. Nick and I chose chairs on either side of him. The kitchen area with its maple cabinets was adjacent to us. Three bananas and two apples filled a wooden bowl on the table.

I scanned the rooms quickly. My eyes focused on the ornate glass-faced gun cabinet. I jerked back around to find Tucker had followed my gaze. "I used to be a hunter," he said, "but Lenora couldn't bear for me to shoot the deer and wild turkeys on our property. Not even a rabbit, although I will say she nearly weakened when a pesky woodchuck kept burrowing under the house."

I tried to manufacture a smile.

"Incidentally, the police checked my guns to see if the bullet came from one of them, thinking perhaps Kirk had used it. He hadn't."

And to check you out, I imagine. Routine. Husbands were always prime suspects.

Tucker brushed his hand across the polished tabletop. "Lenora enjoyed informal entertaining in this room. Unfortunately, because of my work, I missed too many events. She tolerated my schedule, but neither of us liked it." His lips stiffened.

I leaned forward. "You were away a lot, but I never knew her to complain."

"All the same, I can't stop berating myself for being overinvolved at the university this past year and barely available for Lenora's foundation work." He shook his silver head. "I suppose you hear similar things in counseling all the time from grieving spouses."

"More than I'd like." I nodded.

Tucker shrugged. "At least I could bring the foundation paperwork with me and complete it in the city."

"I'm sure you were a big help," Nick offered.

I agreed. Why? Courteous response. How could I know? I disliked when I spoke automatically.

Outside, an owl emitted a deep hoot. What night creatures were present during Lenora's tragic shooting? If only birds or animals had voices to tell us now what happened that night.

"Tucker, would you be willing to repeat what you told me earlier for my husband, Nick? As a lawyer, he may catch something in the sequence of events that I missed. Plus, I could benefit from hearing it again. I admit I was pretty much in semi-shock earlier when you told me."

He nodded. "I realize talking is supposed to help, but does it really? I've been over this several times, and it remains traumatic." Tucker lifted his hands, palms up, in a helpless gesture. "This probably isn't the last time I'll ever have to speak of the horror of last night."

"I understand." Nick averted his eyes.

"Well, I took the train home for the weekend from my job in Illinois, arriving at my usual time, ten-fifteen p.m., just as paramedics loaded Lenora on a stretcher." He turned his head as if to block the picture before completing the account of the chain of events.

"And Kirk's story?" I asked.

"Says he had a seven p.m. appointment with Lenora but arrived late, around nine, due to a flat tire."

"He came for...?" Nick leaned toward Tucker, concentrating his gaze.

"Kirk was to have had a coaching session with Lenora and review his first week on the job for her Second Chance Prison Rehab Foundation."

"She'd been counseling him for how long before giving him the job? Sorry, I'd never paid close attention when Lenora told me about her plan to hire him."

Tucker counted out loud. "Several months, maybe six..."

"If Kirk had intended to shoot Lenora the evening of their appointment, he'd be foolish not to have a better alibi," Nick said.

"Exactly." I spoke the word with such vehemence my face flushed. I hated to think Lenora's protégé would have turned on her.

Tucker shook his head. "The police pieced together a logical scenario. Kirk and she argued about the job, he stomped outside, drove away, but stopped at the road that borders the hill behind our property. He pulled a rifle from his trunk, entered the woods, climbed up, and shot her from a spot behind the house where he had visibility."

"Why all the back and forth?" Nick probably knew the answer but wanted to hear the police theory.

"His intent in all this was to make it look like he wasn't involved. This guy, Kirk, was known to have a bad temper and carry grudges."

"Not good." Nick looked at me.

"Why try to save Lenora afterwards?" I brushed a piece of lint from the tabletop.

Tucker shrugged. "Remorse can be a powerful emotion as well."

Nick stared at me. "We're talking about a crime fueled by passion...anger...committed by an irate man. Jennifer, isn't it unlikely he'd have the self-control to enter the woods and wait patiently for a good shot?"

I nodded in response. "And ridiculous to think guilt could set in that fast when someone is upset enough to attempt murder. And Tucker, Kirk's story is...?"

"Says he arrived around nine and found Lenora passed out in a pool of blood. He called 9-1-1. The police arrived within minutes after he reported the shooting and found Kirk hovering over her bloody body holding a towel against her wound."

"Where was she exactly?" Nick asked.

"Still at her desk. They immediately took Kirk to the station for questioning."

I closed my eyes to block out the vision of Lenora covered with blood.

Tucker continued. "Kirk claims he wanted to call to tell her he'd be late due to a flat tire but had forgotten his phone. When he arrived, the door was unlocked. He walked in because Lenora was expecting him. He used her desk phone to call the police...that part was true."

"Which undoubtedly saved her life," I interrupted. "Kirk waited for the rescue squad at Lenora's side. How noble and tragic as well." My voice caught.

Tucker crossed his arms. "Or an attempt to throw off suspicion. My wife is a wonderful woman. Anger is a terrible motivator."

"What evidence do the police have?" Nick focused on facts; emotion was my territory.

Tucker appeared to pull his words from a point of pain I could only imagine. "No gun residue on his hands, so he was smart enough to wear gloves, although his fingerprints were in the study and the kitchen. The police checked for footprints, but the ground was too dry. From the angle of the shot, they determined where he stood in the woods."

The image of Lenora stripped of her cozy idyllic existence infuriated me. "Have you been to look at the spot yet?"

"I can't bring myself to. The police combed the area but found nothing."

"Then evidence is circumstantial so far," Nick commented more to himself than us.

"But all pointing to Kirk." Tucker clenched and unclenched his fist.

"Tucker, you sound confident he'll be convicted, but," Nick clarified, "circumstantial won't do it, not for attempted murder."

Tucker shook his head in disagreement. "All I know is the police sergeant told me they have what they need to put him away."

"Fresh out of prison, where would Kirk get a rifle?" I asked out of curiosity.

"An ex-con?" Nick shrugged. "With their network of contacts, guns or drugs are no problem. Kirk could have had a rifle stashed somewhere before he went in, possibly even in these woods."

Tucker snarled. "Of course, he denies he had one."

"Tucker, you said earlier today you didn't think Lenora's shooting could have happened during a robbery? Are you still of that opinion now that you've had more time to check?" I asked.

Tucker shot me an impatient look. "I told you nothing was taken."

Nick tapped his fingers on the table. "Makes sense. A sniper attack is unlikely for a robbery. A thief would come into the house, not shoot through a window, and then enter. Too risky."

"Is it possible a former client of Lenora's had developed affection for her which she did or didn't return?" We female counselors work hard to keep male clients from developing inappropriate attachments. "Rejecting a man with an already unstable mind could make him dangerous."

"A disgruntled previous client," Nick agreed. "Makes sense if he knew her habits, realized she was home alone, and psychologically didn't feel capable of killing at close range."

Tucker shifted in his chair. Obviously this thread of conversation displeased him. "Are you suggesting my wife might have been in an inappropriate relationship which she'd called off?"

"Of course not. We'll know more when Lenora recovers enough lung function to be off the ventilator." I hastened to add, "I simply hope, for her sake, her protégé wouldn't have done this."

The unspoken words "*if* she can get off the ventilator" hung in the air. Again my heart hurt for Tucker.

"Truth will come out." Nick used his lawyerly tone of reassurance.

Tucker blew his nose and cleared his throat.

I gave him a moment, then asked if he had the paperwork for me.

He turned, picked up a manila folder from a shelf in the oak sideboard next to the table, and handed it to me. "The complete data on Kirk Corsini from the Second Chance Foundation's files. In addition to giving him a job, Lenora counseled him for personal issues from his past. All her notes are in there."

"Thanks. I'll get this back as soon as possible."

"No hurry. The police have another copy."

"Has anyone else at the foundation worked extensively with Kirk?" The thought had just occurred to me.

"Chuck Denton, Chairman of our Board, Vice-President of Equitable Union Bank, sat in on the interview Lenora had with Kirk for his position. The head of Mr. Denton's bank encouraged his involvement with our foundation as a community service. Mr. Denton may have some insights about Kirk. You can reach Chuck through the bank."

I turned to Nick. "Do you know this Chuck Denton?"

Nick shook his head no.

"He's a helpful guy." Tucker started to stand, then fell back onto his chair. "What will happen to the foundation without Lenora? What will happen to me? This is so awful. Do you think she'll make it through? She must..."

I reached over and rubbed the back of his hand on the chair. "What we can do is pray and make sure she gets the best medical care."

He rose and stood tall. "No doubt about that. I'm seeing to every detail."

"One last thing, as long as we're here, may we briefly see her office where the shooting occurred?" I couldn't leave without going in there.

"Yes, the crime scene team released the site. Follow me."

My blood chilled. Did I want to see the scene of Lenora's shooting? No way. But there might be a clue.

CHAPTER FOUR

SOFT RAIN PATTERED the roof as Tucker led us down the hall and through pine French doors into Lenora's spacious, wood-paneled office. Russet swags imprinted with multi-colored bird designs topped windows framed in white. A massive, antique library table dominated the center of the room. Piles of journals and manila folders clustered beneath it and were scattered in stacks across much of the floor. A shiver ran down my spine. I rubbed my hands down my arms to drive away the coldness in the room.

Tucker flicked on a wall switch. "This is...*was* Lenora's sanctuary. It's been a zoo with detectives and photographers." He sighed and picked up a remaining fragment of crime scene tape.

A hush fell over us as Nick and I examined the hole the bullet had made in the screen, raw edges of mesh turned back ever so neatly.

"I hope the forensics team knew what they were doing," Nick whispered in my ear. "It's not like we're a big city where dealing with attempted murder is commonplace."

Tucker walked over and turned on the desk light. "It still seems surreal."

I remembered reading in a mystery novel about surveying a crime scene in three dimensions. I looked up, down and around, studying the room from different angles.

A huge picture window with smaller windows on each side faced the woods, giving Lenora a great view. It also gave Lenora's attacker a perfect view of the room.

Tucker cleared his throat, interrupting my silence. "Lenora insisted on perfect order everywhere in the house except her office. The cleaning lady rarely set foot in here." He pointed to the carpet. "Lenora used the floor like a gigantic desktop for all her journals and research papers on prison reform and rehabilitation." The first hint of a smile on his face appeared for a second. "Believe it or not, she could find anything instantly."

He picked up a letter opener in his Goliath-sized hand and put it back in the center desk drawer. Tidy man.

"I'll need Lenora's info on her counselees she'd been helping." How I hoped she'd documented thoroughly.

He pointed to a closet on the left side of the room. "Her confidential files are locked in the cabinet in there."

"I can't access them until I get a signed release from each client who wants therapy from me, but I can get names and phone numbers to get started. Under these circumstances, contact info is okay. I'll check her appointment book to make sure I don't miss anyone."

"She kept a separate one for social events and her work calendar in here." He opened the side drawer of the library table desk and pulled out a black leather nine-by-twelve book imprinted in gold with the word "Appointments" above the year. "The police have already examined it."

I reached for it.

He hesitated.

"You do want me to follow up with all her clients, don't you?"

"Of course. It's the right thing to do."

"To save time, I'll take this to get the women's names and numbers, then return it to you." I slipped it into my oversized black bag doubling as purse and briefcase.

"Is there anyone else you can think of? A family member who might have had a motive to shoot Lenora?" Nick was hunting.

Tucker lifted his shoulders. "Lenora got nasty letters rather frequently. We figured they were written by crackpots and pretty much discounted them."

Nick's eyes widened. "Why?"

My chest burned at the idea. My sweet friend didn't mind making enemies. Outspoken she may have been, but gracious always.

"She wrote a weekly newspaper column and occasional editorials about our criminal justice system that drew angry responses. Some neighbors didn't like Lenora providing help for ex-convicts. A few were downright ugly in their indictment of her work with the prisoners."

Nick frowned. "Lenora wasn't afraid to express her strong opinions?"

Tucker had just expanded our search for the shooter to a huge group of potential suspects.

I groped for emotional steadiness. Every time I heard Lenora referred to in past tense, I bit my lip to keep from shouting. *She isn't dead.*

"Yes. My feisty wife even argued with members of her own foundation's board."

"Did she keep these letters?" Nick asked, intent on pursuing this angle.

"I doubt it. Usually she'd get mad, crumple them, and toss them in the trash, but I'll check through her papers." Tucker glanced at his watch.

"Did you inform the police?" Nick's tone demanded an answer.

"I never gave the letters a thought when they questioned me." Tucker bristled. "I see no need to tell them now since Kirk obviously shot her."

"It'd be a good idea anyway." My lawyerly husband preferred full disclosure and I agreed.

"I'll see what I can dig up. It's getting late. I need to get back to the hospital. It's hard to leave her there so helpless. Who knows what kind of care she gets when I'm not around."

"Of course." We were headed for the front door, as I thought of one last question. "Tucker, who would have known about Kirk's release date two weeks ago?"

He responded with a frown. "The whole town. The Recorder carried a feature article last week about the Second Chance Foundation and mentioned Kirk as our first employee. Lenora wrote the press release herself to promote the foundation and included her address for people to send charitable donations."

Nick glanced at me sharply. We read each other's minds. So all these potential enemies had Lenora's address readily available.

"She was extremely vocal about her rehabilitation program," Tucker added.

Was there resentment or pride in his voice? Hard to tell.

I offered a smile. "I'm sure there'd be no stopping Lenora's speaking or fundraising efforts on a program she felt passionately about."

Tucker escorted us to the door. "You'll keep me informed about helping her clients?"

"Of course."

Nick strode briskly to the car, his back to me. "Sometimes women are too naïve. The whole community knew about Kirk and where Lenora lived. I hope you show more sense in similar situations."

I balked at his reference to me but chose to brush it off. "You're right. Not smart with hate letters coming in—better to use a P.O. box."

He jerked the door open. "So had Lenora been foolish in trusting Kirk with a position at her Second Chance Foundation? Did he send her to the brink of her death?"

I settled into my seat and waited as he started the engine. "Why would any man shoot his benefactor? What could she ever have done to motivate such hatred?"

Nick posed no answer. We rode home in silence.

Withhold judgment until hearing both sides, I coached myself as I did in marriage counseling. I needed to know more about Kirk before making an assessment of him. Hopefully, the folder I held in my hand would help.

Lord, his life is precious to You. Let there be no mistakes made and give us wisdom.

CHAPTER FIVE

KIRK'S FILE WAS not my first choice of soothing bedtime stories, but the puzzle of this man's life haunted me. I couldn't sleep until I'd at least skimmed the data on Lenora's alleged attacker.

As I passed Jenny's bedroom door, file in hand, she called out, "Me first, tonight, Mommy."

"Okay, sweetie."

Family was first priority. At bedtime, Jenny, Collin, and Tara waited their turn for me to come into their rooms and "snuggle them up." I spent ten minutes sitting on the edge of the bed with each child—my chance to find out about their daily joys and problems.

Jenny chattered about a new love for roller-skating.

When I rose to leave, she hugged me. "I love you, Mommy. So much."

"Me too, more, now and forever, my muffin."

She mustered an indignant look. "I'm not a muffin."

"That's right, you're my pumpkin."

She broke into a giggle.

Tara bubbled on about the concert she'd be attending as I stroked her bath-sweet arm with lotion. Her body relaxed with my touch.

Collin wanted to know if I felt better. I assured him I did and patted his head. Sweet son.

With everybody tucked in, I changed into blue silk pajamas, then stretched and lifted weights for ten minutes. No rigorous workouts for me, but I did the minimum to keep me toned.

Chintz-covered pillows against the headboard supported my back as I plopped into bed and stretched my legs on our rose-covered quilt. In the background, the murmur of TV news drifted in from the family room where Nick sat in his recliner. I knew his pattern—alternately watching and dozing.

I braced myself, then picked up Kirk's folder. If evidence motivating him to shoot Lenora lurked in here, I'd find it.

On page one the last name, Corsini, was followed by the string of digits assigned every ex-con. The numbers assured he'd be known forever in the government. I read on. *Abandoned by parents on drugs at age seven... Twisted leg from a car driven by a drunk driver at fourteen. Married and divorced.* Thus began a veritable history book of crimes.

How sad. Darling of no one. His most recent penal code violations came next. I skipped through to his earliest convictions, starting with adolescent shoplifting then stealing from a gas station. According to the police report, Kirk claimed to have a gun in his pocket, which he later denied. No gun was found. He may have been faking a weapon. Rigid, pointed fingers did the job nicely, no doubt.

Not many holdup victims will risk calling a thief's bluff with "Show me your gun."

The squeak of the shower nozzle signaled Nick's bedtime routine as I continued flipping through the pages. Ten minutes later, fragrant with Old Spice, he appeared in his worn blue terry robe and sat down next to me.

"What's this?" He picked up a loose sheet and began reading aloud. "Kirk Corsini— conviction for pulling off a three hundred grand jewelry store theft."

"First felony," I said over my shoulder. "His accomplice had a real gun and so did the owner. The shopkeeper was killed; Kirk's accomplice was charged with murder. Kirk became accessory."

"Heavy-duty."

"Unfortunately, yes." I couldn't conceal the sadness in my voice. "Each of Kirk's crimes becomes more sophisticated."

Nick shook his head. "A felon's twisted version of the social ladder. Always seeking more than he's willing to earn by honest labor."

"Glancing at his list of felonies, I couldn't help but contrast it with Lenora's resume, all her personal achievements, service committee chairs, memberships, publications." My voice cracked. "Now Kirk is fully alive and Lenora near death. Does life have a few inequities?"

"God will make all things right someday." Nick sighed. "I believe that's true, but it sounds trite to someone who doesn't believe."

"See the timeline for Kirk's release, his subsequent employment, and Lenora's shooting? Kirk was let out of prison on Saturday and started his job the following Monday. She must have been counseling him in prison to prepare him to start immediately." I opened a small legal pad to make notations.

Nick paged through the file. "Here's a conviction for Kirk's robbery of his second ex-wife's home." He pointed to a paragraph on the page. "This resulted in his most recent prison sentence, followed by parole after serving three years. At least he never personally shot anyone." I jotted down dates and times.

We studied the mug shots next.

"Kirk has a regular album," I noted. "Weird how his hair went from traditional cut to shaggy, then shoulder length as his crime escalated."

"Check out his face, too." Nick's brow furrowed. "He started clean-shaven, then a mustache, finally a scruffy beard. Maybe more facial hair seemed protective—a natural mask for higher level hits."

"Or perhaps he started feeling ashamed. Guilt can be powerful." I pushed my hair back from my face.

"Sounds logical, but it's a stretch." Nick turned a page. "On his discharge shots he's clean shaven again."

"A good sign, I hope, because this file describes a hardened criminal. No wonder he's the prime suspect. How many people believe Christ can change a man inside and out?"

"You have to admit, fast transition is rare even for the Holy Spirit. In my work with criminals, it's not common." Nick plumped up a pillow under his head and leaned back.

"But not impossible. I see some sudden transformations. Think about the apostle Paul."

Nick continued to read. "A parole officer reports Kirk connected with Christ in Prison Fellowship and Lenora's Second Chance Foundation. He credited both for planting seeds of change."

"Seeds. But had they sprouted? For the sake of Lenora's foundation, I sure hope so. Lenora's contact and caring would be huge. I may be optimistic, but I'd sure like to believe he had a genuine conversion."

Nick rolled over. "Me too, but you can't deny it's a big coincidence the shooting occurred so soon after his release."

I flinched. "Red flags all over, I know. Once upon a long time ago, Kirk must have known better. I bet when his kindergarten teacher asked what he wanted to be, he didn't say a criminal."

"How many ex-convicts had Lenora counseled?"

"I'm guessing twenty-five or thirty. She started the foundation about a year and a half ago. The new building is under construction, to be completed in six months. In the meantime, ex-con reorientation sessions were in Lenora's home."

"Her attacker could have been any previously released convict with a grudge. But only Kirk had a motive as far as you know, right?"

"Give me time." I assembled the loose papers and returned them to the folder. "I need the list of the other prisoners Lenora helped. I intend to meet with Kirk as soon as possible, although I'm not looking forward to it. I'm praying for God's wisdom. I don't want to mess this up."

"You won't. You're capable, and you care." Nick edged closer toward me.

"Maybe too much."

He stroked my hand. "Lenora is your good friend as well as colleague. Can you stay objective?"

"I hope so."

Nick took the file from me gently, stretched over to put it on the nightstand, then pulled back the bed covers. "Let's call it a night, Sherlock. Just remember your promise to be careful."

"I will." I crawled under, rolled over on top of him, and kissed his ear. "You can be sure I'm not letting you have all the fun raising our kids."

CHAPTER SIX

MORNING BROUGHT A milk-glass glow to the pond behind our house. When Nick left to drive our kids to school, I plopped on a porch chair to sip my orange juice, watch birds feast at our feeders, and pray for our family.

A Thank You box and notepad centered on the coffee table reminded all of us to express gratitude daily. I'd have hummed a song with the birds except for the thickening in my throat when I envisioned Lenora lying in a hospital bed.

I put away my prayer journal, dressed quickly, and drove through our quiet neighborhood, inhaling the warm, breezy air.

When I reached downtown Lake Geneva, I zipped into the local Starbucks. Soon the fragrance of vanilla-flavored coffee filled the car. When had this brew or black tea crept upon me as a morning necessity?

I pulled into the lot of the Victorian complex housing my three-room second floor office suite.

Once settled behind the mahogany desk I began my job of listening as clients revealed their concerns. I offered insights to improve their lives as best I could. During a break after my third appointment, I focused my thoughts again on Lenora's shooting.

If not Kirk, who could have been Lenora's attacker? An enemy from her past? I knew little about her history prior to our meeting and nothing about her current clients either. Like many professionals in mental health, Lenora worked from an at-home office, giving her clientele the benefit of total privacy.

Who could shed light on the goings-on at Wooded Hill?

I straightened my shoulders and sat back suddenly. Of course, Estelle. I swiveled to the console behind me. She may have observed something.

I reached for my phone, flipped to the "M" in my addresses, and pressed my finger on the number for Estelle Mason, the cleaning lady I'd recommended when Lenora moved here. She cleaned for me, too, but only for special occasions. Nick and I insisted the children assume some responsibility for household chores.

I pictured Estelle, a 250-pound dynamo who operated in only one gear, high, and recollected with delight how chatty she was. In addition to house cleaning and mothering three children, Estelle sold hand-sewn and knitted items and beadwork at craft shows. We often joked about how different we were. I hated scrubbing floors, sinks—you name it—but loved hiking, biking or reading anything, even box tops in a clinch. Estelle claimed she was born loving to scrub and talk.

Estelle picked up on the third ring.

"This is Jennifer Trevor."

"Hello, Dr. Trevor." I couldn't get her to stop calling me doctor. Funny because she said the only doctors she knew took care of people's bodies, and she couldn't possibly imagine how anyone might help somebody by messing around in their thoughts. Estelle wouldn't use my first name either, no matter how many times I insisted. I'd given up.

"Poor Mrs. Lawrence. I heard on the news. Everybody in town knows about the shooting." Estelle's voice faltered. "How's she doing?"

"Her situation is very serious. She's in critical condition at Union Memorial."

Estelle gasped. "I'm still shaking from the second I saw her picture on TV. Did you know I was there the morning of the day she was shot?"

"I didn't, but I certainly want to talk with you about that day, Estelle, and the days leading up to it. It's important. I'll pay for your time."

"Paid to talk?" I could picture Estelle screwing up her face. "Talk's free, Dr. Trevor."

"Your time is valuable; I'll be the judge of paying. How about noon today?" I assumed the police hadn't interviewed her yet or she'd have told me; they might not even know she existed. I doubted Tucker would have thought to mention Estelle.

Her response was silence. I concluded she was pondering something. What was the issue here?

I tapped a pen on my desk, waiting for her answer.

Finally she spoke. "I suppose I could talk with you. Lunchtime works fine. Where do you want me to come?"

"We'll meet at Lenora's?"

"That works good. I'm planning to go same as usual twice a week to keep things up and water the plants, unless Mr. Lawrence orders me otherwise. She'd want her place kept nice."

"That's right."

"Is this about the guy who done it? You know Mrs. Lawrence counseled men and women from the local prison. How could an ungrateful ex-convict do such a thing?"

I chose not to get into that now. "Do you have a key?"

"No bother about that. I've had one for two years now."

"Fine. See you later."

Now if only Estelle could reveal some clue to aid in identifying Lenora's attacker.

CHAPTER SEVEN

A GIGANTIC COCOON of drifting clouds covered the sky as I drove past acres of open farmland guarding the sense of country around Lake Geneva—partly why we moved here from Illinois ten years ago. I inhaled deeply. God's beauty was still evident in the world even if a human beings tried to turn it insane. Did Lenora's protégé repay her kindness with a bullet? It seemed equivalent to Mother Teresa being gunned down by an AIDS patient she'd cared for.

Nudged to pray, I asked for divine hands to somehow reform this tragedy. I whispered, "Lord, heal Lenora and keep Nick and the children safe as they go about their day."

I pulled off the road and put the top down on our convertible. When I reached the top of the hill, Estelle's red Ford truck sat in the driveway with the side door open. As I pulled near, she popped out and waved. Big-boned and vigorous, with the ruddy look of a farmwoman used to physical labor, she'd impressed me the day I hired her. Before I shut my car door, she began chattering. "Poor Mrs. Lawrence. I still can't believe it."

I put my arm on her shoulder. "I know. It will be good for us to talk." We ambled toward the house. In the daylight, the residence seemed more comforting than last night. What's not to like about a rustic country home with wings running in three directions flanked with English gardens?

Estelle sniffled. "Mrs. Lawrence won't want weeds taking over her roses. Gardening is one of her favorite things. I'll be keeping up the yard until she's better."

"I'm sure she'd appreciate it."

I waited while Estelle unlocked the front door. Holding it open with her hip, she gestured me in.

I eased onto a blue, floral-cushioned wicker chair in the main living room and asked Estelle to sit. A mistake. She immediately fidgeted, signaling she wasn't used to sitting in this house.

"Lenora told me more than once how pleased she was to have you, Estelle. As you know I am."

"Housecleaning seems like doll's play compared to the farm chores I did growing up." Her gaze tracked to a crooked picture on the wall of the family room. She jumped up. "I'll just straighten that."

Despite Estelle's large size, she moved gracefully, taking wide strides across the room. She ducked into the kitchen and emerged with a dust cloth in her hand. "You don't mind if I just touch up a few things while we talk, do you?" She swiped at the coffee table top.

I smiled. "I can't imagine putting cleaning in the category of play. I have the greatest respect for dedicated scrubbers." I kept up a patter of small talk a few minutes. It would be best to let her work as we spoke. "I need to ask you some questions related to Lenora's shooting."

She halted mid-step, and her cheeks turned red. "I want to help, sure, but now I can't say anything personal about Mrs. Lawrence. I know she valued her privacy. That wouldn't be right." Estelle planted her two feet firmly on the floor as if the area rug had become a witness stand. "Besides, I never paid much attention to her business."

I doubted that was true. Bless her. Estelle observed everything that went on around her. I prodded. "If you saw or heard anything unusual, Lenora and Tucker would want you to tell me."

Estelle raised her eyebrows and resumed dusting around tabletop bird sculptures before replying. "Why are *you* asking? Aren't the police charging that ex-convict, Kirk Corsini? I never did think Mrs. Lawrence should get involved with felons. I'd like to get my hands on that man." She waved a fist in the air.

Estelle obviously agreed with Tucker. "I understand your feelings, but her attacker may or may not be Kirk. He's only a suspect; we're not sure Kirk or any other ex-convict shot Lenora. Estelle"—I leaned forward—"when a crime's been committed, anxiety rises in many people connected with the victim. We all want quick closure for our own peace of mind. But still we must be cautious."

"Mrs. Trevor, wouldn't Mr. Lawrence know more 'bout her doings than me?"

"Not necessarily, since he wasn't around during the week." I motioned Estelle to a chair again, plunked down across from her and looked straight into her eyes.

"Since you're here twice a week, you know a lot about the things that go on at Wooded Hill."

"I suppose I do, but I don't gossip about it."

"Of course not. It isn't gossip for you to talk with me. Mrs. Lawrence would welcome my help. I like you guarding Lenora's privacy, but there's no time to waste. Mrs. Lawrence is between death and life, but she's a fighter. If she recovers as we all hope, we need to make sure her assailant won't return to finish the job. You can help protect her."

Estelle's eyes widened.

Did I sound reassuring? I respected Estelle's loyalty. She smoothed her smock down over her work pants and nodded. Wrinkles wouldn't dare exist near her.

"What do you want to know?"

I swallowed, relieved. I seemed to be getting through.

"First, you said you were here the day of the shooting?" I picked up my pad and pen to make notes.

"Well, that day stands out because my work days were changed. Usually I do Monday and Wednesday afternoons. But Mrs. Lawrence had to go somewhere Monday, and she liked to be home when I cleaned to tell me anything extra she wanted done. So I came Wednesday and Thursday. I do the linens and the kitchen real good one day and the other, well, I guess you don't need to know about that. Anyway, I was here the day of the shooting."

"Start with that morning."

She pursed her lips. "First she had her ladies' group." I jotted down their arrival time. "Then I remember two men came by. Oh, not at the same hour."

"Can you describe them?"

"I never saw their faces, only heard male voices. You know I'd never stop working to listen, but I couldn't help hearing 'cause the one man talked kinda loud in Mrs. Lawrence's den. He came late morning right after her women's group left, and the other came mid-afternoon. The second one talked regular-like at first but then started yelling."

"Did you see or hear anything else?"

"I heard a muffled woman's voice in the afternoon. I didn't think it was Mrs. Lawrence's, but I can't be sure. I figured maybe one of the ladies from her group had stayed and was in there, too. I didn't notice if they all left after the morning session."

I scooted closer to the edge of my chair. "Think hard. Did you notice anything else about these visitors?"

"Not really. I mean, lots of times Mrs. Lawrence has people in." She screwed up her face. "Hmmm. I did set tea in her office for the gentleman in the afternoon before he came. I remember that. Peppermint. Mrs. Lawrence liked mint."

"Did you hear her say either man's name or did she mention them afterwards?"

Estelle shook her head. "Mrs. Lawrence never told me names, nothing like that."

"Can you think of anything else that might have been, err, unusual, Estelle? It's very important."

She stared off into space, started to shake her head sideways, then stiffened. "One other thing. When the man who'd come late morning left, Mrs. Lawrence came over to where I was cleaning the mirror and said in a tone kind of sad, 'Estelle, what would you say about a man who had a precious jewel but wanted to keep it hidden?'"

"Did you answer?"

"I thought a moment then said, 'I'd think he was afraid of losing it, Mrs. Lawrence, or maybe it wasn't real at all, and he didn't want anyone to know.'"

"Good answer. How did she respond?"

"'Interesting,' Mrs. Lawrence said real deep and thoughtful, and 'Thank you. Thank you very much,' like I'd truly helped her. Kinda surprised me. Made me feel good, I can tell you, for sure."

"Would you recognize the voice of the man who yelled if you heard it again?"

She scrunched her forehead until lines formed. "I can't be sure, but I think so. I'm pretty good about catching differences between bird calls."

I filed that away in my mind and leaned forward. "Did Lenora mention either man after he left?"

"No, but after her morning visitor pulled away, Mrs. Lawrence stomped outside, picked up a rake, and started raking real fast, still dressed in her skirt and silk blouse."

"That's unusual?"

"Absolutely. She usually gardened in jeans and a long shirt with hat and gloves because of deer ticks ever since her friend Sue Ann got Lyme's disease. I worry 'bout that, too. Little Sarah Spooner got horrible sick last summer. Where was I?" Estelle scratched her head.

"Lenora was raking."

"After about fifteen minutes, she went in and made a phone call. Can't say to who, but it seemed to soften her some. Mrs. Trevor, I know you're asking all this, and I hope I'm in the right telling you, but I gotta say I hope you don't think I was ever intruding. I just can't help but notice a bit of what's going on around me."

"Of course, that's what I was hoping, Estelle. What about the cars? Did you happen to look out the window when the visitors left?"

"No, I don't pay no mind to things like that. It wouldn't have been proper for me to be checking out the window."

I didn't like where my thoughts were taking me. Was Lenora involved with another man? Perhaps a current or a former client? I shook my head. Lenora was a Christian. That would be absurd. Still, Christians dealt with temptation every bit as strong as other women.

Tucker had made no mention of Lenora's counseling a man other than the ex-cons or inmates at the prison. No male names were written in her office appointment book.

"I hope I'm helping," Estelle said, filling my pause and finally seeming to warm to her role.

"Yes, very much. How about the ladies' group? Did you happen to see who was here?"

The praise seemed to please Estelle because she was willing to ramble on. I encouraged her by nodding.

"Mrs. Lawrence has her ladies' counseling group every Thursday morning. I know 'cause I cleaned real good on Wednesday to leave everything nice. They meet in the living room and come in and out the front door so I don't see them.

"Did you ever see Mr. Lawrence when you cleaned? Did he ever come around during the week?"

"No way. Just weekends. Weekends were kept private for Mr. Lawrence when he was home from Illinois. Don't think they had much company. I don't know him at all."

Estelle squirmed a little when she mentioned Mr. Lawrence? Why?

"Follow me," I said abruptly. Rising, I led her to the back of the house. "Please take a careful look at Lenora's office—see the papers and mess everywhere? Is this how the room usually looked?"

Estelle scanned the room. "Yep, she liked the house extra neat, but her office was always cluttered—messy if you ask me, really. Yep. This is how she kept it."

"Then there isn't any unusual disarray?"

"No, you never could see her desktop or much of the floor either, for that matter. I could have straightened it up real nice for her, but she never let me touch it."

"Thanks, Estelle, that's all for now. If you remember anything else regarding those men or the women, call me."

"Sure." Estelle twisted the rag in her hands. "Can I tell you something, Dr. Trevor? I'm scared. I don't want to lose Mrs. Lawrence."

"Nor I." I gritted my teeth. "That's not going to happen if we can prevent it, right?"

I emerged from the house into strong wind that whipped my hair. A storm loomed in the darkening sky. Rainstorms in convertibles were not fun.

I proceeded to put the top up. Like a giant accordion it emerged from its creased position and expanded over me. I fastened the corner strips that held it in place before winding down the gravel driveway to the main road.

A woman walked along the side of the road wearing jeans and a misshapen, over-sized sweater. She darted into the field, moving against the wind as raindrops pelted her skin. I assumed she was Lenora's neighbor. She had no umbrella, not even a rain hat. Was she heading for cover? The woman didn't run but kept moving steadily in the direction of a rust-colored barn. Her head tucked down on her chest was the only indication of being pelted by heavy rain. Middle-aged, maybe younger, she reminded me of a stricken bird unable to fly in a fierce wind.

I pulled my gaze back to the road and squeezed the steering wheel. Inexplicably, a sense of sadness washed over me, forceful as the rain against my window.

CHAPTER EIGHT

EVERY MARRIAGE AND family counseling office should have an Ellen, my competent fifty-five-year-old administrative assistant and receptionist. I shuddered to think what disarray my paperwork and calendar would be like without her.

Standing in front of my desk, Ellen fluffed the top of her thinning hair with one hand. "I don't know what to make of this shooting. A woman can't be safe in her own home. What's this world coming to?"

"You're right. It's frightening. I'm concerned for our clients already dealing with anxiety whose worry has intensified." I sorted through the list of names I'd culled from Lenora's appointment book without looking up and passed it to her. "Please call each of these women Lenora has been currently counseling. Inform them tactfully of her condition, if they don't already know, and ask if they wish to temporarily continue therapy with me."

"And if they do?"

"Under the circumstances, I'll need signed and faxed Consent to Release permission forms to collect their files from Lenora's office. I want to know if any are in crisis situations. If they wish to see me, fit them in as soon as possible."

Ellen's face formed into a frown. "As if you aren't busy enough." She had a knack for speaking under her breath loud enough to be heard.

I ignored her response. "Use our standard release form. You know the routine."

Every professional counselor has ethics drilled into them. Clients' files were only examined with their permission. Respecting confidentiality was a huge issue with me. Also, because I treasured my own.

"All I can say is they're lucky ducks to get in to see you with your schedule."

"And that's more than I need to hear."

I let Ellen get away with such comments because she was also my stress protector, guarding me when I crammed my schedule. Occasionally, Ellen overstepped her bounds, turning into a nag. For the most part, I appreciated the vigilance on my behalf, her genuine compassion for clients, and nearly flawless record keeping.

The only time she neglected to be solicitous of my time was during the Windemere murder investigation. As a devotee of mystery stories, she'd have me working to investigate and solve a crime seventy hours a week. I teasingly named her Ellerina Queen.

"Before I call, do you think…" Ellen brightened visibly. "Maybe one of these women shot Lenora. Do I need to be alert for clues? I mean, they'd been at her house, knew where she lived, and could have gotten upset if she confronted them about something. Sometimes I've seen clients leave here angry with you when you're just telling them the truth and trying to help."

"Ellen, absolutely no probing. Just make the calls."

My skin tingled at the prospect of seeing if anyone had a motive to harm Lenora, but I had to handle querying them delicately. A woman could handle a rifle as easily as a man. "Tell each woman she's welcome to come meet me before making a decision about working with me. No charge."

Ellen tossed her head in the air. "I'm sure they'll take you up on it." She snapped her notebook shut.

I chuckled.

Liking all freebies, Ellen assumed everyone else did. "Your pro bono work is three times what it should be."

"Lenora cared about these clients. She'd help me if our positions were switched."

"Right." Ellen huffed and turned to leave.

"If I don't have daytime hours free, add a Tuesday or Thursday night. One more thing, have I told you lately how much I appreciate you?"

Her mouth dissolved into a grin.

When she left to make the calls, I experienced a sense of peace. *Finally I was performing actions on Lenora's behalf.*

Next, I studied Lenora's appointment book and recorded the names listed the past three months, which I considered the most crucial time period. If Lenora's shooting had been a passionate crime of vengeance, a deranged person usually couldn't control the fury to act out by waiting for very long.

The initials R. M. filled the four o'clock calendar time slot the day Lenora had been shot. I didn't have any idea who R. M. was. The name T. Hartford was written without a time, just a notation between ten and noon. Perhaps Tucker would know to whom the initials referred. I wasn't about to rule anyone out as a suspect.

I tried to locate a Hartford with the first initial T online. No luck. I stood, stretched, and walked into my break room, actually a remodeled closet with a small refrigerator and microwave above the one and only cabinet that stood next to a small round table with two chairs. The cabinet held three ceramic coffee mugs, boxes of tea, herbal and regular orange pekoe and black, and coffee.

I reached into my canvas bag for a banana, one of the mainstays of my diet. The golf course scene printed on the bag transported me mentally to pleasant thick green fairways. Not that I was a serious player—I saw the rough more often. I tossed the peel and wiped my fingers on a Kleenex.

Sessions with Lenora's clients along with mine, plus visiting Kirk, would add considerable stress to my life. It couldn't be helped. Where the Lord led, He equipped. How I needed those reminders.

Twenty minutes later, Ellen was back at my desk reporting on her calls. "Sandy Reckland will use her lunch hour today to fill your one o'clock cancellation. She has no objection to having you review her file after her appointment and will sign the release. Nor does Carrie Malone. She's coming in Monday morning. Esther Forbes won't be needing more counseling. She's fine; a flap over a family inheritance is cleared up." Ellen put the names and numbers on my desk.

"Great."

"And get this. The two gals who are coming to see you had counseling sessions on the day Lenora was shot."

"I know, thanks."

I ambled out to the reception area where I kept the cart with carafes of hot water and coffee for my clients and filled a mug with water from the pot on the warming unit. Ripping open the wrap on a tea bag, I swished brown streaks through the steaming water, the extent of my creativity for the day unless I counted the wild thoughts swirling in my brain as creative.

Two clients were followed by a quick lunch of half a cold turkey sandwich, and one o'clock chimed.

I strolled into the reception area to welcome Lenora's counselee, Sandy. I reached out my hand to the tall woman with a Starbucks cup of comfort in her grasp. "Hello, I'm Dr. Trevor. Please come in."

Sandy Reckland clomped through my office door on leather boots with two-inch heels. Her black turtleneck under a fringed leather jacket hardly seemed spring fashion. She tossed her long, brown tresses with quick, jerky movements like a quarter horse. Her tortoise shell and sequined necklace sparkled as she pressed a strong hand into mine.

"I'm glad I could get in right away. It's shocking about Lenora."

"A terrible tragedy." I led her to the Queen Anne chairs. "Please make yourself comfortable."

She dropped onto the chair cushion farthest from mine and flashed a mouthful of bright tooth enamel as she asked for more details about Lenora's condition.

I shared the little I knew, then picked up the manila folder from the coffee table containing her intake and a blank form for my initial assessment. I noted Sandy had left employment info blank.

"What kind of work do you do?"

"MIS."

"Refresh my memory. The acronym means?"

"Management Information Systems. I like a position of power. Computers are always the control center." She grinned and rubbed the back of her neck. "I suppose I should let you know control is one of my issues, according to Lenora. My last session with her wasn't exactly helpful. In fact, we ended early. I was seriously considering not returning."

"Why?"

"Let's just say I didn't like her recommendations."

"Yet you came today? Would you like to tell me the specifics about the issues you and Lenora had been working on?"

Sandy wet her finger and dabbed at a speck on her leather jeans. "Three years ago my husband and I divorced. I didn't have counseling at the time. I went to Lenora a few months back because I was still dealing with that pain."

"It's good you sought help. Ending a marriage can create a sense of loss whatever the initial cause of breakup."

She snapped back in a steely tone and listed a litany of dissatisfactions with her former husband. "I should have known better than to marry him. I'm still dealing with emotional fallout. It's actually also my parents' fault."

Talkative enough at least. "How so?"

"The marital relationship between my mom and dad was horrid. You've heard of mental cruelty? The two tortured each other for thirty years. Dad never allowed my mom to have a single thought he didn't agree with. She paid him back with constant criticism and passive resistance to anything he wanted to do, whether it was where to vacation or when to have the carpets cleaned. When I met my ex-husband, Phil, I thought our relationship could be different. He proved me wrong."

"Your earlier counseling sessions with Lenora were helpful?"

She nodded. "But our last session she said some wrong-thinking on my part may have caused the marriage to break-up. Even though my husband turned out to be a jerk, Lenora said the way I interacted with him further damaged the relationship. I didn't take that well. She had no basis to say I needed to make some changes." Sandy snickered.

How immature Sandy was. *Of course Lenora did. She was trying to help you.* I took a sip of peppermint tea to soothe my irritation. "In counseling we work to help men and women respect each other and relate healthfully. Sometimes that requires saying some hard things."

"Therapy's a lot of crock in my opinion. I could give you a mouthful."

"Why would you say that?" For someone who supposedly didn't like counseling, this gal was in no hurry to stop talking. "What specifically was Lenora suggesting you change?"

"My dislike of men, not just my ex-husband. She inferred I have conflict issues with males at work, too." Sandy's face reddened. "Even implied there might be a pattern, a problem in my attitude and behavior from my childhood experiences. That's what steamed me. Afterwards I had to admit she was at least half-right."

I suppressed a smile. I'd witnessed Lenora's style; she could be direct but kind. If she'd identified Sandy as having difficulty with male relationships, I'd surmise it to be true. "So she ultimately helped?"

"I wouldn't go that far, but she was helping me know myself better. Even though I walked out last time, I'd decided to go back." She looked up, eyes wide to see my reaction. "That's why I'm here now."

People who enjoyed being contrary liked to see the shock they created.

"Good, then we can continue." I met her eyes coolly. Did I really want to work with this woman? She could be a resistant client. Nobody could help someone who didn't want to change.

"Now that you've had a chance to meet me, do you wish to continue with counseling?"

"I'll try a few sessions. Why not?" She shrugged. "My company pays."

I made a note of her willingness and put down my pen. "I have a few questions I'd like to ask you about the day of Lenora's shooting before you leave today."

"Sure." Sandy fidgeted with her hands. "It stresses me thinking Lenora might die when I was just with her the day she was shot."

"Did you observe anything strange while at Lenora's, like phone calls that upset her, anything out of the ordinary, something she said?"

"Not really."

"Did you sense she was worried or scared about anything?"

"Nothing I noticed." Sandy's face had lost its indifferent attitude.

I tried to make my next question sound casual. "Out of curiosity, where were you that evening when Lenora was shot? The police are asking everybody who'd seen her within twenty-four hours of the shooting as a formality," I added quickly to soften the stark question.

Didn't work. She bristled. "In Illinois, on business." Her eyes turned cold. "I travel a lot. That evening I went to a movie and was in my motel by ten. If the police want to know, they can ask me personally."

A nice and neat alibi? How distorted was her thinking? I leaned forward, about to probe further, when Sandy stood up. "I need to get back. How do we set the next session up?"

"Make an appointment with Ellen on your way out." I'd have offered my handshake, but she'd already reached the door.

When she left, I took a deep breath. I wasn't sure what to make of this successful but unhappy woman who went out of her way to be disliked. Could I service her without getting annoyed? Of course. My framed professional licenses on the wall behind me signified I could squelch negative feelings. Yes, I'm well trained, but she'd be tough. I wished frustration toward a client never cropped up but sometimes it did. I wanted their lives to be the best possible, but some were stubborn about changing unproductive behaviors. Christ's command to love reminded me to avoid judging.

I wrote on Sandy's client intake sheet. *Client expressed but didn't emote concern about Lenora's plight. Outwardly hard, appears to guard a fragile shell.*

Had she transferred anger at her parents and the world into a motive for killing Lenora? Had she come in today as a cover-up? Did Lenora's confrontational method lead to deep anger? Did Sandy have a fetish for killing? For that matter, was it safe for me to be around her?

A distinct chill rolled over me. I crossed the room to the opposite wall and twisted the control to turn down the air conditioning.

CHAPTER NINE

AT THREE, I left my office for my appointment with Kirk at his all-expenses-paid residence, the Walworth County jail. The massive complex built with rectangular chunks of stone in two shades of tan spread over several acres. It might have blended into the landscape as a typical business building except for the sign, Law Enforcement Center, and parked sheriff's department cars in the front spaces of the lot.

I shuddered. The idea of a structure constructed to cage human beings deemed too dangerous for the public welfare repulsed me. This would be my first and hopefully last visit.

After I parked, I pulled the hand-sized pepper spray from my handbag after several minutes searching. So much for being prepared to use this easily accessible crime deterrent in an emergency. I dug the silver metal nail file out from beneath my blush then rifled past two lipstick tubes and Chapstick to find my peppermints. I popped a mint into my mouth to soothe my queasy stomach. Best to leave the spray and nail file in the driver's seat of my car. No way would I carry anything inside remotely resembling a weapon. On second thought, I left my purse in the car.

My stomach growled, reminding me my lunch had been light. I envisioned the fast food salad I'd grab when I left.

I charged toward the front door to overcome my reluctance to enter the building, carrying only a small notepad, pen, and car keys, and strolled in bravely. Murphy's Oil and sweat filled my nostrils—same as our local high school during Tara and Collin's basketball games.

A droopy-eyed female receptionist with puffy cheeks and a thin neck sat at a desk in a glass enclosure inside the spacious foyer. At least forty thin black braids coiled perfectly around her head. I waited as she methodically checked the identification of the gentleman ahead of me—I surmised a lawyer. The navy suit moved off briskly and disappeared.

I stepped up to the window, aware of the fluttering in my stomach. She responded to my hello with a noncommittal grunt as I handed over the letter of authorization allowing me to visit Kirk.

"ID?" An expressionless request, no small talk wasted here.

I pulled out my driver's license with my picture ID and quipped, "Bad hair day."

The woman ignored my remark and glanced wordlessly back and forth from the license to me as if the picture might change. Finally her head jerked left toward chairs in the waiting area. I assumed that was permission to sit down. I tried to smile as I said thank you, but it was hard through shaky lips.

Fifteen minutes passed before a handcuffed man in a green cotton uniform appeared with a guard and was led to one of four glass-enclosed visitor's cubicles at the far end of the room.

I was summoned and gestured to sit on the other side. I recognized Kirk's face from his pictures and mentally reviewed his statistics from the file—weight 185, height 5'11. His huge muscular arms reminded me of machinery except with elbow gears. Fuzzy growth covered his arms and decorated his chest in thick curls escaping the top of his open shirt. His head seemed glued on top of his shoulders, like a child's drawing of a stick man.

He sat down warily. Why wouldn't he? After all, we were separated by vast degrees of freedom and lifestyle.

Kirk stared past me then down as his gaze locked on my notepad.

"Hi. My name's Jennifer Trevor. I'm a friend of Lenora's."

At the mention of Lenora, color flushed over his face as his eyes bored into me. "How is she?"

I repeated the latest medical info. "You stopped her bleeding and probably saved her life."

"Yeah, well, everyone thinks I wanted to kill her. The authorities are never going to believe I'm innocent."

Movement in the cubicle next to us attracted my attention. No sound came through the glass, but a quick look at the prisoner's red face and waving arms proved it wasn't a pleasant conversation. I glanced over. Two black eyes met mine, axe blades of anger sharp enough to chop wood. Sweat formed on my brow. I swiped it away. I didn't consider myself a skilled lip reader but figured out his words. *I never had a chance.* He mouthed it over and over to his visitor, the man in the navy blue suit.

A guard dragged the prisoner away but not before he yelled, "Now I'm sucked up into this lousy system." The suited man on the same side of the cubicle as me got the message the session was over and packed his briefcase.

I turned back to Kirk, who'd observed the incident also, and was still watching the retreating figure.

"So that's how you feel? Like a victim caught in the process?"

A shadow flickered across his face. "I don't know how I feel about anything anymore. I was starting to think I was a real person with a job and a future and then this." He waved his arm back and forth. "In my life growing up, the "haves" were the drug-pushers, pimps, and thieves and the "have-nots" were the straights. I try to go straight and look where it lands me."

I held up my right hand in a stop gesture. "No sense wasting time in this pity pit. It's not helpful to you or honest. In your prior life, didn't you define fairness by robbing other people who had more? That's absolutely wrong and besides, it didn't work or you wouldn't have history behind bars."

Kirk lowered his head. "You sound like Lenora."

"I've seen enough clients with 'poor me' syndrome to know it's easy to convince yourself you deserve whatever you can take. It's not right and never will be."

"Okay, you nailed me. Until I reformed, that is. After my third prison stint, I really was going straight. I hooked up with Jesus—made a huge difference in my thinking. Lenora understood." He rested his elbow on the narrow ledge in front of him and looked into my eyes. "I changed, plain and simple and for real."

For his sake I wanted this to be true. I'd heard my share of stories about insincere foxhole conversions but knew real ones occurred too. "Go on, Kirk. The fact is, I need to be convinced."

"It was a big deal to me that Lenora Lawrence cared about me and became a friend. The first I had in a long time, maybe ever." Kirk squeezed his fist into the palm of his hand. "I'd die before letting her down. To think I could hurt her, well, it's just crazy, that's all."

While he talked, I studied him, trying to gage how credible he was. Sincere or insincere? Hard to tell for sure. Maybe Christ had transformed his you-owe-me attitude, but reform is usually a process. Could he have changed so quickly? Or was it the lure of a job with Lenora's foundation that led to his fake conversion?

Lord, give me discernment.

"I'm different, not just here." Kirk pointed to his head. "Here." He stabbed at his heart.

"I want to believe you."

That was as much as I could honestly say. Kirk had an engaging intensity in his outgoing personality. He might have made a great living selling cars. How much of what I hoped was Kirk's innocence came from a smooth professional con act? Did he take me for Miss Sweetie-Pie-Believe-Anything?

No silent sulking on his part, for which I was grateful. It appeared, at least, he'd opened up. I urged him to continue.

He recounted details of his prison Bible study. As I listened I kept seeing the image of my colleague working with him. I respected Lenora's efforts to create a positive change and had no doubt she was an excellent counselor. Her incredible, altruistic bent led to her foundation. But no counselor was infallible. Good counseling enlisted the force of a person's will to motivate change.

One more force helped—the Holy Spirit's supernatural power to achieve more than mere human will. Lenora had experienced the difference genuine Christian conversion makes. How many times had I told my clients, "You can change. You've got to want it as bad as your next breath, work like you're the only one who can make it happen, and pray daily for God's grace to help you succeed."

I studied Kirk as he shifted restlessly on the hard-backed chair. "So I connect with Christ and now this. I'm back in jail and if Lenora dies, I could be in prison the rest of my life. Is this how He treats people who trust Him?"

"Let's keep the blame where it belongs and try to figure out what happened. I get it, Kirk. It'd be stupid to shoot Lenora when she was helping you. In your Bible reading, have you come across Job complaining because of God's apparent abandonment? In the end, Job kept his trust in God, and the things he lost in life were restored. Check out his life."

"Lenora told me to read the Gospels, especially John." He brushed his hand across his eyes.

"Good place to start."

"Now how can I convince the police of my innocence?"

"Convince me first."

"Once and for all, it wasn't me." He raised his voice, and the guard in the corner hurried over.

I jerked my head toward the officer. "Calm down, Kirk."

"Problem, ma'am?" The officer was leaning over me, his badge bright and close.

"No, everything's fine." I stammered.

The guard glared at Kirk. "Keep it down."

To my relief he didn't take Kirk away. No way did I want to end this interview yet.

As the guard backed away, I prayed again for discernment. *Lord, can I believe what Kirk is saying? I don't like to trust my feelings because I know how flighty they can be, but I sense he underwent a genuine reform. You have plans for this man; what are they?*

I stared directly into his eyes. "When I walked in here, I didn't know what to think. I do believe when Christ gets hold of a life, good things happen, not bad. When He's at work, good can come out of even horrible events. If your commitment is sincere, it will be evident, and we'll beat this."

Kirk stared at me. Had his mind registered that he heard me say "we?"

Finally he spoke. "It's nice to have somebody in my camp," he stammered and pulled out a handkerchief to wipe his forehead.

"If you weren't the shooter, we have to figure out who fired that nearly fatal shot at Lenora."

"How can I help stuck in here?"

I lowered my voice. "Were there any other ex-convicts—either ones Lenora worked with or for some reason turned down helping—who might have been angry with her or the foundation?"

"None I can think of off the top of my head."

"When the police finish their investigation, they won't have enough evidence to hold you." *Let's hope.*

Kirk slumped forward. "Thank God." He started to cry.

This didn't appear to be the harsh, self-serving thief whose file I'd studied the other night. I often saw clients' tears during a counseling session. Crying didn't make me uncomfortable, not even these tears seeming to come from the depth of his soul. I longed to pat him on the shoulder but of course, couldn't touch him.

Tears or not, he still had a big test of trust to pass.

I waited several minutes until he collected himself.

"Sorry, not sure where that came from. I've been holding everything in for so long, it just sort of broke out, I guess."

"No problem. The tension of the last few days has to be incredible. Get some rest. I'll be back." I'd wanted to ask more questions, but he appeared wiped out.

I stood and motioned the guard over. He appeared at Kirk's side immediately to lead him back to his cell.

If Kirk had been acting, he was Oscar material.

CHAPTER TEN

THE REST OF the day, my brain bounced like a ping-pong ball between serving clients and focusing on the shooting. If Kirk hadn't shot Lenora, who had? The question reverberated over and over.

My computer database skills were minimal but sufficient for me to perform a basic search on the web for T. Hartford. An hour later I had no success, although I was sure the information was there somewhere.

Frustrated, I called Nick and asked him to arrange for his firm's investigator to locate the phone listing. A couple of keystrokes on his part, and I'd have it. Time was critical. Until the person who attempted to kill Lenora was behind bars, my friend wasn't safe.

I prayed for her again, refusing to think Lenora might never get off the ventilator and be able to provide clues to her assailant.

My cell phone vibrated within the hour. *Nick.*

"Hon, just e-mailed you a list of T. Hartford phone numbers and addresses."

"Good man. Thanks. It would have taken me half a day to do a thorough search and probably still produce nothing. Use all competent help available is my philosophy."

"That's why you married me. See you at home around six. You can give me my reward then."

"A go-between and you still expect a reward?"

"Of course."

I smiled as I put down my phone.

Before I examined the names, I called the hospital. The nasal-voiced ward clerk transferred me to the ICU waiting room. Luckily I caught Tucker.

"How is she?"

"Good news. Her blood gases are improving. They hope to begin to ease her off the ventilator."

"Great."

"They don't guarantee it will work. I'm afraid to be optimistic."

"Nick and I will be praying fervently. May it happen." I shut my eyes briefly. "Do you have another minute?"

"Sure."

"I'm sorry to bother you, but I need to ask you about a name I saw in Lenora's appointment book."

"Who?"

"T. Hartford. Does that ring a bell?"

A brief silence followed. "Yes, I recognize the name. Is he important?"

"So it's a man. I think Lenora was supposed to meet with T. Hartford the day before she was shot. What can you tell me about him?"

"I've never met him, but I know of him. Just a minute, please."

Murmured conversation droned in the background.

Tucker came back on. "The doctor just walked in to give me an update. What I have to tell you about Hartford is a long story. Can you meet me tomorrow for breakfast around seven at Barry's in Lake Geneva? I'll fill you in then."

He hung up before I could say fine. I assumed he knew I'd be there.

"YOU'RE QUIET TONIGHT, honey. Tough day?" Nick talked to my back. We'd just finished dinner. He sat at the table checking evening TV listings in the paper while I cleaned up.

"Just tired." I wiped the counter, clearing away the last particles of food left behind from dinner preparations.

"Let that go for a few minutes. Come sit with me."

"These microbes will hatch into something deadly if I miss them."

"Not a chance with you at the helm of this home. Want some help?"

"No, you cooked." I sighed. "Cleaning is a mundane job—life is filled with ordinary tasks, tedious and soothing at the same time. It's weird how straightening up things at home relaxes me. I only wish I could straighten out people's lives so easily."

"Like Kirk's? Tell me about your visit." Nick put down his newspaper.

"Where are the kids?"

"In their rooms doing homework, I think."

"Good. I can give you the details while the kids are out of earshot. They don't need to hear. The laundry can wait. Let's sit in the living room."

We settled side by side on the sofa. I slipped out of my faux suede slides and lifted my legs onto the coffee table. "Kirk seemed nice, after he loosened up. To start with, he acted like a zombie. I think because he was so scared. When he realized I sincerely wanted to help, he relaxed a bit and started talking."

"What's his story?"

"Says he never would have hurt Lenora. Her kindness made a huge impact on him. She's like a holy angel in his mind. He assured me she was his prison savior."

"How?"

"Softened him up, opened his eyes to opportunities around him. Got him to attend Prison Fellowship meetings that really benefitted him. Claims he made a decision to let Jesus transform him and he sees life differently now." I heard Jenny whoop with glee in the background. She must have finished her schoolwork.

"Good for him."

"I agree. If it's for real and Kirk seriously made a commitment to Christ, he's a brand new creation. Let's hope he's not using Christianity as a shield."

"Don't you think he's genuine?" Nick's question plunged into the recesses of my mind.

"I don't know. He seems sincere, but how can I be sure without knowing him better?" I ran my fingers across my forehead. "He's still a strong suspect. I read the notes Lenora had made for his job performance eval—pretty severe."

Nick's eyes widened. "What were his issues?"

"Not enough compassion. Lenora wanted him to convey more caring when he spoke to fellow ex-cons. Apparently he came across as rather judgmental and harsh."

"Makes sense his reformation would be a process." TV noise exploded from the family room. "Turn it down," Nick yelled before resuming, "and included would be forgiving himself for his former lifestyle."

"Well, if he didn't shoot Lenora, there's no shortage of potential suspects. Those regular editorials she wrote on prison conditions pushed buttons. Hopefully, Tucker can come up with actual hate letters she received if she kept them—which is doubtful."

"*And* if they're as severe as he stated." Nick leaned back, stretching his arms overhead. "People don't usually shoot you because they disagree with you."

I blinked. "No? Watch yourself, Nicholas Trevor. I expect perfect agreement at all times about everything." I playfully pounded his shoulder.

He yelled, "Husband abuse!"

I giggled. "Thanks. I haven't laughed all day. It feels good."

Nick wrapped his arms around me and squeezed "I know another way to make you feel good."

"Show me."

And he did.

CHAPTER ELEVEN

THE NEXT DAY I awoke at six and, while still reclining in bed, made a silent morning offering of thoughts, words, and deeds of the day to God. I prayed His protection on Nick and the children. My morning routine, down to a science, took twenty minutes including a quick shower, three minutes to apply makeup base and my favorite coral lipstick and blow dry my whip-it-and-go hair. I dressed in a beige linen suit with a white silk shell, dressier clothes than usual because I was scheduled to give a presentation to the Rotary Club on family mental health at noon.

I caught my image in the full-length mirror on my closet door. Too drab. I hunted for my blue, green, and beige scarf and draped it across my shoulders then rummaged in my jewelry drawer for a gold circle pin to hold it in place.

My movements were stealthy so as not to awaken the children. Today was one of my twice-a-week early-exit days while Nick reluctantly got the kids off to school. Playing Mr. Mom wasn't his favorite role. I was out the door for my meeting with Tucker before he and the children woke up.

Lake Geneva, our upper crust resort town of seven thousand people, has a gorgeous spring-fed lake at its center. The population swells like a pregnant woman every nine months to ten thousand-plus. Fontana on Lake Geneva and Williams Bay are Geneva's saucy little lakefront sisters, equally charming on a smaller scale.

I drove past the lake's vibrant waters that seemed to mysteriously slide into the sky at the horizon. Never did I tire of seeing this natural exquisite beauty. I often praised the Divine Artist who blends the colors of our world with such precision.

I parked halfway between the rustic Frank Lloyd Wright prairie-style library and the public Riviera Ballroom still touted as the place where big bands appeared during the war. The building now housed shops on its lower level. Together these structures assured continuing public access to the lakefront for locals and visitors.

My eyes roved the beach where resident ducks hunted for breakfast. There couldn't be a better place in the world to live. I breathed in the delicious air as I strolled toward Barry's café, following the smell of coffee.

Inside the packed restaurant I spotted Tucker in a rear booth. The thick aroma of bacon and eggs brought back memories of my deceased aunt's kitchen. She lived down the block as I was growing up and fed me every chance she got. How I loved her big breakfasts.

Tucker sat immobile, staring at an unopened morning paper. His left hand absently rubbed his coffee cup like a genie's lamp as I slid in across from him. The vinyl seat chilled my legs beneath my short skirt.

When he looked up his mouth curved partially into a semblance of a smile. "Thanks for meeting me this early. I don't want to miss seeing Lenora's doctor when he makes morning rounds. I need to be there by eight thirty."

"No problem. How did Lenora's day go yesterday?"

"She's still not out of the woods. We get more test results back today."

I searched his eyes, which remained expressionless. "It must be horrible seeing her so helpless—such a vivacious woman."

"Yes. Plus going home to an empty house without the energy her presence brings to it is like nothing I've ever experienced." Tucker cracked his knuckles. "I've always been okay alone at our Illinois apartment during the week because I'm busy at my job, but I'm not accustomed to being in our Wisconsin house without Lenora."

A harried teenaged waitress scurried over, balancing carafes of decaf and regular coffee near each hip. "Coffee, ma'am?"

"Decaf please." I slid my cup and saucer closer.

"Refill?" the waitress asked Tucker.

He set his palm over his cup. "I'm good, thanks."

As a semi-health food devotee, I ordered oatmeal, a bran muffin, and juice, fighting my urge for bacon. I sipped my coffee.

"Jennifer, it occurred to me yesterday that perhaps the bullet was meant for me."

I gulped, swallowed wrong, and coughed. "Does someone have a vendetta against you?"

Tucker lifted his shoulders to his ears and dropped them. "Not that I'm aware of but I can't understand why anyone would want to hurt Lenora." He sounded bewildered and angry at the same time. Who wouldn't be with a spouse on the precipice of life or death?

"I agree it doesn't make sense. Hopefully, she'll be responsive soon and able to tell us why someone would want to shoot her."

"If only... I so long to hear her voice."

I rested my elbows on the table, cradling the steaming coffee cup under my chin with both hands. My questions about T. Hartford could wait a few minutes. Brimming with sympathy, I asked Tucker, "Would you like to reminisce about her? I'm a good listener. I know very little about your history together. You met at the university, right?"

He nodded. "I was one of her students, although I'm five years older. When I came into her class, we connected instantly. Lenora had opened her home several evenings a week to students. I went every time and often stayed until the early hours of the morning. We had great discussions about similar interests. We both loved nature and the arts and dabbled in politics." Tucker looked up with wide, smiling eyes. "Did you know my wife was a radical feminist before she became a Christian and tamed down?"

"Radical? The label doesn't fit the Lenora I know—levelheaded, strong-willed, conservative is more appropriate." I added more sugar to my refilled coffee and stirred it.

"Lenora's early writings reflect her extreme positions. I respected her for her boldness." Tucker's conversation became more animated. "She weeded out students who didn't agree with her philosophy. Every topic somehow became a feminist issue to her. She was one tough lady."

He paused as the waitress set my breakfast platter in front of me. The smell of American fries at a nearby table made me wish I'd ordered potatoes too.

"Anything else I can get you?" the gal asked.

"Not right now, thanks." I resisted temptation and returned my attention to Tucker. "Did her strong feminist views make waves on campus?"

"Some. Certainly the rigid standards for academic performance she imposed on her students did. You asked me about T. Hartford." His chiseled mouth formed a rueful smile.

"Yes, you said you recognized the name."

"He was one of two male students who never finished their master's program on Lenora's watch." Tucker paused and rubbed one cheek. "Lenora was the person who recommended dropping them from the program. A couple of years later, she regretted the hoopla from that decision."

"Why were these two men excluded by her?" My words turned sharp, demanding. I wanted details. Motive was stamped all over his words.

"As a matter of routine, private interviews were held with each student. Lenora's standards were strict. She said she didn't believe Hartford had the compassion and patience necessary to be an effective counselor and refused to advance him for a practicum or even for continuance in the program. Fact is, she didn't like that he was an out-spoken macho male. Her decision bore weight. Unfortunately, there were hard feelings."

That sounded like the Lenora I knew—very principled, whatever her beliefs might have been at the time. My antenna perked up. "How do you know this?"

"Lenora was quite vocal about it. She said he complained to the dean. After his expulsion, he made a formal appeal to be reinstated and wanted her removed."

"What happened?"

"As a tenured professor, Lenora was safely entrenched. To question her rejection would have reflected poorly on the administration's endorsement of her as an instructor, so the chairperson supported her."

I leaned forward. "And Hartford...how did he respond?"

"Got rather squirrelly about it. Followed Lenora around and made threats. The police gave him a severe warning. That was the end of it, as far as I know."

"What about the other guy?"

"He never made a fuss. Didn't seem to care as much."

"How long ago was this?"

"Seven years, maybe eight. Shortly after we married, she went into private practice, and we moved up here and never heard from either man again as far as I know."

I pulled out a tiny notebook and pen from my purse. "Do you recall his first name? T. Hartford is all I have."

Frowning, Tucker took his time before answering, "Terrence, Tyler, Thomas…Hartford…yes, I believe Thomas was his first name."

"Thanks. I'll check this out. If he's still vindictive, we have another person with a motive. Unresolved bitterness can grow stronger over the years. I'm assuming they had some kind of meeting since his name is recorded in her appointment book. Have you told the police about Thomas Hartford's past stalking?"

"I'd forgotten about him until you asked. No need to bring him up anyway."

"I'm surprised they didn't check this out. They must have seen his name in her book just as I did."

"Why should they probe further when they have Kirk right at the scene with a clear motive?"

"I understand and certainly don't want to dredge Hartford up unnecessarily, but I'm not convinced that Kirk is Lenora's enemy. I'll see if I can come up with something more specific linking her former student with Lake Geneva. No sense dragging up the poor man's pain for nothing. While we're on the subject, is there anything else in Lenora's past that might be of concern?"

I would have sworn a shade dropped over Tucker's eyes before he answered. "Not that I'm aware of."

"Did you know Lenora's first husband?" I asked nonchalantly, trying to stay cold and logical.

"No. She was divorced before we met." Tucker waved the waitress over. "I'm ready for more coffee now, then the bill, please." He waited while she filled his cup then he added, "I gather from what she said, he was the argumentative sort. Although knowing Lenora, I'm sure she could hold her own and then some. Her first husband's alcoholism and infidelity were hard on her, but you probably know about that."

"Lenora and I lost touch for several years when I went into private practice. Soon after their divorce I understand her husband died in a drinking-related car accident. I never knew much about him, even though I'd asked her."

"How did she answer?" His big eyes scanned me like a laser.

"I still remember her words, 'Whatever's true, noble and good, I choose to speak of. He was none of those.'" I leaned back and pressed my fingers into my neck while contemplating her words. "She'd become a Christian by then and didn't want to rehash her past. I get that."

"Sounds like my wife. Lucky for me, she was willing to risk marriage again."

I looked up sharply. "Before you, she'd been quite against it. You must have been quite persuasive."

Red, the color of beets, flooded Tucker's face visible around his beard. I worked at buttering my muffin to avoid staring. He'd always seemed too distant and crotchety for my taste. What had Lenora seen in him? The man's usually granite features would have fit nicely on Mt. Rushmore. Maybe he was her rescue and fix-up project. I recalled her happiness during their private wedding ceremony. She hadn't verbalized any problems since. To each his own? I squared my shoulders.

Tucker sighed audibly. "We've had a great marriage. Moving to this area was her idea and a super one. Until now." He diverted his gaze from me to the copper kettles strung along a black iron rack suspended from the ceiling, then reached for a paper napkin to blow his nose.

I pushed my empty plate aside, giving him a moment to deal with his emotion. "What about your background. Anything there you'd like to share?"

Tucker shot me a surprised look. "Not much to tell." He refolded his newspaper. Perhaps he didn't like the question. Finally he offered, "I'd been married once before, too."

My eyebrows lifted. "I thought you were a bachelor when you and Lenora married."

His eyes held a sheen. "My wife ran off three months after the wedding. Left a note saying she didn't want to settle down after all. I guess being married to a stuffy research professor was too boring. Looking back, it was for the best. We had little in common. As an analytical researcher, I'm probably not the world's best communicator."

I gazed down and smoothed the vinyl cloth that had lifted at the table edge, holding back my agreement.

To my relief he didn't seem to notice my lack of response. "With Lenora, that changed. We wanted the same things out of life."

I imagined her excellent counseling skills drawing him out. "Was it okay with you that Lenora changed from being the strong-minded atheist feminist you first knew to a strong pro-life Catholic convert?"

He shrugged. "People change. I make jokes about her 'do-goodism,' but she knows I'm proud of her generosity to anybody in need. I'll admit though, she's more trusting than I am."

No surprise there. Lenora deeply loved God's people. "So you didn't share her enthusiasm for her foundation?" I could see into the open kitchen from our table. My eyes fixated on the one-handed egg crack of the counter chef adroitly preparing scrambled eggs.

"I approach life on the practical level. Change, like what Lenora believed happened to Kirk, well, I'm skeptical. And now with good reason."

Out of nowhere came a niggling wish. I longed to have Lenora's personal assurance that things were okay in her marriage, but that wasn't possible.

I checked the rooster clock on the wall. "I've got to run. Thanks for the info about Hartford. I'll let you know what I find out." I rose. "One more thing. Can I get a list of all the convicts Lenora has worked with this past year plus any who requested help that she had to turn down?"

"You're wasting your time, but I'll get the names. I'll double-check the list, based on my recall, to be sure it's accurate."

My head jerked up surprised. How would he know and why wouldn't it be correct?

"I don't want to email or fax such sensitive data. Stop by later."

CHAPTER TWELVE

I WHIPPED TOGETHER a spaghetti dinner for my family of five with the help of my personal chef, Ragu. Afterwards, with the children absorbed in homework, I tracked down Nick in front of the TV. "I need to run over to Tucker's place."

"What for?"

"To pick up Lenora's counseling notes on the gals I'll be seeing now that I have their permission."

"You want me to go with you again?"

"Thanks. I'll be okay."

Tara pranced into the family room exuding teenage oblivion to anyone but herself. Her sun-streaked brown hair held enough mousse to stick straight out an inch from her scalp.

Without pausing to check if we were in the midst of a conversation, she announced, "I need a ride to Ellie's. We're working on school stuff. Her mom will drive me home if one of you takes me over."

Nick pointed at me.

Tara shifted full focus in my direction. "Please, Mom."

Our girl could be sweet as honey when she wanted something. I doubted the schoolwork needed immediate attention, but Tara liked flitting about. I'd get an onslaught of reasons to oblige her in Nick's inherited persuasive style if I said no.

"No problem, I have an errand too, but don't make a habit of working at friends' houses on week nights. Can you be ready to leave soon?"

"Like now." Tara grabbed her books while I collected a sweater and my purse. She followed me into the garage. The large steel door lifted with my finger push on the button.

The second I put the car in reverse, Tara reached for the radio.

I put my hand over hers before backing out. "Whoa. Let's talk for a few minutes instead, sweetie. How was school today?" I tapped the remote on the visor, and the garage door groaned down.

"Fine."

Jennifer, what were you thinking? You teach parents not to ask questions with one-word answers?

"What's your homework tonight?"

"Studying for a test. I hate the subject. It makes me feel dumb. I'm no good at numbers or shapes, but I *want* to ace this test."

My competitive tiger. School studies seemed irrelevant to my crisis-filled counseling life, but I struggled to relate. "Go for it. Just remember A's are not absolutely necessary." I strategized with her while encouraging her. "You're wonderful in our eyes whatever your grades as long as you try your best in every subject."

Tara grinned. Her wobbly self-image sopped up my comment. *Lord, help me remember my children's emotional needs.* If only I'd heard more affirmations during my childhood, entering adulthood would have been much easier.

After a pause, Tara's tiny voice sliced through the air. "About Lenora, Mom. What happened to her made you so sad. It scares me that caring a lot for people means you can get so hurt. I've decided it's best not to have really close friends." Tara tossed her ponytail back and crossed her arms.

I reached over to press her hand and let mine rest atop hers. "You might want to rethink that. I read a book called *Confessions* by St. Augustine. It describes how he mourned the death of his close friend, Aeschylus. Augustine thought he'd never be joyful again, but in time he was. He honored his friend by living fully after his initial sadness passed."

"It's too hard."

I smoothed my palm over her fingers. "Friends are worth the effort."

"Maybe." Tara pulled her hand away, released the band holding her ponytail, and shook her hair loose. "Can I turn on the radio now?" She bent over and began fiddling with the dials.

"We're here." Tara's head popped up as I pulled into the blacktop circular drive of Ellie's ranch home. I kept the car idling while Tara walked up the steps and waited until Ellie opened the front door.

Tara waved at me, cupped her hand and shouted, "Her mom's driving me home, remember."

"Don't be late," I yelled through my open window.

TEN MINUTES LATER, I steered up the Tucker driveway as the trees splashed moving grotesque shadows inside my car. Soon the house emerged like a huge, lurking octopus. The sensor light came on at the garage where I parked. Tucker's car was nowhere to be seen. *Great, he's probably still at the hospital, and I'm alone here.*

A gush of cool air blasted my face when I stepped out. Goose pimples peaked on my skin. I'm a scaredy-cat in unfamiliar situations, but this was a familiar place. Why would I feel weird? Because I rarely came at night? Of course not, I knew why. Whoever shot Lenora that fateful night meant to kill her. I pictured him waiting in the woods. *Stop thinking about it, Jennifer.* My jeans and jacket blended into darkness as my Reeboks moved noiselessly along the path, cleared of leaves by strong winds. Why had I worn black?

I forced myself to move up the walk. Trailers for horror movies popped into my brain. I snapped my eyes shut to block the gore. How could I turn off my imagination now?

Self-talk. *Be not afraid, fear cripples. Replace panic with deep breathing and peaceful thoughts.* How many times had I recommended methods to reduce anxiety? "After all, you are a counselor, Jennifer." I spoke aloud. "Don't be a wimp. Tucker will be here soon. Get these names and go."

The problem with self-talk was my other voice spoke, too. *Idiot. Why didn't you arrange to pick these up in the daytime?* I smacked my forehead with my hand and answered out loud. "I couldn't get away. Besides, Tucker wouldn't be home. And since when is daylight totally safe anyway?"

I charged up the cedar steps leading to the porch, trying to manufacture confidence with speed. How silly was that? A ray of light flowed into the yard behind the house, probably from a kitchen window. Was Tucker home after all or did a timer control that light?

A spider's lavish web had attached to a wide black cow bell mounted next to the front door, illuminated by another sensor light. Bad location. I hated to be a home wrecker. I pulled the bell cord. A loud clang sounded. I waited. No one appeared.

Just in case the clanging hadn't been heard, I fist-knocked the door. No response.

A wooden swing on the porch provided a good vantage seat for waiting, after I brushed off a few twigs and leaves. Surely he'd arrive any minute.

To pass the time I scanned the night sky, locating the Big Dipper. As a child, stargazing brought consolation and comfort. I'd ducked into the back yard and hunted for it. I also sought out the Morning Star I'd read about in Scripture. I never found it, but the dipper was always there.

The groan of a motor and flickering headlights came up the winding drive.

"At last," I said aloud.

The car pulled into the graveled half-circle and parked. When the driver emerged, I strained to see, but my view was blocked by night shadows.

The sensor-controlled light in the parking area flashed on.

A lump formed in my throat. Instead of Tucker, a man of average height appeared. Who was this?

My isolated woodland setting made me squeamish. I cringed against the back of the swing, wishing I were invisible as I pulled my jacket tighter around me. In the dark, he couldn't see me. Not yet. And I wasn't going to call out. Primordial female fear kept me from announcing my presence.

The man stepped over to my empty mini-van and peered in. He walked around, checked the back window, then turned and surveyed the dim house and yard before stepping briskly toward the deck.

He spotted me and did a double take. "You startled me." His voice was cool, professional.

I startled *him*? "Likewise."

"I came to see Tucker. Isn't he home?"

I noted with some relief his business suit, button-down oxford shirt—surely not the latest in sniper attire. Although killers did wear suits in mobster movies, they weren't this attractive with a square jaw and intense blue eyes. He was a cross between Tom Cruise and Paul Newman in his prime. Thick hair, slicked back straight off his forehead, receded to leave half-moons at each temple.

My observation skills had kicked in, perhaps because we were at the scene of a recent crime. Was this man safe? Despising my hint of a stammer I responded, "I expect him any minute." I wanted this guy, whoever he was, to know we weren't going to be alone long.

He peered at me intensely. "You're Dr. Trevor, correct?"

He knew me? My spine prickled all over. "Have we met?"

Before answering, he mounted the deck steps and stopped at the rocker across from me. "I'm Chuck Denton, a member of the Second Chance Foundation's board. You were introduced at one of our fundraising dinners. We didn't have a chance to chat. You left early."

"Probably for kid duty." I forced a smile. "I have three." I proceeded to recite their ages as if he'd want or need to know. Being chatty—nerves, no doubt. I recognized his name at least from foundation literature. But I wasn't ready to shake his hand. Courtesy could wait for different surroundings.

Denton looked around. "It's weird being here after what happened, isn't it?"

"Exactly what I was thinking." I cleared my throat. "Tell me about your work on the foundation board."

"Pretty low key. We meet three times a year, not much real responsibility. We wouldn't be described as a working board because Lenora runs the show and does it very well. Or did." He glanced down as if apologetic for saying her name aloud.

I chuckled. "That's my colleague. She's a fireball."

"Right about that. Have you heard about her latest project?"

I shook my head. "I never could keep up."

He described in detail the halfway house being built for ex-convicts. "Unfortunately we're experiencing objections from some sectors of the community opposed to having former inmates in their neighborhood. That's got to change. There are several million people in prison in this country and ninety-seven percent of them will need a transition place when they get out."

"It's admirable Lenora saw the need in our community and stepped up. Terrible what happened to her though."

"A travesty," Denton agreed.

Tucker, where are you? I am done with small talk and need to get home.

Despite Denton's smooth talk, or maybe because of it, I wasn't getting good vibrations from him, but then I was off my familiar turf in the dark and he was a stranger. Still, my uneasiness deepened by the moment. I babbled on. "How long have you served on the board?"

"Six months. It's nice to be involved, even if I didn't volunteer. My bank requires community service from its officers."

"Good public relations."

"Yes, although we're taking some flack on this issue with the proposed house. I keep trying to smooth things over."

"How do you do that?" In spite of myself, I was intrigued.

"Mostly I talk up the value of the foundation as a charitable organization and help with fundraisers to garner financial support. When I was growing up, I had it pretty easy. It feels good to do something for guys not as lucky."

Denton appeared to be enjoying our small talk. I didn't. I wished I were home.

His positive words belied his tone. Something about his compassion level didn't register. I keyed in on discrepancies. I was trained to evaluate truth in clients' personal revelations. A headache began a drumbeat around my temples as I tried to figure this guy out. Why would he lie? I peered anxiously at the road. Where was Tucker?

Lenora knew compassion couldn't be faked. Had she thought Denton genuine?

To my immense relief, Tucker's car came shooting up the drive. He exited, slammed the door, and hurried over.

"Sorry I'm late. I wanted to stay until Lenora was settled for the night. She was more restless than usual. Have you been here long?"

"About thirty minutes. Mr. Denton kept me company."

Chuck Denton stepped forward, extended his hand, and made sympathetic remarks to Tucker. He ended with. "I wanted to extend my condolences in person. I'm so sorry about Lenora."

"Thank you. Come in, please, both of you," Tucker invited.

He led us into the kitchen. Tucker opened the briefcase he'd carried in. "Here's the list you wanted, Jennifer; I made two copies." He handed me two clipped pages but held another setback. "These are for the police. They called today for this info, also."

No need to tell Tucker I'd talked to the police chief, urging a wider investigation.

"Good. I'll check them against the list Nick had scrounged up for me to make sure we missed no one."

Tucker lowered his gaze. "I hesitated to give this information out."

"Why?" Denton asked, clueless about how personal these issues were.

"I don't want Lenora's other prison protégés dragged in unnecessarily."

"The police are discreet," I assured him. "And you know as a professional counselor, I will be too. Lenora's other client files will be safe with me. I'll be back for those as soon as I get every Consent to Release form signed."

Tucker lifted his eyebrows. Why? He knew I'd require them. He seemed reluctant to let anything of Lenora's go.

Denton interrupted us. "I need to be on my way." He handed me his card then turned toward Tucker. "If I can assist with anything, Tucker, please call." He hesitated. "I mean it. Anything, let me know."

"Thanks. That's very kind of you."

"It's what neighbors are for." Denton patted Tucker's back.

Out of the corner of my eye I noticed Tucker stiffen visibly at his touch. Strange man.

Tucker turned to me. "By the way, sorry you had to wait outside. I keep the place locked since the shooting. We rarely bolted the doors before."

"Understandable. I'm hoping Lenora will use more caution when she gets home." I spoke positively about her recovery for my sake and his.

"Not that locks would have helped protect her from a sniper like Kirk."

"Or whomever," I corrected.

"Right, mustn't prejudge. For all we know the shooter could have been someone from my past wanting to shoot me."

This was the second time he'd suggested he could he have been the target. What in this man's life made him think someone might want to murder him? Besides, couldn't the sniper see Lenora at her desk? Maybe the image was shadowy, and the sniper merely assumed the target was correct.

THAT NIGHT, AWAKE and waiting for Tara to return, I slipped out of bed, leaving my husband snoring softly. I couldn't fall asleep when our daughter wasn't in her bed where she belonged. When I looked at the clock, my stomach lurched. It was eleven-fifteen.

At eleven-twenty I called Ellie's. No answer. A shudder raced down my spine. Every nerve tingled.

Tara tiptoed in at eleven-thirty and began chattering the minute she saw me. "Ellie's mom had to do an errand at Wal-Mart. She said to tell you she's sorry we're late."

"Ten-thirty is your curfew on school nights. You should have called. We'll discuss this tomorrow."

Clearly the pressure from not knowing about Lenora and her shooter had heightened my paranoia.

CHAPTER THIRTEEN

THE NEXT MORNING, eager to get started on my research of ex-convicts Lenora worked with, I called Ellen into my office.

"Here's a list of the individuals. Get any current employment information available. Some addresses are hopefully accurate, others are incomplete or blank; we need relocation information, anything you can track down. The police will be checking these names, too, but we'll do our own investigation. With privacy parameters, we can't expect them to release information."

"Smart move on our part." Ellen grinned.

My pseudo-sleuth office manager loved when I said "we" and "our" and "us." She beamed at me. "I'll do my best."

I pushed up my sweater sleeves. "Tracing the ex-convicts still on parole with early release dates shouldn't be a problem. Those that served their sentence and have since taken off can easily slip out of the tracking system."

"What shall I say when I call?" Ellen's face, normally pale, looked radiant. In spite of the serious nature of our discussion, I chuckled. My gal read mystery novels like an addict.

"Just confirm the basic info. I'll make contact next to find out if any prisoner heard via the grapevine about a vendetta against Lenora before or since getting out. And I'd like to know if they have an alibi for the night Lenora was shot. Now I need my next client's file. Why isn't it on my desk?"

Ellen cupped her hand over her mouth. "Sorry, I forgot."

While waiting for my appointment to show, I called Tucker for an update on Lenora's health.

His deep, throaty voice sounded lighter. "The doctors tell me she's making progress."

"Great news."

"Now if she can sustain it."

"I have a question about the man I met last night at your house, Chuck…"

"Denton, a nice neighbor. He usually keeps to himself. I was surprised he came over. A good guy, an officer at the bank downtown and helpful to the foundation, although, he has some difficulties at home that limit his involvement. His wife's been ill, and he has a daughter to care for. What else can I tell you?"

"What's his wife's name?"

"Angela."

"I'm wondering if she's the woman I saw out walking the other day. Have you met her?"

"No. Angela's a recluse. According to Denton, the poor woman had a nervous breakdown before they moved here. Why?"

"Wouldn't it seem natural for Lenora to either befriend or counsel Angela Denton?"

"Didn't happen that I'm aware of."

"Okay, forget it. Could you request permission for me to visit Lenora? I'd like to be with her and pray."

"Sorry, still no visitors except immediate family."

"Let me know the minute that changes." I knew I failed to keep the disappointment out of my voice as I said goodbye. I longed to see my friend. The death of both my parents after extended hospitalizations was still a fresh memory. I opened the file on my desk and switched my focus to my next counselee for her benefit and mine.

Lenora, of all people, would understand.

NICK CALLED AS I was putting on my coat for lunch. "Glad I caught you."

"What's up?" My voice was terse, as I had barely enough time to get to Panera for a bowl of soup.

"Guess."

"Nick Trevor, you like games and quizzes more than me, remember."

"C'mon, try."

"Good news or bad?" It had to be good, or Nick wouldn't be teasing.

"Not sure how to answer that, but Kirk's out on bail."

I eased onto my desk chair and dropped my keys. "That fast? I mean, I'm glad for him, I think, just surprised at the timing."

"Nothing to delay it. No gun, no solid evidence, and he's got a decent lawyer acting on his behalf."

"Who put up the money?"

"Some guys from his church. Another guy from my men's group at church, Thad Turner, is giving Kirk a place to stay until this blows over and he can get another job."

"What about Kirk's work at the foundation?"

"Tucker won't let him back. He's pegged Kirk as guilty. You can understand his reluctance."

"Do the police really think Kirk's innocent?"

"Not necessarily. They couldn't hold him in jail on circumstantial evidence, but he's still a suspect."

"What's Thad's phone number? I want to stay in touch with Kirk to continue what Lenora started. I'm concerned about him getting despondent over her."

"I'll find out and e-mail it."

"Don't forget. I have a late client and won't be home until after dinner."

"Got it covered. The kids talked me into pizza. Afterwards I'll drop them at church for youth group in time to get to my class action briefing appointment. I can pick them up later."

"Thanks. A few peaceful hours alone sounds heavenly."

CHAPTER FOURTEEN

THE NIGHT AIR thickened into sticky fog by the time I hobbled through my front door shortly after seven. The misty weather matched the state of my brain.

I tossed together a dinner salad, layering pre-cooked chicken strips, diced pepper, and tomato wedges over chopped romaine. I drizzled it with peppercorn ranch and dug in.

Watching a house makeover on Home and Garden TV entertained me as I ate. Those work teams astounded me with all they accomplished in days. Where were contractors like this when I needed them?

After dinner, my body craved exercise. I switched into a gray sweat suit, laced up my yellowing, leather tennies comfortably creased in the right spots, and did a couple warm-up leg stretches. I slipped neon-orange bands over my wrists and selected my cap with the headlight. Having three kids gave me impetus to model safety habits.

The moist overhang of sky had lifted enough for me to run. Streetlights streamed decent visibility despite the giant shadows cast by huge elms. I breathed in the rain-fresh air of the woods as a delicious peace washed over me.

A few more warm-up stretches on my driveway and I headed off past my neighbors' homes, spaced on half to one-acre lots. Thick woods bordered both sides of our road. I could easily run the route blindfolded. As my ears adjusted to the sounds of the night, a rustling echoed through the trees, hopefully raccoons or woodchucks. My pulse picked up and then went down a few notches when I spied three deer lope across the road fifteen yards ahead of me. I paused in awe of the grace of these amazing creations of God.

I resumed jogging toward the unpaved area of new construction and had run about a mile, when crackling branches behind me jolted me from my pace. I turned but saw no one. Yet a sensation of eyes poking holes into my flesh unsettled me.

The running noise stopped when I did and restarted when I took up my pace again. Weird. A bead of sweat rolled off my upper lip. I tasted salt.

This path is in a safe neighborhood of custom homes, I reassured myself. I run here twice a week. All the same, prickles ran up my back. I've worked with rape victims enough to learn there's no such thing as a totally safe place. I considered turning back, but it would be shorter going forward to complete my circle.

Settle down, Jennifer. I hated the vulnerability women dealt with simply by being female. I faced real danger without flinching, but the unknown could put bumps on my skin.

I kept an eye on the path ahead of me, checking behind me every few minutes. I saw no one, yet the steps grew closer. My neighbors, mostly older people, were seldom out after dark.

When I made the turn onto Winston Street, a loud crack exploded behind me. I jumped. Was that a gunshot?

I picked up my pace but halted when my shoe struck a fist-sized stone on the path. I tripped and hit the ground hard with no time to break my fall. Pain seared through my shoulder, but worse was my jack-knifing ankle. Over the thumping of my heart I heard the pounding of feet running the other way.

My right hand stung. Daggers of pain ran up my ankle. Indentations of gravel were pressed into my palms. I tenderly dabbed at my forehead. To my relief no sticky, bloody substance, just a burgeoning goose egg on my temple.

I pushed down on my left hand, struggling to my knees. That was as far as I got. I commanded my body to get up but couldn't. How long I stayed there, I wasn't sure, but several minutes at least. Every time I tried to stand, I started sweating and breathing heavily then dropped back down in intense pain.

I searched my pockets. Why hadn't I grabbed my cell phone? Once again, I'd been in too much of a hurry. I chided myself, wasting energy.

Lights danced in the road. A car approached from the south, slowed, and then pulled off to the side of the road. My heart caught in my throat as a shadowy, darkly clad figure rushed over. I drew back until I saw it was a woman around my age dressed in jeans, tee shirt, and a denim jacket.

Concern darted across her face. "Are you okay?" she asked in a husky voice.

"Not really." Bathed in the glow of her headlights, I rubbed my ankle. "Nasty sprain I think. How graceful am I not!"

She smiled gently with soft brown eyes. "Been there, done the same thing."

"If there are no protruding bones it can't be too bad, right?"

She swiped at strands of brown hair, loose and shoulder length, blowing against her face as she bent over to help me up. "Lean on me. Can you put any weight on it?"

I winced with pain and shook my head. "Apparently not. It may be broken."

"You need to get it looked at."

I leaned against her car, nauseous from the sudden, intense pain. *Jesus, help me.* "I'll be all right in a minute." I said it aloud, more to reassure myself than her.

"Lucky I came along. I was driving back after dinner and saw you."

"Do you live nearby?"

"No. I'm here on a work assignment and stayed a few days extra for a little vacation." She held out her hand. "Name's Chris Lepsell."

"Jennifer Trevor." I offered a limp handshake. With every passing minute there was more certitude I needed medical attention. How would I get it? Nick was at a meeting. His calls would be fed into voicemail. The kids were at church youth group. Not only could I not get home to my car on my own, how would I drive to the clinic?

"I'm staying nearby at the Abbey Resort. I can either take you home or to the hospital ER if you'll direct me."

"Thanks. That's very kind of you." I studied my rescuer. Straight nose and intense eyes framed by smooth olive skin. About fortyish and around a hundred and sixty pounds. Her teeth were small and slightly yellowed. I smelled cigarette smoke on her clothing. Funny, I always noticed teeth and noses first on faces. "Williams Bay Mercy Hospital isn't far. If you're sure you don't mind, I'll take you up on your offer of a ride."

"Sure."

No sooner had I agreed than I panicked. This woman had shown up out of nowhere. I'd heard of people being kidnapped after a contrived accident and held for ransom. For someone terribly frightened ten minutes ago, I was being extremely trusting.

Stop the paranoia from TV news, Jennifer.

What choice did I have? No phone. No nothing.

Chris helped me into her car. I made nervous banter as I twisted in the passenger seat trying to find a comfortable position.

Another vehicle approached and slowed down. The driver stared then whipped his head in the opposite direction and sped up.

"Hopefully it's only a sprain, but a doctor can tape it up far better than my husband could." I huddled as close to the door as my seat belt would allow.

Chris turned the key in the ignition. "Now which way?"

"Turn on 67. Take it through Williams Bay to the corner of Highway 50. You'll see it on your right." Bile rose in my stomach, and I bent over clutching my arms across my chest.

"Are you okay?"

"A little queasy but I'll be all right."

Next time I looked up, we were at Mercy. Chris had driven directly to the ER entrance. Three wheelchairs, lined up under the overhang, waited like a welcoming committee.

Chris got out, grabbed a chair, and helped me into it while I assumed the role of a ninety-year-old invalid. I was too busy dealing with pain to protest as she pushed me to the registration desk. I breathed a deep sigh, grateful for assistance.

A curly-headed, fortyish blonde intake clerk with a harsh face that contrasted with the smiley face circle pin at her neck wasn't thrilled about registering me when I told her I didn't have my insurance card on me. Lack of medical I.D. required a check in the bowels of the computer bank to confirm I was a reasonable risk for bill payment. She sighed non-stop while her hands busied themselves on the keyboard.

A young man ran in behind me and dropped on the floor moaning. He managed to say, "I need to see someone immediately. I think I have a kidney stone."

The clerk glanced at him and said very calmly, "I'll be right with you."

I was about to tell her to make him a priority when she finished checking me in.

"Next time remember to run with your medical card between your teeth," Chris quipped as a nurse wheeled me to a curtained-off cubicle twenty minutes later.

A row of beds were separated from one another by canvas drapes on ceiling rollers. Nurse Sheri and an aide who appeared from nowhere helped me onto one of the narrow slabs covered with a white sheet. Hospital furniture designers must think only twig-like people needed medical attention.

The aide promptly swirled yards of white curtain with one swift tug along a thick aluminum track, shutting me off from the other curtained cubicles. Good thing. Voices chattered in the reception area. Things were starting to hum around here.

A dark-skinned female doctor, who appeared to be about thirty but could have been fifty, breezed into my cubicle. I described what happened in response to her questioning. She probed my leg, my ankle, and foot. I tried to decipher the long Indian name sewn on the pocket of her white jacket.

By now my anklebone looked like a ball of Silly Putty had been stuck under it. She ordered x-rays of my head, too, and used scary words like "possible concussion." I tuned out the possibilities of additional injuries running in my head.

"My head's okay; it's my ankle. I don't do concussions," I insisted.

She said nothing, turned her back on me, and disappeared.

I squeezed my smarting, blood-spattered hands into fists. They still hadn't given me so much as a Tylenol for pain.

The aide returned and wheeled me off to x-ray. I closed my eyes while pictures were taken. My first quiet moment to think. Had I been incredibly foolish or was someone chasing me? Could that *crack* have been a gunshot? I was certain those were footsteps running behind me. A sudden chill ran down my spine. Chris had appeared out of nowhere. Was that simply providential or strange?

The aide pushed me back to the reception area to wait for the doctor to check my x-rays.

Chris put down the People Magazine she was leafing through.

I tried to make small talk. "You said you're in this area for your work? What do you do, Chris?"

She hesitated a moment before answering. "Investigator for an insurance company."

"Sounds interesting."

"Not really."

"What kind of investigating?"

"Mostly confidential stuff."

"I see." Something about her seemed guarded. Was it my imagination? Before I could probe, the doctor sauntered in and interrupted us. "X-rays are fine. No ankle break or sign of concussion."

I inhaled deeply.

"We'll get you taped up and you can get out of here." She scribbled a prescription and shot off rapid-fire directions about heat and ice. "The nurse will give you initial meds to get you started. You'll need something for pain."

As if on cue, a nurse scurried over and handed me two aluminum foil packets with capsules inside and a disposable cup filled with water. "You're free to leave after you take these, if you can manage to walk on crutches."

"No problem. I'll call my husband to come get me. He should be home by now."

Chris jumped up. "Don't bother. I can drive you."

I hesitated. "Thanks, but let me try Nick first."

His voicemail came on. Annoyed, I ended the call. "Okay Chris, I'll take you up on your offer."

Outside, thick blackness covered the evening sky. I got the hang of the crutches fairly easily, and Chris guided me into her car. "Nothing like the first sweet breath of outside air after being in a hospital. It must be like the scent of heaven. And I insist that you're an angel." *I hope so, anyway, because I'm trusting you.*

She laughed. "Hardly."

"Where's home for you, Chris?" I fumbled a bit but managed to strap on my seat belt.

"Ohio, Buckeye State."

I mumbled a response, gave Chris directions, and leaned back against the headrest as exhaustion set in. My effort at conversation was over. I drifted into a light sleep. Whatever the doctor gave me for pain was working.

When the car stopped, my eyes opened, and my house came into view.

"I'm incredibly grateful for your help. I might still be crawling around out there somewhere. Tell me your last name again?"

Chris pulled out a hospital flyer entitled Blood Pressure and You. "I don't have a card with me. I'll write it on this. You may not remember tomorrow." She noted her name and room number at the

Abbey Resort. "I'll be here about a week. Let me know how you make out."

"Sure will." I folded the sheet into quarters and stuffed it into my pocket, making a mental note to send a thank you and flowers.

Chris came around, opened my car door, and put her arm around my waist to steady me into the house. She left after I repeatedly assured her I'd be fine.

In the comfort of my kitchen, I hobbled to the fridge, stuck a handful of ice cubes in a plastic bag, and rolled a washcloth around it before flopping onto a chair. I draped the cloth across my ankle.

By ten fifteen my ankle had swelled like I'd pumped it with an air compressor. *Lord, You know I don't have time to be laid up. What am I going to do?*

Nick and the kids came back at ten thirty and found me on the chair in the living room. They fussed over me when they saw the crutch at my side. I reveled in their tender hugs and solicitous attention. Tara brought me a pillow. Jenny said not to worry. She could go to bed on her own.

"Sweetie, what a night." Nick laid his hands gently on my taped ankle and prayed for a complete and rapid healing.

"Yes, heal me up quick, please, Lord," I added when he finished. "And Lenora, too."

I've witnessed enough of the healing power of prayer to believe God still heals, but His heavenly timetable and method wasn't always the same as mine. And I knew sometimes healing was heaven-side.

When Nick and I were alone, I confided my fear during the run. "I was in a vulnerable position when I went down. Why didn't the runner show up then?"

"The woman, you said her name was Chris, perhaps her sudden arrival scared off the person following you."

"Or, I imagined everything. I have been under immense strain lately."

Nick assisted me onto the bed and assured me nothing irregular had happened. If only that were true. I snuggled joyfully in his arms, grateful for pain pills but remained unable to throw off the fact that the night had clearly been a warning.

CHAPTER FIFTEEN

MY PRESSING QUESTION as I rolled around in bed at seven the next morning was whether I could handle my client schedule at the office. My ankle pain had subsided, but I was nowhere near a hundred percent. I moved my foot, wiggled my toes, and decided the discomfort would be manageable. My brain hosted a light layer of fog from the pain pills but not enough to keep me from being functional.

I reached for my iPhone on the bedside table and opened to my calendar.

The sound of Nick washing up in our bathroom made me feel guilty. Poor man had to be tired. He'd managed to keep my ankle iced off and on during the night and brought me painkillers every four hours.

He emerged, clad in a towel. Moisture steamed into our bedroom with him.

"Oh no you don't, Mrs. Trevor. Back to sleep with you. You need lots more rest."

"Thanks, hon. I think I'll be fine."

"Thinking won't cut it."

"Nonsense. I intend to go to my office. Kirk's due in. Don't forget, I sit most of the day. If it's too uncomfortable, I'll cancel my afternoon appointments and come home." I added that to pacify him.

Under protest, not the least bit disguised and mumbling all the while, Nick drove me to my office.

Ellen mouthed more words of concern as she rearranged chairs so I could keep my ankle elevated. I promised to take my meds every four hours to keep the pain and my caregivers at bay.

Providentially, my second client of the day cancelled. I had no doubt how to use this unexpected free time. "Ellen, bring me my file for T. Hartford."

She hurried back and peered over my shoulder as I opened to the list of eleven possible numbers. "Can I help?" Ellen glowed. "I could come up with a good story to get information. We need to be sneaky to find out anything."

This was clearly feeding Ellen's inclination for detective work.

"No, but thanks, amateur sleuth. I can handle the calls, and I refuse to lie. You know I despise deceit."

"If you don't fudge a little, how can you find anything out?"

I closed the folder and held her eyes with mine. "I'll start like this: 'Hello, Mr. Hartford. This is Jennifer Trevor. I'm contacting University of Wisconsin Whitewater Counseling Program alumnae. Is it correct you attended the University?"

"And if he says yes?"

I smiled. "Haven't got that far but you can be sure I'll pray about what to say next. Now, it would be lovely to chat, but I'm sure you have work waiting at your desk."

Ellen shuffled out, shoulders drooping, as I picked up the phone.

My first calls to T. Hartfords on the list had disappointing responses. "Sorry wrong number." and "No one here by that name." Two phones were no longer in service.

On the sixth call, to Woodstock, IL, a leathery-voiced, sweet older man said in response to my questions, "Sure, me and my son, T. Hartford. Named after me. We both attended University of Wisconsin. Fine school it used to be; not sure about it anymore." He referred me to his son, T. Hartford Jr., in Virginia. He would have continued talking, but I hurried him off the line.

When I called the son's number in Norfolk, a male voice answered. "Thomas Hartford here."

A chill crept up my spine. I squeezed the phone. "Hello. I'm researching what graduate students from the University of Wisconsin are doing after leaving the University counseling program."

"I didn't graduate." His tone was icy and abrupt.

Bingo. My heart skipped. Before he could hang up I hurriedly responded, "No problem. That's not a criteria."

"Strange. Nobody cared about me when I was there. Why now?"

I prayed for the Holy Spirit's guidance and heard myself opting for transparency. "My name is Dr. Jennifer Trevor." I gave him Lenora's name and described our relationship. "You were her student?"

Hartford sucked in air before answering, frosty and sarcastic. "In another world."

"I understand you had a professional conflict with Lenora. I'd appreciate hearing the details from your perspective." I tried to sound kind but professional, praying he'd talk.

"Whatever for? What is this about?"

"I'm investigating Lenora—"

"I'm not discussing Lenora with you or anyone. If you're digging through University records for a class action lawsuit against the woman, I'm not interested."

Great. How to get past his defenses? "It's nothing of the sort."

Giving him the complete status on Lenora, straight and simple, remained my only chance. "Mr. Hartford, Lenora's been shot. She's in critical condition even as we speak."

Dead silence.

"Are you still there?"

"That's an unfortunate circumstance, but it has nothing to do with me."

"I understand you and another student had grievances against Lenora."

"Many years ago. I prefer to forget the incident and suggest you do the same." Thomas Hartford spoke with authority. A shame I couldn't respect his wishes.

"You saw her recently... I'd like to talk with you in person about that visit. We're trying to reconstruct the time period before she was shot."

"Why should I consent to such a thing?"

"It's in your best interest. I don't believe the police know about your association. I expect you'd prefer me in your living room rather than them. Your cooperation will be a sign you have nothing to hide."

Silence again. Was he evaluating my words like a poker player?

"What did you have in mind?"

"Thirty to forty-five minutes, max. I'll be in Virginia the end of the week and would like to come by your home. Is seven thirty Thursday night convenient?"

"I can't believe I'm agreeing to this, but I will see you. Make it eight. We're having a house party. I can slip away, briefly." He emphasized the last word before hanging up.

I jotted the time on my calendar. This trip to Virginia with Nick could fit into my schedule. I would need for Ellen to rearrange a few appointments.

The rest of the day flew by. By five I was exhausted, nowhere near done with my paperwork and still had another appointment.

At five thirty my cell phone vibrated. "Where are you? I thought you were leaving early." Nick's voice sounded testy.

"Didn't you get my voice mail? Kirk's coming in for a counseling session. I'll be home at seven." To soften his irritation I added, "Honey, good news. Want to guess? It's your turn."

"No way, not with the world's most unpredictable woman."

I chuckled. "I'm accepting your invitation to travel to Virginia Beach with you for the American Justice Center Legal Conference."

"That's great." Nick was obviously pleased. My man loved having me travel with him whenever I could. "What made you change your mind?" Suddenly he sounded wary. "Last week you said you had too much going on."

"Well, I do have an additional reason. While you're at the conference, I've arranged a meeting with Lenora's former student, Thomas Hartford."

"Isn't that the man whose name was in her appointment book?"

"Yes. I'll drive to Norfolk to question him. It's only thirty minutes from Virginia Beach."

"Why do you need to meet with him? Talk to him on the phone."

"It's a long shot but worth checking. I want to watch his reaction in person to assess him as a suspect. He had a beef against

Lenora—festering wounds and resentment from an old grudge. He could have hired the man who shot Lenora or done it himself."

"If that's true, you could be in danger."

"You don't understand psychology. His vendetta against her was for a particular situation. I doubt he's a serial shooter. Don't worry. Besides, lots of other people will be around. He'll have a party going on while I'm there."

Nick scoffed. "Oh, that's very reassuring. You're a married woman and the mother of three children who need you. Will you please remember that?"

I sighed. When Nick got like this—hungry, tired and annoyed that I wasn't home for dinner—there was no talking to him. I understood, but still didn't like his response.

"I'm sure this visit is just routine to rule Lenora's former student out."

For his sake and mine, I hoped Hartford was innocent.

CHAPTER SIXTEEN

KIRK WAS TEN minutes late for his appointment. He'd been late for his meeting with Lenora, too, the day she was shot. A prickle raced down my spine. I'd just counseled a woman who'd been raped in her office. Not conducive to settling my nerves.

I filled a cup with water to rescue the ivy plant on my bookshelf and poured liquid life over its suckling roots.

The distressed client who'd just left still suffered panic attacks two years after the tragedy. Once a violation occurred, it was difficult but not impossible for a woman to ever feel safe again. I used every which way I could to reassure her she could move on with her life and ended with a prayer that seemed to soothe her. *Lord, help her; she needs inner healing.*

I settled into my chair, resting my elbows on the desk, to write up her progress notes. My sympathy surged out to women who have experienced physical violation. Some never wanted to leave their house afterwards. Although staying home alone didn't make them feel secure either. It was as if there were nowhere safe.

My recent feeling of panic during my run was still fresh. The lump at my temple had flattened, leaving a black and blue effect as if I'd been stamped with an inkpad. As long as I wore flat shoes, I could walk without limping, though my ankle remained slightly swollen and tender.

I now identified fully with the panic feelings clients described. I tried to verbalize what came over me—smothering fear that what happened to Lenora could happen to me. I shook my head. *Mustn't dwell on that.*

I'd finished writing and was pushing the file aside as the door opened and Kirk strode in behind Ellen. He eyed my office as if sizing it up for a prison break, circling the room twice before choosing the chair closest to the door.

In response to my hello, Kirk's face worked itself into an ugly glare. I noted his day's growth of beard. Maybe he didn't feel like he belonged to the daily-shave class yet. At least he'd dressed neatly in a short-sleeve broadcloth shirt and belted black jeans.

Ellen scurried back to her outer office. I fought the urge to follow her.

Instead I said, "You seem uneasy, Kirk. Are you okay being here? I mean, it's not scary is it? You've had counseling before and have an idea what to expect at least."

He shot me a cold stare. His voice when he finally spoke resembled a growl. "Truth is, I don't buy this counseling crap. How can talking fix hurts from the past? Words aren't worth a..." He caught himself. "...a darn."

I forced a smile. *Then two of us are not completely eager at this moment, Kirk.* I kept my reaction, hardly a professional response, to myself. "I hope you'll give our counseling a chance and begin to trust me as you did Lenora." I felt like a pediatrician talking a child past normal immunization age into getting shots.

"Whadda you expect you can do?" He spoke with the enthusiasm of a rapper at a violin concert.

I picked up my notepad. "Let's get underway and see." I swiveled my chair closer to him. "I know the basic data on your adult life from the foundation's file, Kirk. A brief walk through your earlier years might be helpful. Let's start with your first clear memory?"

Kirk's face darkened. He sat silent a few seconds. "That's easy. Dad beating Mom is my strongest. Sorta became his weekend sporting event." His tone was almost matter-of-fact, but his pain was palpable.

"How terrible for her and you, Kirk. Did she ever report him?"

"No. A couple of times neighbors reported a ruckus. Whenever the police came, Mom would deny what happened, never pressed charges. Dad musta known she wouldn't 'cause he kept at it."

I shook my head. "How sad." Stories like this were way too common.

"When I was fourteen I had enough size on me and got the nerve to fight him. I'll never forget his look the night I pulled him off Mom. He threw me across the room, but I came right back at him and let him have it good. He woulda known the day was coming, if he wasn't so dumb."

"Was he a drinker?"

"Binged mostly on weekends. Drunk, he was no match for my size and strength."

"What happened after you beat him up?"

"Scared the… I mean, scared him good. I didn't just beat him; I threatened to kill him if he touched her again. He left, and we never saw him again. As far as I was concerned, he died that night because I wished him dead and wanted him to be." Kirk narrowed his gaze, maybe checking to see if I was shocked.

"Then what?"

"My mom, my sister, and me stayed together a couple of years. Funny thing, after a while I became as much of a tyrant as my dad, except for I never hit either of them." He lowered his head. "When I was fifteen, Mom had enough of me. My sister was older than me, and she'd already taken off. I don't remember much else about family stuff."

"Have you been able to forgive your dad for the way he hurt you, most likely not even knowing the harm he was doing to his children?"

"Forgive?" He rubbed the hair on his forearm. "You had to bring that up. When Lenora visited me in prison she talked about forgiving all the time. Said I had to or I'd be drinking poison every day. Wouldn't ever be free inside or be able to help others."

"And?"

"Dunno. I had a lot of thinking time in prison. Even went to a retreat inside. A priest heard my confession and helped me see that my old man was doing the best he could. I let it go at that." Kirk looked up sharply.

"And your mom?"

Hardness formed in his facial expression. Had it reached his soul? "Moms are supposed to be kind and gentle and loyal. Mine wasn't."

"She gave you life, didn't abandon you, kept you fed and cared for until you could provide for yourself. That's huge."

"Isn't that what moms are supposed to do?" He fiddled with the stretch band on his watch, an old scratched Timex, snapping it in and out.

"Not all do." I shook my head slowly and sighed. "But we try to forgive them."

"Mine turned me out as soon as she could. I read in the Bible respect is what kids owe parents. I tried to forgive, but I'll never forget. You make it sound like something simple. It's not." Kirk twisted in his chair as if trying to wiggle out of his emotions.

"I don't mean to make it appear like it is. Relationships are tough, but they do get easier when you strip layers of blame away. It's incredibly hard, but if you can focus on the good God puts in people and choose to forget the bad they did, you'll be a lot healthier and happier."

"I said I forgave her. Lenora knew 'cause I told her."

"Good. Did you have any other family close by? Aunts, uncles, grandparents?"

"None I knew. Hey, my immediate people were problem enough."

"How did you support yourself when your mom put you out on the street?"

Kirk pushed up his shirtsleeves revealing a curvaceous, tattooed purple lady decorating his muscular forearm. He flexed his muscle, and she moved. "I fended for myself, whatever it took. I never went hungry. I worked the streets with a buddy. I learned fast, had to or I wouldn't survive. It's not my fault I got screwed up. What else was I supposed to do?"

This wasn't the time to bring up homeless shelters or church outreaches. "Kirk, you certainly had a lousy childhood. I don't want to minimize that. However, I don't buy the victim theory. You're responsible for choices you made messing up your adult life. A bad start isn't an excuse. People shake childhood abuse and dysfunction to become solid adults. We all stand before God to give account of one life—ours. Lenora must have told you this."

"Yeah, I heard it." Kirk looked me square in the eye for the first time. "Plenty."

"What about other female relationships in your life?"

"I had a few girlfriends I crashed with off and on. Even got myself married in Chicago after a spell, but it didn't last."

"Why?"

"Let's just say, my career got in the way. Angie stood by me for a year, then left. Who'd want to stay with a loser like me?"

"I'm sorry."

"Said she'd take me back in a minute if I'd straighten up but wasn't gonna put up with what I made her live through no more." Kirk brushed the back of his hand across his eyes.

"Sounds like a good woman."

His tone softened. "She was. Not 'till Lenora came along did I get it. Lenora helped me; I gotta admit. Talked to me about stuff like self-dignity, achievement, and God making me for a purpose. By then it was too late for Angie." He looked down.

Lenora's warm voice echoed clearly in my head. My eyes blurred with tears, but I forced myself to concentrate on Kirk. "Where's your ex-wife now?"

"She died in a car accident six months ago." Kirk pronounced each word slowly like it was a knife cut. "Wouldn't have been in that car if it weren't for me. Woulda been home where she belonged."

"I'm so sorry. You can't blame yourself for what happened to your wife." I dropped my pencil and bent to retrieve it to hide the image flooding my face. *I hope you're not responsible for what happened to Lenora either.*

"I realize now how much she mattered to me. I'd give my right arm to have her back." Kirk pulled out a handkerchief and blew his nose. "I ended up in prison soon after Angie left me. They treated me like scum in there because I'd raped a woman once when I was drunk. Nobody'd talk to me."

"When did you run into Lenora?"

"Inside the joint my last time." Kirk shifted his legs toward the left side of his chair.

Guilty reaction? The words popped into my brain.

He studied his hands. "Is she doing any better?"

"Still touch and go." I swallowed hard and rubbed my palm across my forehead, hating that my vibrant friend was connected to a mechanical breath-maker. "Tell me about your sessions."

"She'd listen to me rant. Eventually Lenora linked me up with a guy from Prison Fellowship. He told me about this Jewish carpenter named Jesus who loved sinners of all types, no exceptions, and already died to serve my sentence for everything I did wrong. Weird, huh?"

"And wonderful." I fingered the cross I wore around my neck.

"The guy gave me a Bible. I read it cover to cover, several times actually. First book I ever finished. The words of Christ got through to me, and I became a Christian. Lenora helped me understand what I read. She kept telling me, 'You're a human being created in the image of God; you're worth something. It's time to start acting that way.'"

A thrill swept down my spine. "Absolutely."

"Yeah, so look what became of her. Check out the two women in my life who tried to help me. One's dead; the other's in a coma. I feel like I should wear a warning sign. Contact with Kirk Corsini is dangerous." He patted his breast pocket where a pack of cigarettes was sticking out. "Is smoking okay in here?"

"I'd rather you didn't, if you don't mind."

He folded his hands in his lap. "I need to quit anyway. You should know helping me, something bad might happen to you. You better be careful."

His words startled me. Was that a warning or a show of concern? "I'll take my chances. Regardless, my welfare is not your responsibility. You do need to take charge of yourself, though."

"Sure haven't done a good job of that, have I? The police are itching to pin Lenora's shooting on me and put me away for life."

"If you're innocent, you can fight and win, Kirk."

"What chance do I have?"

"With God, there's always hope."

He sighed. "You sound like her. Lotta times Lenora told me 'You've always got a prayer.' Now she's on her deathbed. What kinda God would allow that?"

An answer popped into my head, but I chose not to say it aloud. *One who sacrificed His own Son for you.* Instead I asked, "Kirk, is there anything else I should know about your life story?"

"That's it. Not much of a story."

I smiled. "Bad choice of words. Let's talk about the evening of Lenora's shooting." I looked down, scanning the file in my hands for his arrival hour at Lenora's.

"All I know is I was set-up. I just got out of prison a couple weeks before."

"Who might have been aware ahead of time you were going to be at Lenora's the night she was shot?"

He shrugged. "Nobody I know. Had to be someone from the foundation."

"Anybody hold a grievance against Lenora? Did she help any convict who then turned on her?"

Kirk twisted in his chair. "I been thinking 'bout that. Most people I know liked her, 'cept maybe one. Russell might have held a grudge. She wouldn't give him a small business loan. Said the foundation wasn't set up that way. He got pretty mad. Truth is I didn't blame him."

"She'd have wanted ex-cons to learn personal financial responsibility. Giving money doesn't foster that." I jotted down Russell's name.

Kirk saw me writing. "I doubt he'd hurt her though," he added hastily. Kirk's hands began to tremble. "Lenora's gotta make it out of that hospital. If she dies, I'm a goner." He cleared his throat. "She's gotta recover and tell who really shot her. I don't mean to sound as if I don't care about her. It's not like that."

"I bet there's a lot of things you don't mean. It's good to be aware of what you say and how people interpret things, Kirk."

"People like Lenora shouldn't get hurt when they're so good to others. Forget about me trying to forgive the guy who shot her."

"Why are you sure it's a guy? Do you know more than you're telling me?"

"Would a lady do something like that?"

I tilted my head. "I don't see why not."

CHAPTER SEVENTEEN

THE NEXT MORNING, I called the hospital first thing. Tucker had added me to the list of people who could receive updates on Lenora. To my delight she could have visitors for brief visits even though still on a ventilator and heavily medicated. Maybe my presence in itself could cheer her, plus I wanted to pray for her in person.

With the van windows rolled down, I inhaled the fragrant autumn leaves. Nick's favorite season is fall. Mine is summer, full bloom, and total life. Fall reminds me of change and death. *But signifies new life to come,* God nudged into my thoughts.

I passed a girl in a farm field, probably six or seven, picking poppies. Around her age I'd plucked poppies from our garden and twisted them into necklaces. Flashy red fire gems I wore with my shoulders back, head high and haughtiness worthy of the Hope Diamond. I'd also stuff a handful of stems into my fist and hold them like a bride's bouquet, thinking they were more exquisite than any in the florists' windows. Having alcoholic parents meant I spent a lot of time alone with my imagination.

The present thudded back as I approached the medical center. The hospital was undergoing expansion. Construction trucks were everywhere. Finding a spot in the visitor's lot took twenty minutes.

I'd already sent a flowering plant to Lenora's room but didn't want to visit without bringing another reminder of life. The sweet clerk inside the hospital gift shop appeared to be at least eighty. Her powdery skin was smooth like chalk, and her hair the color of honey. She greeted me with a warm smile. Permanent smile lines around her eyes etched a history of good humor.

Her ID tag read, Alda, Hospital Volunteer. She finished cleaning her eyeglasses, straightened to full height, smoothed her pink smock, and stepped from behind the cash register.

I smiled at her. This is what I wanted for Lenora and myself, too. To grow old while still serving people.

"May I help you?" Alda leaned forward to be of service.

"I'd like to take you home to be my grandmother."

She laughed in a voice smooth as exquisite silk. I asked her recommendation for a bouquet of their freshest flowers.

"You're in luck. We got a shipment of roses this morning." With fluttery hands, she opened the cooler behind her and pulled out a bumpy pea green vase filled with delicate peach roses circled by baby's breath.

"What a perfect arrangement. I'll take it." I rubbed my fingertips across a smooth rose petal.

Alda counted my change twice. "Sorry for the wait. I don't want to have any errors in the gift shop cash register during my shift."

"No problem." I savored the peaceful interlude of a few moments to transition myself mentally for my visit.

At the hospital information desk, an elderly gentleman with a congenial air directed me toward the elevator row at the end of the hallway.

The silver doors opened when I approached. I pressed eight and held my breath until the steel cables reached my floor. At what age had riding in an elevator stopped being a thrill?

Following the maze of arrows, I found the ICU wing. A curly headed blonde ward clerk pointed me toward Lenora's location and gave me permission for a ten-minute visit.

A sense of dread dropped over me, and my chest tightened. I mustered my willpower to tiptoe into the eerie maze of electronics maintaining Lenora's life. One machine's control panel looked intricate enough to fly a plane. It rhythmically inflated her lungs like balloons being pumped for a children's party. I forced myself not to cry. Lenora's face appeared twenty years older than when I'd last seen her.

I couldn't hug her with the apparatus attached but planted a light kiss on her cheek. Her skin was hot and lifeless. I cringed.

A tan vinyl and chrome lounger beckoned me from the corner. The sooner I got into a sitting position the better.

Lord, let her live. Lenora's dying wouldn't be right. Only a full lifespan was acceptable for my friend. Yet God's idea of what's best often differed from mine. I didn't pretend to understand the timing of death. Life on earth with no aging was my preference and then entering heaven all at once with those I loved.

Wishful thinking. God was in charge. The fact that He lengthened ancient Hezekiah's life fifteen years as a result of prayer inspired me, so I always prayed for more life. I sensed a hovering dark presence in the room. With authority I said, "Death, you cannot have her. Get out."

A teardrop formed in the corner of Lenora's eye. Did I imagine it? I called for the nurse.

A ruddy-complexioned woman in white slacks and yellow sweater appeared. "Was that you buzzing?"

"She's crying. See." I pointed. "Does that mean my friend's coming out of her coma?"

"She's heavily sedated to keep from struggling against the machine. The tear must be an autonomic response."

"I don't think so." My voice sounded loud and frantic. "How long must she be on it?"

"I'm sorry. You'll have to ask her doctor." The nurse gave me a sympathetic smile. "Are you aware you can only stay ten minutes at a time?"

I nodded.

She approached Lenora's bed to straighten the sheets and reposition the pillows, making her more comfortable before leaving the room. Reports of people emerging from a comatose state who said they'd heard every word spoken around them popped into my mind. Was there a tiny chance Lenora could hear me and understand? I ignored her physical state, forgot my emotions, and spoke normally.

I stroked Lenora's arm and in fact chattered like a Chatty Kathy doll, first about the Second Chance Prison Foundation and then work. I wished she could turn my way, instead of being immobile, confined by mechanics. Resting my hand on Lenora's, I prayed, "Lord, make every cell in Lenora's body as healthy as it was the day of her birth."

Silence settled into the air. I sensed the presence of the Holy Spirit with Lenora and me like a third friend. I relaxed in a chair, closed my eyes, and sought comfort and healing for Lenora in this frightening place.

I lost track of time. Too soon the nurse returned. "Time's up." She smiled.

A heavy weight descended on my shoulders. "Couldn't I remain a bit longer?"

"If you wait fifty minutes, you can visit for another ten."

I checked my watch. The paperwork in my briefcase could be done here as well as at the office. Now that I was finally with my friend, I wanted all the time I could get.

"The waiting room is just off telemetry." The nurse spoke kindly and gestured toward a door down the hall on the left.

"Fine. I'll be in there."

The eight-by-ten room, mercifully empty, would serve well as my office for an hour. I sat on a comfortable tufted chair, clicked on Fox News for the murmur of background noise, and pulled out paperwork to review.

I began to read but soon the page blurred in front of me. My head drooped toward it, and I jerked upright. As I floated in and out of sleep, eventually I stuck my work back into my case and leaned back. The strain of this visit had been greater than anticipated.

Almost an hour passed before a nurse slipped in. "Excuse me, Ms. Trevor. You can return to Ms. Lawrence now."

I shook my head groggily to clear my mental fog. "Thanks." I stood, stretched, and took a deep breath before following her to Lenora's room. This time the hulking ventilator seemed less intimidating. Was it possible to get used to things like this?

"Not to worry, Lenora," I said when we were alone. "You're going to be fine. Tucker is holding the fort until you return. The sooner the better."

Lenora's eyes were open, focused on the ceiling. If she understood, she gave no indication. I chattered on anyway. "You'll be off this contraption soon. Modern medicine is phenomenal; you're getting excellent care here." I searched my mind for other phrases to encourage her. "Tucker is holding up well but is very concerned about you."

I stared at her glass-like eyes for any glimmer of recognition.

Nothing.

"The foundation needs you. I'm making myself available for your clients, but I know they'd prefer you..." I paused. "Squeeze my finger if you understand any of this."

The beeper on Lenora's IV pole went off, startling me. Still she didn't squeeze my finger.

The nurse hurried in and switched bags of IV fluid. As she adjusted the flow, she explained to Lenora what she was doing. Nurses were expected to speak to comatose patients as if they were alert. I'd been doing the same thing, so it didn't surprise me. "Lenora, your brother called to check on you. He sends his love."

I stared at the nurse, my mouth agape.

Focused on her patient, the nurse continued. "He wanted a report on your condition." She turned on her rubber soles, brushed past me and out the door.

I jumped up following her into the hall.

"Lenora doesn't have a brother," I stammered. "She always jokes about being an only child."

"That's weird. Musta been some kind of mistake."

"Did this man leave his name?"

"No. Said he'd call back later..."

"Please listen carefully. This is very important. The caller could be the sniper checking on her physical status. Tell your supervisor to contact the police. They need to get a guard here immediately. Now that this person has confirmed her location, Lenora may be in danger."

The stunned woman hurried off with bulging eyes. I returned to Lenora's room.

"Lenora, dear." I kissed her on the forehead. "You keep fighting. My time is up, but I'll come again. We need you with us. I love you."

My lips quivered. Why had I never told my friend I loved her, when I truly did?

Trudging down the corridor toward the exit, I passed several other glassed-in telemetry rooms, each with a mechanical arsenal fighting the hovering enemy of death.

Family members moved in clusters in and out of loved one's rooms, startling at every beep of the IV.

I felt guilty for all the times I let minor troubles bother me in relationships with people I loved. At every moment, day or night, beloved people in hospitals were fighting for life.

Lord, except for Your grace, how could we endure such emotional and physical pain? How horrible to be suspended between life and death as Lenora is. Heal her, please. Dying isn't a bad thing; I expect heaven to be wonderful, just not yet for Lenora, Lord, not like this.

A client's wife had shared with me that her husband raised his hand before dying to reach out to someone invisible, saying, "At last you've come…" Then he smiled and died.

I tossed my head. *No more thoughts of death, Jennifer.*

ONCE IN MY van, I whipped out my cell and called Tucker. He didn't pick up so I left a voicemail message warning him to be on the lookout for a phantom brother.

When I reached my office, I called the hospital to make sure a guard would be located outside Lenora's room. The ward clerk told me that wasn't going to happen.

"Why not? What about the phony brother's call?" I explained how serious the threat was.

"Please calm down, Dr. Trevor. The head nurse concluded the nurse on duty must have misunderstood or there was a mix-up of patients' names. The brother's call was probably for another patient. We have a Laura on the floor, too, who does have a brother." The ward clerk failed to convince me.

I set my phone down.

No way did I believe Lenora was safe. Was I being paranoid or wise?

CHAPTER EIGHTEEN

"ONE OF THE ex-convicts goes by the name Russell."

My assistant Ellen looked up from reading a G. K. Chesterton mystery while sipping Diet Coke during a break in our tiny staff room. "He may know something about Lenora's shooting."

I grabbed a Grannie Smith apple and bit into it. "I need to connect with him. Kirk mentioned a Russell as a possible suspect."

Ellen was instantly alert.

I scanned the other names on the five-page report I held in my hand. It listed the ex-convicts the foundation had been involved with the past two years. "Five women and nine men had finished serving terms of various lengths."

Ellen's eyes glistened, eager as a beagle's. She leapt into her self-chosen role as the female Watson to my Sherlock Holmes, but she wasn't him, and Sherlock I was not.

"Ellen, please set up a meeting with Russell ASAP." I gave her a thumbs-up before tossing my apple core across the room into the wastebasket, a la the amazing Michael Jordan's slam-dunk.

I headed back to my office. As my desk phone rang, I picked up my pace. "I'll get it," I called back in the direction of Ellen.

"Hello. This is Chris Lepsell. Is Jennifer Trevor in?" Her words were quick and clipped.

"Chris, my road rescuing angel, how nice of you to call." I rifled through some business cards on my desk.

"Jennifer? I expected to have to fight my way through your receptionist."

"You would have, but she's away from her desk. How's your vacation time going?" I scooped to pick up a card I'd dropped.

"Great. I'm between tennis and golf and decided to check up on you. How's the ankle?"

A memory of pain glinted in my mind. "A little stiff but otherwise doing amazingly well, thanks to my prompt medical treatment. Again, I thank you." I stacked papers on my desk, regretting a tad I'd picked up the phone. Not that I didn't want to chat with Chris, just too busy now.

"How's your friend Lenora?"

"I saw her yesterday—first time since the shooting. She still can't communicate, but she's being weaned gradually from the ventilator. They won't totally remove it until they're sure she can breathe independently."

"Not being able to speak must be horrible for a counselor."

I agreed. "When she's off the ventilator, I'm hoping she can tell us who tried to kill her."

"And get out of the hospital with its risk of germs and back home."

"Actually, I'm concerned if it's safe for her to return home before her assailant is behind bars."

"Sounds like you better hurry that up; you're running out of time." Chris' voice sounded robotic to my trained ear, but then she didn't seem to be a particularly expressive person.

"You've got that right. Once she's home, I don't envy Tucker. Keeping an independent dynamo like Lenora calm and quiet as she regains her stamina won't be easy."

"You're no slouch yourself. Bruised, bloodied, but back at work."

"It's that Puritan work ethic I can't shake."

"I've the same problem, although, today is no indication. I can handle being a lady of leisure for a few days, then I'm ready to work again. Which is good, by the way, because I'm also attached to three meals a day and a roof to keep off the rain, all of which require a regular paycheck."

I laughed. "I know the feeling."

"I can't complain. My skin is two shades darker than when I met you, courtesy of the spa. I've enjoyed every minute. Is there anything I can do to help in your investigation while I'm around? I do investigative stuff in my insurance work. I admit, I'm just a bit bored doing absolutely nothing."

"How nice of you to offer." My eyes dropped to my desk, where my right hand rested on the prison list. Funny how you can pick up a little nuance. During the pause in our conversation, Chris' breathing became uneven as I deliberated, and she waited for my answer. "I'll keep you in mind, but things are too muddled at this point for me to delegate."

"You still think the original suspect, Kirk, is innocent?"

"You know his name?" I was startled by Chris' knowledge and by her question and didn't try to hide my surprise.

"I read it in the paper. You'd just said he was a reformed convict."

"In Lenora's eyes only, may be the case."

Even though Chris had read about the situation, I couldn't confide in her. She was virtually a stranger. All I truly knew about her was that she was kind. I closed the call on a positive note. "It's sweet of you to check up on me, rescuer, but now I must get back to work."

"Sure. I think it's cool you're making this huge effort to help your friend. Keep at it."

"I will. You're pretty good at helping people yourself. Sure you're not an angel, after all?" I joked.

Chris laughed. "No wings last time I looked."

Ellen entered my office and waved her hand for my attention. "Gotta go. Stay in touch." I hung up and turned my attention to Ellen. "Have you arranged a meeting with Russell?"

"I finally got through. He'll meet you for lunch tomorrow at noon but only if you'll drive over to his town. He doesn't have a car."

"I can manage that."

She gave me a note with the details and map to the restaurant. "Lenora's former counseling client, and your next one, Carrie Malone, is in the outer office filling out her intake forms."

"Send her in as soon as she's completed them."

I picked up a pen and began to conjure up possible questions to ask Russell. No way would I meet this man anywhere but a public place. Who knew what sort of person Russell was?

CHAPTER NINETEEN

CARRIE MALONE CLUTCHED her duffel-bag-sized purse to her chest like a toddler's security blanket. Short blunt hair with straight bangs framed her face. She couldn't weigh more than a hundred pounds. Her eyes darted around my office.

Conflict marred my emotions. Sadness for her, yet eagerness to quiz her about the day Lenora was shot. Being disrupted in the midst of productive counseling once a relationship had been established with a therapist could be difficult at best, traumatic at worst.

This was true of Carrie Malone, Sandy Reckland, and whoever else was at Lenora's for counseling the day she was shot. A few nursery rhymes came unbidden to mind. First, Three Blind Mice. Would these women be like three blind mice that had seen nothing? Or like the three little pigs that had seen the big, bad wolf? If so, could one of them have knowledge leading to the identity of Lenora's assailant? I was desperate to find this person before she was attacked again.

Carrie extended a skinny arm to give me a weak finger-squeeze handshake. "I'm glad you had your secretary call, Dr. Trevor. I couldn't sleep all night after I heard about Dr. Lawrence. It's terrible. I sure appreciate what you're doing."

"The news shocked me as well." I offered her tea or coffee, both of which she declined. I took a sip from my mug of mint tea while glancing over Carrie's paperwork. I used my vocal chords more than average and needed lots of liquid.

Carrie's previous intake form from Lenora read: "Twenty-four years old, two children, ages five and three, married at eighteen.

Primary presenting problem: 'Husband constantly puts her down—verbally abusive, unfaithful, threatens divorce.'"

"Carrie," I began. "I have your records here. I appreciate that you authorized their release, but I'd like you to tell me in your own words why you originally went to see Lenora for counseling."

Her face reddened, and she lowered her head. "Three months ago my husband, Rob, said he no longer wanted to be married. He was leaving me the end of that week. At the last minute he changed his mind and decided to stay. I suspect his girlfriend changed her mind about him, but I never said nothing except I was glad. Things never have been good between us. We argue all the time."

"What sort of issues cause the conflict?" I probed gently.

Carrie turned her palms up in a helpless gesture. "I never know what will set him off. The way I talk isn't right or the kids do something and he blames me. He starts yelling I'm no good, and he never should have married me. His mother never did like me, and she tells him he made a mistake marrying me, and he wants me to know what she thinks of me, that kind of stuff. It goes on and on."

"Has he ever physically harmed you?

"Nothing big."

"Small ways count too."

"I get nervous if he's been drinking. Rob's into bodybuilding and health so he doesn't drink often, thank God, 'cause he gets bad then." She raised her eyes toward the ceiling. "I know a lot of the badmouthing he does about me is true," Carrie confided. "I am dumb."

I clenched my teeth and pressed my automatic lead pencil so hard the point broke off. How I hated these kinds of statements. Like many women, deep down Carrie felt she somehow deserved her husband's diatribes and abuse. "Carrie, I bet you're a lot smarter than you think you are. How are things with you and your husband since you started counseling?"

"Still not good. Soon after I began my sessions with Lenora, I made some changes. I try not to let Rob talk down to me no more. I told him we're through if he ever hits me again. Lenora said to say it and mean it. I do now. I'm stronger than I was before counseling."

"Excellent."

Carrie flicked her lower lip with her tongue. "And I said he had to sleep in the rec room if he was going to stay out past midnight. He can't be waking me and the kids up all hours."

"Good, you used your God-given mouth with wisdom and grace, telling him he must stop these behaviors. I'm delighted Lenora helped you establish better boundaries. We can continue to build on them."

"Yeah, that's what she said I needed to do; it's still hard for me. Rob didn't like one bit me using tough love like Lenora taught me. Next, she wanted Rob to come to counseling with me, but he wouldn't. Even called her himself. I heard him yelling on the phone. It kinda worried me."

"Why?"

She cast a glance at the door. "This is confidential, right?"

"Absolutely."

"For a second, only a second, mind you, when I heard about Lenora being shot, I thought…well once he'd told me he'd kill Lenora and me if she didn't stop filling my head with nonsense." Her eyes fastened on mine. "I know he didn't mean nothing by his threat to her."

"He said that to her?" My pulse picked up. "Were the police informed of this?"

"Lenora said she wouldn't report him, but it better not ever happen again. You won't tell the police now?"

"Carrie, if Lenora's in danger, I must. Remember the form you signed? Our conversation is confidential, unless someone's life is in danger."

Her face drained of color. "Rob'd never hurt Lenora; he's all talk. He's that way all the time with me, and like I said, he's getting better."

"I hope so, for your sake and his."

"Lenora wasn't scared. She still said he should come for counseling. He finally agreed." Carrie's smile flashed as if someone had promised her a world cruise then her mouth drooped. "That was shortly before this happened."

Alarm bells flashed in my brain. Was he really all talk? Had his change of heart been all show, a diversion from his real intention to hurt Lenora?

Carrie hunted for a tissue. I returned my focus to her and gestured toward the box on the table between the wing back chairs. She took hesitant childlike steps, painful to watch. The word phlegmatic described Carrie's personality. Her gentle, laidback disposition and timidity made her vulnerable.

Rob's rage sounded scary.

"Carrie, I want to be sure I understand the extent of your work with Lenora. You saw her for individual counseling how many times?"

"Around, let me see, seven, and I would like to continue with you. I don't want to lose what we started."

"Here's what I have in mind. I can't see you as an individual client more than once or twice due to time restraints, but if I form a small group with some of Lenora's other current clients, would you be interested?"

Her ponytail bobbed up and down. "I like counseling. We talked about what's right and what's not in a relationship. When I went to my first session, Rob wanted me to let his new girlfriend move in, and I brought that up."

"How upsetting that he expected you to put up with something so hurtful."

"Lenora encouraged me to tell him this other woman couldn't come, and I wasn't leaving either, but he could go. I'd be getting a lawyer. Lenora told me everything we have is half mine."

"That's true."

"That got to him. The idea that I owned something and could hurt him financially scared Rob. It may sound crazy, but I don't think he ever thought of that before. I know I didn't. He started being more respectful, yelling at me less, and going hunting with the guys less. He didn't like what Lenora was telling me one bit, but he was shaping up."

Carrie's eyes widened like she still couldn't quite believe the change in her husband.

"Tough, tender love really works," I said.

"I used to let him do whatever he wanted. As a Christian, I figured I had to submit to whatever."

"That's not what the Christian faith teaches." My face flushed. The confusion Christian women had over the teachings on submission could be terribly harmful to them and their spouses. "God alone is worthy of the surrender of your will. He always can be trusted to guide you for your good."

"That's sorta like what Lenora said. I used to always give in to Rob whatever. No more."

"Good, you're to be loving and kind, but not a doormat. Scripture says submit to one another, and husbands should love their wives as Christ loves the church, meaning be sensitive, kind and unselfish."

"I like that." Her cheeks brightened like a flower opening to the light.

"God wants you treated with respect. It's definitely not His will that you let your husband beat up on you emotionally or physically. You're infinitely precious to God and so is Rob. God doesn't want you to allow him to sin against you."

"Funny, Lenora said the same thing. I still need courage to work on that stuff. That's why I came to you."

"Then you'll continue counseling with me," I flinched, "until Lenora is back?"

She nodded.

"Good. Based on what you've told me, I'd like to have you and Rob come in together for marriage work as well as have you join the group." I explained what we'd cover in our sessions.

"Sounds great by me. I guess I don't need to warn you, Rob's pretty hotheaded, but he means well. I'll try to get him to come. I hope he will. I love him, but he makes life difficult for us."

"That's what we'll work on."

She smiled shyly. "Good."

"That's settled. Now if you don't mind, I have a couple of questions I'd like to ask about events on the day of Lenora's shooting."

"Shoot," she said, then blushed. "Sorry, poor word choice."

"I understand you were at Lenora's house earlier on the day the shooting happened? Is this correct?"

"Yes."

"Did you notice anything unusual?"

"Like what? I don't know what you mean."

"Any difference in Lenora's behavior or in the surroundings? Any calls she may have taken or made while you were there?"

Carrie pursed her lips and rolled her eyes toward the ceiling. "Umm, now that you mention it, Lenora did seem a little jumpy."

"How exactly?"

"When a dog barked outside, it startled her. She got up and closed the window. I only noticed because usually she's so calm."

"This is important, Carrie. Do you have any idea why she'd be anxious?"

She shook her head from side to side. "I sure don't know."

"Was anyone else there?"

"I saw the cleaning lady carrying trash out." She paused. "A man in a big black car was going down her drive when I drove up. I figured he was the appointment before me."

"What can you tell me about him?"

"Nothing much. It was an overcast day. Sorry. I just had a glance."

"Did you notice what he was wearing?'

"I think a suit coat or sports jacket. He didn't look like a gardener or nothing." She bent her head, rummaged in her purse and pulled out a pack of Juicy Fruit. "Want some?" she offered.

I declined. She unwrapped a piece and stuck it in her mouth like an extension of her tongue for a second. She squeezed the wrapper neatly into a ball and dropped it back into her purse.

I looked at my watch, amazed how fast our fifty minutes had gone. I made some concluding remarks. "Thank you, Carrie, that's all. Before you leave, have Ellen schedule a joint appointment for you and Rob to meet with me later this week if possible."

"If he won't come, should I keep the time anyway?"

"Yes, but let's hope he will." I smiled and patted Carrie's shoulder as I led her to the door. *Precious woman, guard her Lord.*

"Keep in mind, Carrie, treasure yourself and others around you are more likely to treasure you, too."

How sad that the man she loved and married had an abusive tongue and dominated her. Even Christian men had to guard against meanness at home. Carrie's situation could change if Christ got Rob's attention.

If men didn't deal with their lust and anger, they destroyed the people they professed to love and anyone else who got in the way. Satan prowled about looking for relationships to devour.

Rob Malone obviously disliked the impact Lenora was having on his wife. Might he be Lenora's attacker? He certainly deserved a slot on my suspect list. I was eager to meet him.

CHAPTER TWENTY

Pulling into my garage, I couldn't shake my concern over Carrie. I tried not to bring counseling problems home, but tonight this was impossible. After dinner, when the kids started to watch an old Bob Hope movie, I whispered, "Nick, can we talk?"

"What's up?" He closed his paper and looked up.

I put my finger to my lips and led him to the velvet-covered chairs in our bedroom. "Today I counseled a Christian gal who submits to a husband who abuses her. She married young, has been a stay-at-home wife, and her self-confidence is nil."

"I'm sure you told her Christ didn't encourage women to be namby-pamby. He wouldn't want people to submit to evil."

"I like the way you say that. We need more follow-up to make sure this is clear to her."

"I've got something else you'll like." He wiggled his eyebrows.

"Sweetheart, the kids are still up."

"They're busy."

"Later." I brushed my fingers across his lips. "Back to my subject. I hate how Satan deceives people into thinking they're not holy, dearly loved, and a sacred dwelling place for God's Holy Spirit."

"Would your client allow herself to be pushed around if she truly believed that?" Nick stood up. "Biblical principles are simple and powerful, but people have to know them and use them. We've both met hypocrites who only mouth them." Nick lowered his head. "I spent years doing it. I hope people can now experience genuine Christianity through me."

I stood and wrapped my arms around him. "They do, sweetheart."

"You shouldn't have done that. I'm not leaving this bedroom."

"Tara needs your help with her math homework." I released him. "And I need to make some calls."

Nick snapped his fingers dramatically. "Foiled again. Why is she watching a movie if her homework isn't done?"

"She talked me into it. Promised she had time later."

"Why are you such a softie?" He rubbed my cheek.

I shrugged. "Probably guilt over being too busy at times."

"Only in your imagination." Nick narrowed his gaze at me. "She gets plenty of attention."

"Plus, she seems to resent my authority, and I hate to make waves."

"Because she'd like to take over running this entire house and every one of us. It's her strong will that makes her pushy."

"Let's call it her Take Charge syndrome, healthy if channeled properly, otherwise disaster." I shrugged one shoulder.

"Good luck doing that. Look who she's got for a mother. I'm still working on your channels, woman." He embraced me and nuzzled my neck playfully.

I gently shoved Nick out to look for Tara.

When he left, I called Tucker, connecting immediately to my delight.

Tucker rattled off an account of Lenora's status almost robotically, as if exposing his feelings again might be too painful.

Getting an "unchanged" progress report weighed heavy on my heart, as it must have on his.

"Tucker, don't give up hope. We'll intensify our prayers. In the meantime, I'd like to examine the foundation records on other former prisoners Lenora worked with."

"I already gave you the list. Wouldn't the detailed files be confidential?"

"Not the Second Chance Foundation's files. I want to check on a man named Russell. Any information on him I'd appreciate. Would the data be in her home office?"

"Probably, but I don't know when I'll have time to go through the papers and get them together."

"I could collect them when Estelle's cleaning. She can let me in and you won't have to be there."

"Let me see what I can arrange and figure out when I can get back to you." He hung up.

When he can get back to me? Annoyance washed over me. The person who shot Lenora remained at large. In my opinion, her danger was intensified. So far I'd accomplished very little. Was I asking too much of him?

I shifted my focus to the delight of being Mom and went to tuck the kids in bed. *Tuck*—I like the word with its comfy-coziness, evoking images of safety, being tucked away from harm. I don't remember when tuck-in at our house had become a ritual and a favorite part of my day. It's amazing the things children are willing to share with a seated parent just before going to sleep.

Jenny, my youngest, needed the most shuteye so I went to her room first.

"Hi, sweetie." The outline of ballet dancers in pink and yellow tutus on one wall of Jenny's bedroom had been drawn with broad black strokes by my artist friend. Her bedspread had figures of dancers in pink and orange lacy costumes.

I bent over her bed and used my index finger to form a cross on Jenny's face, starting with the forehead to the chin and then moving my right hand from ear to ear. As my finger touched her soft skin I prayed aloud, "May God bless you in the name of the Father, Son, and Holy Spirit."

"Mom, I've been thinking, why don't we just take every gun away from everybody who has one so what happened to your friend couldn't happen again?"

"Guns aren't the problem, Jenny." I tucked the covers under her chin. "Firearms can be used safely for protection and for hunting."

"I'm glad, Mommy, 'cause if we took away the guns, we'd have to remove all the knives in the world, too, and then how would we cut our food?"

I smiled. "That's right. We trust God to keep us safe and live without fear. Time for our story. What will it be? *The Adventures of Tommy Smurlee* again?"

"Yeah."

I read Jenny a chapter of her favorite book even though we'd read it through three times already.

I headed into Collin's room and prayed with him for his chemistry exam the next day. "I studied Mom, but the teacher writes questions weird. I mean, it's like he deliberately tries to trick us."

"You prepared as best you could, sweetheart. That's all you can do. You know the motto?"

"Do your best and keep the joy, no matter what," he repeated by rote, then grinned. "Love you, Mom."

"You too, son." I brushed the hair from his forehead and blessed him tenderly.

Lord, how I love the children You entrusted to me.

Tara pounced on me the minute I entered her room. "Mom, I need new shoes for my drama performance on Sunday. I saw the cutest pair at Mitchell's. Can I get them?" I assured her the black shoes she already owned would be fine, ignoring her protest. I rose from her bed, leaving the nightlight on.

She spoke into the semi-darkness. "Ellie and Kara ignored me at recess. I heard them talking about me and laughing."

I returned, sat down on her bed, and hugged her. "I'm sorry. That wasn't nice. Girls can be mean."

"They sure can, even though I'm nice to them. Ellie came back and apologized though before it was time to go inside."

"Sweetheart, life isn't always easy or fair, but God is. He's always there to give you comfort and strength and all the love you need."

"I wish I could see Him."

"Someday you will. We all will." I smiled. "You need a princess blessing." I touched her head, her ears and then her chin as I prayed, "God bless my precious princess and fill her with wisdom and joy. Thank you."

I sighed and headed toward my room. *Lord, I have pain of my own tonight; I could use some wisdom and joy, too.* I took an extra-strength Tylenol then collapsed on the bed between the sheets and waited for the release of sleep. Fortunately, it came quickly.

I dreamed of biking through a gorgeous forest with Tucker and Kirk. We came to a fork on the trail, and Tucker and Kirk sped off to the right. I raced to catch up, or I'd be lost forever. As hard as I peddled, my bicycle wouldn't move.

Lord, what does that mean?

CHAPTER TWENTY-ONE

THE LUMINESCENT DIAL of my alarm clock read 4 a.m. A thousand pinpoints of darkness floated around me. Something had startled me into wakefulness. What was it?

As my mind began to focus, I remembered loud cracks. A tree falling or could those have been, I gulped, shots that ripped through my barrier of sleep? I sat up. Only half conscious, I stretched my hand toward Nick's side of the bed, feeling for his body.

He wasn't there. Nick usually slept like a stone. Had the noise, whatever it was, awakened him? Where had he gone?

I staggered to our walk-in closet and grabbed my robe from the hook. I belted the satin sash around me as I tiptoed down the hall.

The children's doors were still closed. I was grateful they hadn't awakened. At the end of the corridor, light filtered from the dining room.

I eased up and peered inside. Nick had his back toward me and was standing at the window.

"What were those loud noises?" I asked, my voice quavering.

"Rifle shots."

"No way. Are you sure?" I inched next to Nick until our shoulders touched. "Somebody's up early hunting squirrel."

"I doubt it." I detected the concern in his tone.

I clutched my robe tighter.

Nick never turned around. "The shots were too distant to involve us, hon, relax. I've already been out to check, and everything seems fine."

"Despite your reassurance, it's obvious you're worried."

Nick turned and enfolded me in his arms.

"I don't get it. If somebody wanted to scare us, the shots were too far away to be threatening."

"On the other hand, close enough to give us a shock." Nick rubbed his forehead with his palm. "Perhaps that was the intention."

"I hope not. I'm making some tea. Want some?"

"Yes, thanks."

I dragged myself into the security of our familiar kitchen as a pouring rain began to pound on the skylights.

Nick left his post at the window and followed me. He heated water in two mugs while I ripped open two tea packets and pulled out chamomile herbal tea bags. I was hungry but couldn't handle a regular breakfast. Granola or oatmeal needed a steadier digestive process than my stomach could handle under the circumstances. I retrieved two blueberry muffins from the fridge, heated them in the micro ten seconds, then set them on napkins.

We sat on padded stools at the snack bar, listening to the rain in silence.

Finally, I said what we probably both were thinking, "What if the sniper is after us now?"

"Better not be." Nick's voice was hard.

I shivered. I longed to put my brain into Scarlett O'Hara shutdown mode. "Let's not think about this anymore. Until tomorrow, at least."

Nick patted my hand and announced sleepily, "It's almost morning, darling."

"Don't remind me."

We spoke reassuring words to one another between sips of hot tea. I hoped the chamomile would calm me down.

After I downed my last swallow, I yawned and drifted back to our bedroom, leaving Nick to turn off the lights. Once under the covers, I pulled an oversized pillow over my head. If there were any more distressing noises, I'd be insulated.

Nick slipped into bed and snuggled next to me. At age twelve I bought a huge, plush teddy bear with babysitting money, a little old typically for stuffed animals maybe, but not for a girl who never had one. Now I got to sleep with a real one, and I sure needed him tonight.

The alarm went off at seven. My brain was groggy, but I forced myself to get out of bed. As Nick and I went through our morning dressing ritual, we recapped last night's terror. No way did I want to instill fear in the children. I'd pretty much dismissed the incident by the time I got them off to school.

When I left, Nick stayed behind to finish a brief he needed to deliver on his way to work.

I was okay until I pulled out of our garage, started down the drive, and screeched to a halt. The dead bodies of two raccoons had been placed neatly side-by-side near the end of our driveway with their insides coiled next to their carcasses. I parked on the side of the drive and walked over, dodging the rain puddles. I'd never seen a pile of intestines, let alone an orderly coil with a note in the center.

Even before I read it I sensed it implied these innards could be mine.

The animals' deep-set brown eyes rimmed in black stared straight ahead, frozen in death. Perhaps it would have been kind for me to try to close them, but I couldn't when I felt like vomiting. I stared at the soggy, blood-streaked 6 x 8 card with its capital letters written in permanent marker. *STOP MEDDLING. WE DON'T WANT EX-CONS AS NEIGHBORS.*

Needing a place to sit down fast, I returned to the car and pulled out my cell to call Nick at the house.

My voice was shaking as I related, "I found last night's victims." I described the carcasses and the notecard. "Should we bother to call the police? There's no chance of fingerprints after all this rain."

He assured me he'd make the call and handle cleanup. Fine by me. I could easily let myself be a fluttery female upon such an occasion. My hands trembled. The implication on the card seemed clear—the next bullet may be for you. It would be hours before I could clear my head of the sickening image and the threat bright as a neon sign.

When I entered my office suite, Ellen was pulling files for my morning clients. I quickly evaluated whether to tell her what had happened during the night. The therapeutic value of communication was rated high. Would this make the horror more manageable, less grotesque and traumatic? Maybe. I proceeded to describe the double-death in our driveway.

Ellen's eyes widened and stayed that way. She stammered several times. "No way. A peculiar coincidence, wouldn't you say?"

"If you believe in them." I clenched my teeth.

"Jennifer, you could be the sniper's next target."

"Stop." I groaned. "Ellen, I know it's easy to get into the drama of the event, and I appreciate your concern, but this could also be a vague threat by someone too cowardly to speak in person about his or her social concerns. Now let's get to work."

Nick called mid-morning. "New testimony's come up on a current case. I won't be able to go with you to meet this Russell guy. I need to be in court. Can you postpone it a day?"

My stomach clenched. "I have a window of time open today. Not to worry, I'll be fine."

"I don't like you going alone, especially after what happened last night."

The knot in my stomach tightened. "Nick, those dead raccoons are not going to make me melt with fear."

"Humor me and try to reschedule." Worry was in his voice.

"I'll see if I can postpone. But if I can't, I'm going."

"You are incorrigible and stubborn." Nick exhaled his breath loudly. "Be careful then."

Ellen was unable to locate Russell to change the appointment.

I had to decide. I took a moment to pray for the Holy Spirit to give me wisdom. To go alone or blow him off? A reformed ex-con out of prison, Russell wouldn't want to put his freedom in jeopardy by any shenanigans with me. I concluded I'd be safe. And the sooner I saw him the better. Patience wasn't my strong suit. I had to get to the bottom of Lenora's shooting so normal life could resume. I didn't want Nick or the children in danger. How harmful could it be to meet in a public place?

I would soon find out.

CHAPTER TWENTY-TWO

THE MORNING ZIPPED by. I wrote my client notes in record time, prior to leaving. I'd arranged free time from eleven to two.

When I passed Ellen's desk, she dumped her fears on me again. Worst of all, they echoed mine.

"What do you really know about him? What makes you think this Russell's safe?"

"I'll be fine. He's reformed and harmless. The last thing I want to do is to show prejudice toward a man because he has a prison record."

Ellen frowned and opened her mouth to reply, but I glared at her and made a zipping motion across my lips before striding outside.

The weather was the perfect snapshot of a fall day in Wisconsin. Crisp leaves, freshly painted by the Master Artist, sailed along on brisk breezes. The sky sparked memories of my blue-chiffon senior prom dress trimmed with lacey clouds of white.

I set my GPS, named Emma by Nick for her lovely English voice. Emma led me to the town of Kerr without any trouble. I pulled out the note with the name of the restaurant and circled the block twice to find the downtown business section before realizing I'd already driven through it.

I backtracked. The town had a total of six buildings; two were boarded up. The window of one had a six-foot "For Rent" banner. I located Hannah's Restaurant on a side street in a weathered building lettered with "Home of Chicks" on the front with "Hannah's Restaurant" painted over it. A plywood "Bowling" sign hung above the side door on the right half of the building.

Cement blocks speckled with blobs the color of hens' eggs formed the skeleton of the building. I entered the cracked blacktop lot in back.

Out of the corner of my eye I saw what looked surprisingly like Chris Lepsell's car turn the corner and head down the block. Weird. I shook my head; there was more than one car like that. Why would she be around here? I selected a parking place and glanced about before cautiously opening my door and heading for the storefront. I inhaled deeply and ventured inside.

Old stale smoke, bitter coffee, and a strange smell, a cross between sardines and onions, attacked my nostrils. After my first whiff of Hannah's, I realized this wasn't going to be my favorite lunch spot ever.

Plus, I could think of more fun things to do with my free hours than meet with this ex-convict, Russell, but if it would help me find Lenora's attacker, I was game to dine with him here.

The interior walls, dirty yellow-green, were either a strange paint shade or a uniquely colored mold. One wall had scattered nails framed by whitish rectangular outlines where plaques or pictures once hung. The only frame left held a yellowed Covenant of Good Service that gave me no comfort.

Asphalt flooring in assorted patterns, predominantly beige, had been laid in a motley style, probably leftovers from other jobs. Some people shouldn't make decorating decisions.

A dingy chalkboard announced the day's luncheon specials and was covered with enough dust to make me suspect the specials hadn't changed all month. Hamburger, grilled cheese with or without ham, and potato soup were my choices.

Five patrons clustered on stools at the counter. I smiled in their direction but received only stares back. Six chrome-edged table and chair sets with split red vinyl had served years of bowling leagues, judging by their condition.

May Russell be on time and may this be fruitful. I didn't feel like waiting around long.

The sign on the far wall announced the restroom location. I walked over to use the facilities, passing six well-polished bowling lanes—the only thing in Hannah's with a shine, unless you counted one man's bald head. Nobody was bowling, so it wasn't obvious if the lanes were functional or not.

Inside the ladies' room two rusted sinks, one grosser than the other, both had a steady drip. I washed my hands and exited fast.

The clock above the swinging kitchen door, in the shape of a red cactus ringed by white numerals, had both hands pointing to twelve.

At the far end of the counter sat a heavy-set lady, the cook from the looks of the stained butcher-type apron covering the front of her jeans. "Heartbreak Hotel" by Elvis streamed over the speaker, which seemed to have transfixed the woman as she sucked an unlit cigarette.

I flashed a weak smile and approached with all the warmth I could project. My dad had taught me as a child to respect every person I met, regardless of his or her personality, or lack thereof, or unusual appearance. He'd read me enough O. Henry stories filled with strange characters to instill his interest in all types of people into me. I usually could start and enjoy a conversation with anyone.

"I'm meeting someone and need to be sure I'm in the right spot…is this the only restaurant in Kerr?"

The cook gave me a cold stare before drawing words slowly from her ample mouth. "Family Diner went outta business last year. There's the Mexican grill but ain't nobody eats there. This gotta be the spot."

"Thanks." I chatted with her about the weather and moved on to discussing the town.

All eyes were on us. I ignored stares from the other customers, mostly coffee-drinkers. Did I dare eat here?

Why had I jumped at the prospect of a meeting with Russell? If I'd given this more thought, I'd have insisted on more details before I drove here. I should have tried harder to connect over the phone.

I gingerly perched on a worn gray vinyl chair at the nearest table.

A waitress, around fiftyish with red hair that almost matched the clock, sauntered over, pulled an order pad from a hip pocket, and popped a pencil from behind her ear.

"Hi." I gave her my best smile.

"Yeah. What can I getcha?"

"I'll have iced tea in a to-go cup."

If Russell didn't show, I'd skip lunch and be on my way.

The door opened and all eyes turned as a woman with two boys around the age of ten came into the restaurant and headed straight for the bowling lanes. Soon the sound of a ball rolling down the alley reverberated, followed by smacks of falling pins.

From the sound of conversations around me, everyone in the place knew each other. A friendly bunch except cool toward strangers, judging by the hard stares still coming my way. I kept one eye posted on the door.

At fifteen past twelve, a six-foot man with a mop of curly black hair strode in, slamming the door behind him. He checked the place with rapid eye movements and waved at me.

Russell had arrived.

And I wanted to be somewhere, anywhere else.

CHAPTER TWENTY-THREE

Russell's noisy entrance added a momentary spark of interest to the eyes around me. He flagged me to a table toward the back of the room next to the bowling lanes.

Gritting my teeth, I picked up my iced tea and followed him.

"You're the only person seems outa place, so you must be Dr. Jennifer Trevor."

I produced a smile in an effort to be cordial. "And you're Russell?"

I started to extend my hand, then withdrew it. He never offered his nor seemed to notice my gesture. So much for manners.

"Got that right." He abruptly pulled out a chair for himself and pointed me toward the empty one across from him.

Where had he gotten the money for all the tattoos covering his neck and both arms? The man was a walking art show, if you liked body ink. Personally, I didn't. I struggled not to stare at the curvaceous, tattooed lady covering his entire right arm. My mind took a side trip. How long had he sat having his skin jabbed for her?

The lower half of Russell's face wore the shadow of a black beard. Probably one of those guys who could shave every three hours and still look unkempt.

Russell yelled to the cook, "Fried egg sandwich and fries, Mel."

He looked me up and down.

I recoiled from his gaze. I totally disliked being stared at. "Let's get to the point of our meeting, Russell. You have information about the attack on my friend Lenora Lawrence?"

He leaned closer and spoke in a low voice. "Yeah, I do. Kirk is innocent."

My skin bristled. "This isn't news. Kirk already told me, for what it's worth. Even if I'm inclined to agree, there's no proof either way."

"I know for a fact. Kirk and me were for real goin' straight. He was busting his buttons over his new job. He wouldn't have ditched it for nothing. Shooting the dame was outta the question, get what I mean?" His face was inches from mine. I drew back and squeezed my hands together in my lap to hide their shaking.

"That's not what the police think." I blurted the words out, wanting to sound brave.

"They're wrong."

"Okay, if you're so sure Kirk didn't shoot Lenora, who else had a motive?" I reached for my notepad in my purse. "Another ex-prisoner?"

The waitress appeared from behind me and plunked down Russell's food. He wolfed down half the fried egg sandwich before responding.

"I got ideas. I'm looking into it." His fingers dripped pungent bacon grease, and he paused to lick them. "I figure it coulda been some loser the Lawrence woman helped or a thief off the street. I got buddies out there asking questions since it happened. Or it mighta been somebody inside horning in on her foundation money. I'm not saying nothing definite until I'm sure. Just want you to know I'm on it."

I stared at him. Did he think that was worth a trip here?

Russell swiped grease from his mouth with a napkin. "You can be sure of this—the person who shot Lenora is dangerous. You better be careful, lady."

"Thanks for the warning."

What kind of game was this? Ring the woman around, promise her info, then tell her nothing. My shoulders slumped. "That's all you have to say? Kirk's innocent 'cause you know, and you're on it. I came all this way for nothing." I nearly choked on my tea.

Russell leaned forward. "I wanted you to come 'cause I got something else to ask you in person. Kirk promised I'd be one of the first guys helped in his new job. I need a bankroll to start a small car repair business. I want the foundation to float me a loan. I expect you've got an in. If not, I might give you an opportunity to have a personal stake in my business yourself."

"Lenora is a colleague and friend, but I have nothing to do with decisions about how the Second Chance Foundation monies are distributed. I do know it isn't a bank." I crossed my leg, swinging my foot back and forth to dispel my annoyance. "I can't believe you deceived me into coming to hear a business proposition."

The waitress strolled over with more coffee for Russell. Tension coupled with the rumbles of my stomach. I ordered a bag of Fritos to stop the thunderous sounds my insides were starting to make.

The combination of the restaurant smells started nauseous waves in my throat. I spiked my iced tea with sugar, then gulped it.

"I wouldn't call it tricking ya." He shook his finger in my face. "Hear me out."

I opened the bag of Fritos the waitress dropped in front of me and started munching.

Russell gave a glowing report of his behavior and his mechanical skills. "I'm a guy worth investing in. That's gotta be obvious to you. I can't believe the other broad refused to loan to me when I asked her."

"Lenora already turned you down?"

"Yeah."

His self-eulogy created steam in my nostrils. "Did it occur to you that you're a suspect?" I used my diminishing self-control to remain civil. Forget annoyance, I was at fury stage. Something kept me sitting.

Russell planted his elbows on the once-red checkered vinyl tablecloth, picked up a fork and beat it against his open palm. "Well, I'm gonna try to get Kirk off, 'cause Kirk's gonna put in a good word with Lenora when she's outta that hospital and see what he can do. I've been working at a gas station for a couple of months. I'll be dead by the time I got enough saved for a shop. I figure my plans go down the tube with Kirk."

"I'm sorry, but I can't help you." I stood to leave. "Perhaps some community resources can finance you. I'm sure you're mechanically capable, but if Lenora already turned you down, Kirk wouldn't be able to do a thing for you either, provided he even stayed out of prison and kept a job with the foundation."

"Community resources for an ex-con? Get real, lady. But you're lucky. I'm still gonna help."

I sat back down. "Why? You told me you have a grudge against Lenora because she wouldn't help you. So why would you care about her? Besides, how do I know you didn't shoot Lenora? Why should I trust you?" My stomach was still aflutter, but I found strength from my anger.

Russell leaned his chair legs back and put his hands in his pockets—a kingpin on his home turf. No wonder he wouldn't come to my office. He was in control in his own territory.

Russell slapped his hand on the tabletop. "I'm going to tell you something, lady." His voice grew louder. I sensed the staring eyes of the other customers again. "Life inside prison was pretty darn good. Don't think I sat in a cement cell like maybe you saw in the movies, lady. I had planned rec-time and access to TV's inside and outdoors with movie channels. You name it. I had a desk and bookshelves. Athletic equipment and sports opportunities—volleyball, handball, weights. I even took college courses. You know what it cost taxpayers?"

"Plenty," I said, irritated.

"And in prison I didn't pay a nickel for nothing. Now I'm out and trying to be a decent, responsible guy and can't get a start. I coulda done without the frills at prison, if that money coulda gone for a decent small business loan when I got out."

"Russell, you talk like the world owes you something. What you make of your life is up to you and God."

I glanced behind me. Everybody was listening as well as watching us.

"If I don't get any breaks on the outside, you think I'm gonna worry about going back to prison?"

"Are you threatening me?"

"Let's just say, I lived a whole lot better in the can with a prison-rights group watching out for me and lawyers wanting to represent me for free. All I had to do was snap my fingers. If I don't get help from the foundation, I'm going to get the money another way. And it'll be your fault and Lenora Lawrence's."

My back stiffened. *Patience, Jennifer. Ignore his threats. Lord, help me salvage something from this meeting. I need wisdom fast.* "The fact is,

Russell," I said as compassionately as I could. "The foundation's work is on hold since Lenora was shot." I checked my watch. "I need to get back to work." Crumpling the empty Fritos bag in my hand, I reached into my purse. "Here's my card if you come up with some real information about Lenora's shooter. Not that you've told me anything in the first place."

"I'll still be looking into it. Don't forget what I said about that loan…"

I sensed the Holy Spirit nudging me as I said, "I'll mention your request to some other non-profit organizations. Perhaps the foundation can help you when things settle down." I couldn't permanently dash all his hopes.

I might have expected a smile or a thank you. Instead he glared at me. His expression sent a chill down my spine. I didn't like having this man for an enemy.

Outside in my convertible, I shook my head. How could you be so stupid, Jennifer? Clearly Russell had a strong motive for shooting Lenora and a huge capacity for anger.

I glanced in my rear view mirror. He stood outside the bowling alley writing down the number of my license plate. Great.

What was that for?

CHAPTER TWENTY-FOUR

THE FLUORESCENT LIGHT gave the green walls a sallow, clandestine glow like an underground nuclear lab. The fragrance of scented deodorants mixed with sweat hung thick in the air. Fourteen women, mesmerized by soft rock music, followed the gyrating movements of a skinny aerobics instructor in her class.

Exercise at the Y was one of my favorite ways to spend lunch hour. The gray steel building minutes from my office had a side-yard flower garden with stepping stones proclaiming donor names. Nick had generously put our name on one.

On my way into the locker room, Mary, the mother of Tara's best friend, Ellie, waved at me. I quickly changed into black nylon shorts and a white tee shirt screen printed with *"You go, girl,"* a memorial from a race for life Mary and I had run.

I reached the classroom as the instructor began. She led our group of sixteen through a low-level workout for half an hour then switched to weights for strengthening. As my body loosened up, my mind broke free, too. Weird. An elusive thought kept tickling my brain—I'd missed something obvious about the attack on Lenora.

After we finished, the group of gals headed over to the machines. Mary called to me from a rowing machine in the back of the bodybuilding section. I positioned myself next to her to do abdominal crunches on a slant board.

Between exertions we puffed and chatted about kids and a new local coffee shop. I thanked her for giving Tara a ride the other night.

"My pleasure. Sorry we were late. Another gal, the Denton girl, Joann, was over too, and I drove her home as well."

"No problem. I only wish Tara had called. She can be forgetful. Want to switch to the elliptical equipment?"

"Sure."

I grabbed my towel and wrapped it around my neck. "I don't think I ever heard Tara mention Joann."

"Probably not. Joann doesn't get involved in many activities. She rarely goes to anyone's house."

"Why is that?" I mounted an elliptical machine.

Mary climbed on one next to me. "Her mom likes her home most of the time. I understand the mom keeps to herself. I've never seen her at school events. She's sick a lot. I know Ellie never goes to Joann's house, but we've invited Joann to come for dinner several times. Sweet girl."

"Your Ellie's tender and caring."

"Tara's no social slouch either."

"I'm not so sure about that. Lately she seems to think only about herself. I doubt she'd invite a gal to dinner she didn't already know well. Perhaps it's my fault. I haven't exactly modeled hospitality for her. With my work schedule we don't have company often." Slivers of guilt appeared. I squashed them with my familiar phrase. "Oh well."

"Who can do it all, except the gals in TV sitcoms?" Mary laughed.

"I may die trying. Then Chuck Denton is Joann's Dad?"

"Yes, do you know him?"

"Only just met him. He's on the board of Lenora's foundation."

"I'm surprised he has time. It's challenging for him caring for his daughter with his wife ill so much and him working full time. Anyway, that's the rumor around school. Joann never says a word about what goes on at home. Gotta run, errands call."

I stared at her retreating form, deep in thought.

CHAPTER TWENTY-FIVE

CARRIE'S HUSBAND, ROB, stomped into my office, exuding enough energy to heat a house. Carrie scurried in behind. His black leather baseball cap topped a black stringy ponytail a foot long hanging down his back. Manicured nails, slightly rounded, extended an eighth-inch beyond his fingers.

It's impossible not to have some preconceived notion of a client after a session with his wife describing him.

Big, hefty, masculine Rob was what I expected.

He wore sterling silver rings on three fingers of his left hand. The buffalo band on his right thumb caught my eye. A walking jewelry store.

I estimated Rob's height at five feet six. His dark skin suggested Spanish ancestry or perhaps Indian. Expensive black leather tasseled loafers and thin dress socks told me he spared no expense on himself. His muscles were toned well enough to be featured in a fitness club ad.

Rob heaved his right shoulder against my door, shoved it shut, and grunted a response to my hello. I got an instant impression he was indifferent to conventional courtesy and liked to set his own rules. I wasn't thrilled to have him in my office obviously disgruntled. Family members had shot counselors before. Like Lenora? I shuddered.

Carrie, all ninety-five petite pounds, wearing washed-out khaki slacks and a red and white striped blouse tucked in at the waist, trembled as she sat. She'd crisscrossed a once-white sweater around her shoulders and clutched a large tan vinyl purse under her left arm like a lifeline.

I wanted to reassure her things would go well, but could I be sure?

"Dr. Trevor, you need to know Rob made a huge fuss and refused to come at first. I was scared to insist, but I did it."

"Did what?" Rob demanded, glaring at her.

She shot back. "Told you I won't live like this any longer. Said we're through if you wouldn't come for help with our marriage."

Good for you, Carrie. Tough love. As nervous as she was, this had been a courageous statement. "I'm glad you're both here. Hopefully, we can resolve some of the issues distressing you."

Rob gave me an icy stare. "Yeah, she's lucky I came. I'm a patient guy. All she does is nag since she started counseling with that other broad. I'm not gonna say I haven't considered walking out on her."

"I'm keeping an eye on you. How can I trust you? You'd take off with the TV and VCR and the only car that runs. Everything is half mine if we can't work this out."

"She keeps saying that. I'm sick of it." Rob jabbed at the air in front of Carrie, as if I needed help figuring out who "she" was. "She went to see a lawyer after she talked to Lenora Lawrence. You better believe I gave that woman a piece of my mind."

"You were gone four whole days. How did I know you'd ever come back?"

Carrie, brave soul. Her words and tone meant she was learning healthy assertiveness.

Time to intervene. "Rob, talking about your relationship in a counseling setting can help make it better. What's wrong with that?"

"I don't like being set up to do anything," Rob ranted. "Carrie knows that. I didn't like that pushy Lenora woman. For that matter, why should I trust you?"

Carrie glowered at him and spoke on my behalf. "Dr. Trevor is a friend of Dr. Lenora's who's helping. I'll be doing what she says. If you don't want counseling, I'm getting it anyway."

He answered through clenched teeth. "I didn't like what that Lenora was talking my wife into. No wonder the woman got shot. Probably had it coming."

Carrie's eyes widened. "Rob, how could you say that?"

"The violence against Lenora was a terrible act, Mr. Malone." I couldn't let the hostile reference to Lenora pass. I worked to stifle my fury at his insensitivity. "Your response is inappropriate to say the least. If the police heard you, you'd be considered a suspect."

"Settle down. I didn't mean I'd do something to the dame," he muttered.

"That's how you are, always unpredictable and exploding." Carrie looked close to tears. "One day you say I'm wonderful; the next day you're carrying on with another woman and want to leave me. Then two weeks later you say, 'I didn't mean to hurt you.' All the time, I'm supposed to let you do whatever." Her tone rose with increasing emotion.

"Carrie, I'm working on this."

"That's what you always say. God doesn't want me sworn at or treated with…with dis…disrespect. I'll divorce you. I really will. I don't have to take this."

"I don't need counseling, let alone six weeks of it."

My turn. "Rob, I set the six-week time period because it's often the absolute minimum necessary for covering basics of communication and conflict resolution."

"Carrie and I can work this out on our own."

"Have you ever had a broken bone? Physical healing often requires medical help and time. Healing of relationships benefits from professional help and the process of time, too." *Lord, help me motivate Rob. How stupid and incomprehensible a man's pride can be.*

"I know how to talk. Carrie doesn't listen—that's the problem."

"Me. You're the one…" Carrie thrust her finger at Rob's face.

"Often marriages headed for a split can be turned around once relationship skills are learned and when spouses become sensitive, loving partners. Carrie's moving into a healthy emotional state."

Carrie nodded. "That's 'cause God's become my source of love and security. I can make it without Rob if I have to do. Rob says he's Christian but doesn't live it."

"Carrie, you'd still like to strengthen your relationship with Rob, right?" I liked to clarify and keep my counselees' goals in front of them.

"We're fine like we are." Rob reached over for Carrie's arm. "Let's go."

She grunted and pulled away.

I stared straight into his eyes. "Give counseling half a chance, okay?"

"All right, I'm here, so do it. Let's get this over with." He jabbed a finger toward me. "Just remember"—his voice was intimidating—"I don't want nobody messing with my brain or Carrie's. Understand?"

I refrained from saying, "Let me tell you something…" God gave me extraordinary patience with resistant clients. "It's true I may ask you to make some changes during counseling, but they'll be good for you, too. Rob, Carrie's been hurt by your relationships with other women. Would you like her to see other men?"

"Whadda you talking about? They mean nothing."

"Then end every one. You can't fool around and be married. Fidelity is a serious issue. Remember, God hates divorce. Even past adultery can be resolved."

"If she's a Christian, she can't divorce me."

"As a last resort, only if a man or woman is in an abusive situation, God allows divorce." Carrie dug into her purse for a Kleenex and blew her nose loudly.

Rob seethed. "Abusive, whadda mean? Talk like this makes me want to walk, Carrie."

I studied Rob. His quick, deep anger startled me. Had he tried to remove Lenora from his wife's life so he could go on with his freewheeling lifestyle? If so, the attack backfired and made Carrie stronger.

Carrie switched her focus to me. "You can tell from his ways he's not ready to change. I'm only asking for better treatment." She pointed her finger toward Rob. "You leave me for one more wild night and you won't see me or your kids anymore."

The beauty of counseling was I get to be a couple's objective voice. *Time for me to take charge.*

"Carrie, is Rob a good father?"

"Yeah," she conceded.

"And do you honestly believe he loves you?"

"Yes." She folded her hands in her lap.

"You want him to be 100% faithful and more considerate of your needs?"

Out of the corner of her eye, Carrie glanced at Rob, probably to see if he was paying attention.

He was.

The tightness around her mouth relaxed. "Rob's the only man I ever loved." She spoke quietly, looking down at her hands in her lap. The words appeared to soothe Rob's gruffness like moisturizer on dry skin.

I thought of the biblical proverb: *A gentle answer turns away wrath*. "May I ask how often you tell him you love him?"

She raised her shoulders. "I'm not sure."

"It's been a year at least," Rob answered.

"Rob, what are your feelings toward Carrie?" I turned toward him.

"I'm not used to saying stuff like this..." His voice became quieter. "I do, I guess, I love her..."

"You guess. And what about the other women?" Carrie wailed.

"I've fooled around a little, flirting a bit...all guys do. It means nothing, just physical stuff. I don't want to lose Carrie."

"Rob, the majority of men don't flirt with other women because it can lead to dangerous situations. The worst is destroyed trust. It's more macho to be faithful," I said. "Infidelity is incredibly hurtful. I've dealt with the aftermath enough, I know."

"That's right. You can't be going out on me no more." She folded her hands dramatically across her chest. "I'm special, Rob Malone."

Attaway Carrie.

"I told you I'd quit fooling around. Stop picking," Rob snapped.

"Can I believe you?"

"Because I said it." The vein popped out on his neck.

I'd made my point.

"Rob, how often do you take Carrie out?"

"Out? She's always grocery shopping, cooking, or taking the kids to school. That's all she has time for." He shrugged his muscular shoulders. "I can't remember our last date. Not 'cause I don't want to. Carrie's always busy with the kids or housework or too tired."

Carrie jumped up. "Do you ever help with the kids so I'd have energy left to have fun?"

"Do you ever ask?"

"I guess not much." She eased back into her seat.

I shifted to face Carrie. "Why?"

"I don't think men are supposed to work 'round the house. My dad never did."

"Did he and your mom have a good marriage?"

"No."

"Or do fun things together?" I asked.

"Gosh, no." Carrie's eyebrows shot up. She got my point.

Did Rob get my point? His expression didn't give me an answer.

I forged on. "Married people with kids often forget to take time to be together or don't want to spend the money. A date can be an hour or two and doesn't need to be expensive. Go for a walk or coffee and dessert at least once a week. I hope you'll make time to be together a priority. I'll give you several conversation topics designed to increase emotional intimacy. If Rob wants to go out occasionally, go with him and agree together on where you'll go."

Rob started to mumble then quieted. "All right already. I got no objection."

"Good. Any other concerns?"

"I got one," Rob fired quickly. "I don't like Carrie telling all our private stuff to people."

"I'll talk about whatever I want, right?" Carrie looked to me, still needing huge doses of reassurance.

"If your goal is positive and constructive. When you're stuck on an issue, counseling can help but skip the gossip with friends. You and Rob can help each other, not tear one another down. Enough people and life events will do that for you."

"I'll stop bad-mouthing Rob if he treats me better." Carrie looked at Rob sheepishly.

He squirmed. "Whatever," he said.

"Okay, moving on. You both say you're Christians. That's not just a Sunday thing. Talk to God throughout the day. Ask every morning for God's blessing and protection on your marriage and your kids."

"We ain't never done that." Carrie fiddled with her ring and sent Rob a sideways glance.

"Will you give it a try?" I pressed.

Rob shrugged. Carrie nodded yes.

"And you might try holding hands and saying a prayer in bed every night before falling asleep."

Rob shook his head. "I stay up later than her."

"Then grab her hand when she says good night before she goes to bed. You can adapt and make these suggestions work for you, Rob. You're a smart guy."

He chewed down hard on his gum. "Maybe."

"Good." I picked up the Marriage Enrichment folder and whipped through my papers until I found the ones I wanted. "Here are emotional intimacy suggestions and a handout called Conflict Resolution—how to fight right without destroying each other." I handed over both papers. "Please read them before our next session."

"Cool," Carrie said.

Rob scratched his chin. "I'll do the dating and try the praying 'cause that's easy, but I'm gonna have to think about coming again. I'm a busy guy. I don't have time for all this." He waved his arm in a half-circle.

"You better," Carrie insisted.

"I'm not giving in about everything. I should be the boss of what we do."

Time for me to interject. "The goal in marriage is not 'Rob wins' or 'Carrie wins' but that both of you get your needs met and respect one another."

Rob stood up. "Okay, we're done for today. I'll be in the car. See ya." He waved his hand as he walked past me. I preferred to think that meant he'd be back.

"Carrie, use tough love wisely. Rob hasn't been sensitive to you for a long time, but that's no excuse for being overly demanding or unkind to him now that's he's beginning to try."

"Okay."

I scheduled another visit with optimism, and she hurried out. I'd have been pleased about our session except for one gnawing fact—Rob's taking satisfaction in Lenora's shooting. His viciousness disturbed me.

I tried to picture him as Lenora's assailant. Trekking through wooded terrain he'd manage with ease, but I couldn't see him waiting patiently to fire.

But then, I'd been wrong about people before.

CHAPTER TWENTY-SIX

AT TWO A.M. I awoke to Nick's snoring punctuating the silence of our bedroom. I tossed in bed, fighting a fruitless battle for sleep. Drowsiness played with me, bringing me ever so close before luring me away with thoughts of Lenora. I gave up, rolled out bed quietly as to not awaken Nick, and stumbled into the den.

Behind the closed door, I lit my desk lamp, inhaling the scent of Genji shower gel I'd used earlier. I pulled my well-worn *Orthodoxy* book by G. K. Chesterton from the blue bookcase I'd streaked with white glaze years ago when the process was considered trendy.

Philosophy should induce sleep, right?

After twenty minutes, I gave up and picked up the file box containing Lenora's private papers.

The soft light in the room helped dispel the creepy feeling of invading someone's life unknown to them. It seemed like I was holding binoculars to her window. What would I see? My only consolation was knowing she'd want me to do this.

I reviewed the most recent entries in her appointment book and worked my way back. *Lord, did I miss anything?*

I checked again for names that had been marked out, which I'd glossed over before. Now, examining more closely the remaining parts of the letters and tediously comparing all three cross-outs, I concluded the first letter and the last letter of each were A. I ruled out males because Lenora's private practice client load was predominantly female. I picked up my Ipad from the desk and searched an online for a list of girl babies' names beginning with A.

Alicia, Amelia, Amanda, Angela. This name had been written and inked out in every Wednesday the three weeks before Lenora was shot. "A" may have been a new client scheduled to come who changed her mind.

Angela Denton? Why no phone number next to the name? Lenora had written numbers next to her other appointments. Recording a number was common office procedure. Perhaps she had the number memorized or the person had no phone? Or maybe it wasn't safe to call? Clients sometimes didn't let family members know they were seeking professional counseling. If Lenora had worked with Angela, why hadn't she recorded any notes about Mrs. Denton in her files? Surely she would have written an initial assessment at least.

I scoured the appointment book for any other references to "A" but found none. Might this entry have been for a social visit rather than a counseling session?

I stuck my hand into the file pockets on the front and back cover. Two post-it size notes were stuck deep in the back one. One doodle, half-printed read, "Need to finish report for the American Jail Association, good project for Tucker if he'll do it. He's been moody lately." Hmm. Insight into their relationship?

The other note read: "Ask Tucker about the foundation account? Didn't the Landers family bequest come in? Balance seems off?"

The notes niggled at me. I disliked being suspicious, but for all I knew, he could be a gambler misappropriating funds and selling Lenora's home out from under her. Why don't women run background checks before they marry? Maybe a return to the good old days of arranged marriages or hooking up with someone from your own hometown might be a good idea. Then you'd have knowledge of what you're getting plus mutual history.

Jennifer, don't be ridiculous. Men don't shoot their wives because they found them moody and irritable. Still the reference to the account intrigued me. Was Lenora referring to a simple clerical error? What of the other note? Did Tucker resent Lenora's occasional working on weekends? Is that why she wanted to keep him busy? Few marriages escaped periodic stone-in-the-oyster-shell irritations. Rather than make pearls, the majority of people ripped out their grit with divorce.

Lenora had jotted in an appointment with her personal lawyer set to take place the Thursday after she was shot. Why was she seeing him?

I pondered Tucker's weekday living arrangement in Chicago. Long-distance intimacy could wither fast.

When it came to abusive behavior toward wives, I had seen so much that I was suspicious of husbands until proven innocent. Tucker appeared to show deep concern for Lenora but was that only since her shooting? Judging from his doting behavior and comments now, perhaps he regretted some measure of neglect in the past.

He and Lenora were apart more than they were together. I'd seen too much infidelity not to wonder. Not that he seemed a ladies' man.

Emotions people exhibited during trauma weren't always reliable. When I experienced excruciating pain, I often giggled. How crazy was that?

Could I, for a moment, suspect Tucker? Then again, why not? Did he actually have Christian morality or the mores of society? Anyone was capable of evil. I'd come a long way from my naïve, pre-Christian days believing everyone was basically good.

But he wasn't even in town when Lenora was shot; his alibi was airtight. I snapped shut the box and clicked off the light.

Nick was still asleep when I rolled my body against his back, hoping to entice him to wakefulness. He turned over and encircled me with his arms.

"What's wrong?" he murmured sleepily.

"Nothing you can't make right, darling. I can't sleep." I began to kiss his neck.

He rolled over and began to snore.

CHAPTER TWENTY-SEVEN

BY THE TIME I'd finished with my clients the next day, my subconscious had formulated a step-by-step plan for the evening, starting with a call to Tucker.

"Call before you visit." My mother's training served me well.

I caught him planning to leave for dinner in half an hour. "I'll be right over. I need to get something." I hung up before he could object. Not that I liked going in the first place, preferring to stay home with my family. Their energy and laughter appealed more than the scene of any crime, but I now had signed permission slips which enabled me to collect Lenora's group files to continue the counseling sessions with Carrie and Sandy.

Tucker answered my first knock. Gray circles ringed his eyes. He looked haggard. Sinatra crooned "I Did It My Way" over the radio. The words used to send a ripple of determination through me until I began to prefer doing things God's way.

Tucker's shoulders slumped unbecomingly. He reminded me of an elderly chief. Shouldn't he be surrounded by Indian braves?

"Are you okay?" The words shot out of my mouth.

"Sure." He appeared flustered. Commenting on his demeanor seemed to make him more uncomfortable.

"Thanks for waiting. I am counseling Lenora's gals. They consented. I'll need their recent files."

"You want to take them? Must you?"

"It's best. I'll add my notes to hers. Is there a problem?"

You'd have thought I was asking for the keys to his house. People acted strange during trauma, but this? "Remember, you wanted me to help. I'll be careful with them."

He sighed. "All right."

Tucker snapped on lights and led me through the great room. Even during the day, shadows filled the room. We walked past the open kitchen and breakfast room where I'd visited with my friend sitting on the lovely antique wicker furniture in green chintz spattered with peach and pink roses. Lenora should be perched there, exuding her brilliant enthusiasm. White enameled cupboards contrasted with the natural knotty pine walls in the main sitting room with its stately brick red fireplace. So Lenora.

Entering Lenora's office, I went directly to the six-foot-long carved library table desk. Inside its drawer, I hunted for a pen to write down today's date and notate the files I was removing. Nothing but whiteout, rubber bands, and markers. I remembered a pen in my over-the-shoulder bag.

Tucker hovered on my heels, acting like a guard at King Tut's tomb. Why the tight surveillance? Was he worried what I might find? Strange. I paused in my writing.

I approached the file cabinet, opened the top drawer, and worked my way through the alphabet, keeping these thoughts to myself. Nothing there but studies on prisoner behavior.

"Tucker, you're making me nervous."

"Sorry. I want to help."

I decided to test him. "By the way, I came across a note from Lenora about the foundation account."

He stiffened and avoided my eyes. "Nothing but a bookkeeping error. I made a deposit into our personal account by mistake and straightened it out as soon as I realized."

"That's understandable." A draft of cold air wafted through the open door.

"Lenora was peeved with me; I'm usually thorough. We'd laughed about it. She said she didn't want to have to fire me." Now his eyes riveted on mine. "Certainly you don't think I'd do something unethical..."

"Of course not. I wasn't implying anything, simply asking what happened."

"Good." He looked relieved. For Lenora's sake, I hoped he was innocent. She loved this man.

"Forgive me." He'd invited me to help, hadn't he?

Tucker turned down the music and settled on a green chair near the desk. I surmised noise helped fill the void of Lenora's presence.

He glanced at an envelope on the desk, and his eyes filled. "Just seeing Lenora's handwriting is painful. Her arms are now stuck with IV needles, and I wonder if she'll ever be able to write another word."

I walked over and gave him a spontaneous hug.

Clearly uncomfortable, he turned a blotchy pink. I made a mental note not to try that again. How could a woman who loved Battenburg lace and floral chintz, elegance and excitement, marry a cold persona like Tucker? Had he been a "settling for less than" as some women chose to do when faced with growing old alone?

Journals under Lenora's desk were stacked into cardboard file boxes. My friend had often joked about being a pack rat. Now I observed the extent for myself.

Several wire bins on the desktop overflowed with correspondence and yellow pages torn from legal pads. Filing apparently wasn't her thing either.

I rifled through, finding nothing of significance in the first two. To my delight, the third held Lenora's current counseling folders. I tucked the three I needed under my arm and straightened up.

"Done?" Tucker perked up as he said the word.

"Yes. I'll be taking off. How about you? Do you travel to the city tonight after your dinner?"

Tucker cleared his throat loudly before answering. "I resigned from my research job yesterday."

"What?" My eyes widened. "Why? Couldn't you have taken a temporary leave of absence?"

"Not with the deadline looming on our current project. It required someone full time. Right now it's hard for me to think about anything but Lenora. Funny, she always wanted me to spend more time on foundation work, but I was too busy. Now it's all I have." He lowered his eyes.

A ripple went through my chest. Why are men reluctant to show their feelings after years of talk shows about sensitivity issues? I gritted my teeth and approached Lenora's bookcase. A tiny wooden box on a shelf caught my eye. The top, painted with the words, "The Secret of Success," intrigued me. I lifted the lid and read, *Work hard, laugh much, and live well.* The saying fit Lenora.

Tucker's eyes followed me. His voice became a whisper. "We married too late for children. Lenora joked I was her kid. I have to admit she helped me become more childlike and taught me to enjoy life." He tensed. "Jennifer, am I kidding myself? Do you think she'll recover? I'm afraid to get my hopes up."

"Hope is never wasted. Many people are praying for Lenora's healing. Prayer is powerful. I'm concerned about you as well, Tucker."

"I'll be fine. I'm going back to the hospital after dinner. I just need more rest."

"Lenora needs you well and strong when she gets home."

He lowered his head. "I know."

His tone sounded forlorn. Did he not think she'd recover? And if she did, would she still be gifted with intelligence? How could any of us know God's plan for her future? I steeled my nerves. Hope and prayer were the only weapons in my arsenal on her behalf.

Outside the window the woods hedging three sides of the Tucker estate seemed less ominous in daylight, but still, the property gave me the heebie-jeebies. Lenora loved this isolation. She'd said time in nature kept her from being burned out by people.

As Tucker closed the door behind me, a song on the radio blared again. Had he changed his mind about leaving immediately?

CHAPTER TWENTY-EIGHT

SANDY RECKLAND DECLINED the comfy wingback in favor of my straight wooden chair with a padded seat, tucking her feet around the rungs. "My back's bothering me, and I can't get into the chiropractor until tomorrow."

I made a note on the physical assessment section of her intake form. Back pain. Symptom of stress? "I'm glad you came anyway. I hope I can help. I collected your treatment history file. Let's start with a review of your initial goals when you began counseling and now."

"They're the same—improving relationship skills."

"With family, friends, work?"

"Mostly work. I'm at a primarily male corporation. My associates have been known to complain that I'm too aloof, hard to approach. I keep my distance, that's all. It's okay for a man, but let a woman try it and she's labeled a people-hater. Women are supposed to be warm, fluffy, and friendly with everybody. I'm smarter than most men there, but they get the promotions." Her face lit like a blowtorch. "It makes me furious."

No need to use descriptors, Sandy. Anger is written all over you.

I wrote on my notes—resentment issues regarding men. "Lenora noted in your file that you weren't willing to try new behaviors that might contribute to better relationships."

"Because I didn't agree with her. She said I overreacted to the opposite sex, and she wanted me to release the deep-seated aversion I have toward men, work on becoming comfortable talking honestly with them. I told her she was wrong. I just keep my guard up because we're in competition."

"Might your aversion not be competitive but a fear of men, period?"

"I'm not afraid. I choose to protect my emotions until I meet a man I can trust. What's wrong with that? I just never have. And in the meantime, I refuse to pander to the male ego."

"Lenora mentioned to you that could be a cop-out?" Associating my words with Lenora helped me make my point without alienating Sandy.

"You bet. Said I wasn't being honest with myself." Sandy rubbed her chin.

"True?"

"Maybe."

"Have you dated since your divorce?"

Sandy flushed and shook her head. "I'm not a lesbian, if that's what you're thinking. I intend to marry someday. People always want to fix me up with guys," she ranted. "I don't know why. What's wrong with being single at my age?"

I lifted my palms as an imaginary shield to deflect her wrath. "I only asked the question."

"I'm going to have a business card printed that reads, 'Personal Life Private.' All new acquaintances ask, 'Are you married?' When they find out I'm not, they assume I'm pining for a guy and want to arrange a date. They always know just the person." Her complaining seemed a well-formed habit.

I chuckled. "I agree. Matchmakers can be insensitive."

Sandy removed her jacket. "It's warm in here." Her tight turtleneck accentuated the pudginess around her middle when she fiddled with her Harley designer belt buckle.

I smiled. Maybe I was getting through to her. "I'll turn the fan on." I pulled out Sandy's yellow social history form and frowned. It was blank. "Why didn't you fill this out?"

"I don't like anyone digging into my past."

"Let's see. You dislike counseling and resent people implying that the single life is inadequate, but you admit you'd like to marry eventually if you meet a kind, loving man. You've had relational problems in the past you don't want to talk about. How would you like me to help you, Sandy?"

She leaned back. "You're like Lenora, direct. I hated her boldness, too."

"Hate's a strong word."

"Deal with it. Don't think it gives me a motive to shoot Lenora."

Thank you. I'll give it more thought now that you brought it up. Where did her anger come from? I eyed her closely.

"I believe in violence when it's called for. I carry a concealed weapon and don't care who knows. I have a license which makes it legal here but, unfortunately, not everywhere."

"You're armed because you're fearful?"

"It's just smart. The crime rate dropped after people were allowed to protect themselves. If it comes to my life or somebody else's, I'll fight to stay alive but only shoot in self-defense. You can be sure of that. Anyway, maybe I got a little ticked off, but that's not a reason to go after Lenora Lawrence."

A line from Shakespeare's Hamlet ran through my head: *My lady doth protest too much...*

How had Sandy connected with Lenora? Did they know each other prior to establishing a counseling relationship? I asked.

"No need to go there. I'm her, what do you call it, her counselee, period."

"I'm wondering why, since frankly you appear rather resistant to the process." Might as well be truthful.

"I have my reasons."

I looked at the wall clock behind Sandy's chair. I positioned it so I never have to check my watch directly when with a client, which seems rude. It was easy to lose track of time during counseling sessions. It was best when I wasn't tightly scheduled and could ignore the clock, a utopian idea. Real life didn't cooperate.

"Unfortunately our time is up for today. How about continuing counseling in the small group?"

"I'll think about it and get back to you."

"My secretary will call you when we get the group time nailed down, and you can let me know then."

She grunted an okay.

Was Sandy truly motivated toward self-improvement? For her sake, I hoped so.

She shrugged and stood up. I noted her height, approximately five-foot-ten, on my initial assessment form. Height and weight I record if I believe they may affect a person's emotional state. For Sandy, being almost six foot could limit the number of men available to date. Although some shorter men are comfortable dating taller women, most are not.

I recalled the driver's account of a man walking on Old Bend Road the night of Lenora's shooting. With a cap over her head, Sandy's build and stride could be easily mistaken for a man's. How much hatred did she have?

Stretching back in my desk chair, I extended my arms overhead and stretched before I summarized her notes: *Major issue—unsatisfying relationships with males, perhaps females too. Pent-up anger needs release.* The question weighing most upon me, I wouldn't write in her file.

Had Sandy released her anger on Lenora?

CHAPTER TWENTY-NINE

MY *JOURNALING THROUGH Trauma* group ended at four p.m. Sweet group of young women, all traumatized by the actions of a loved one either through divorce or abuse. After five months, I saw real progress in each of them.

I'd earned a social break. How I treasured special moments with girlfriends, few as they were at this time of life. I smiled as I placed the call—recent research confirms that women thrive on time with female friends as much as exercise. I combined both with Mary, my warm and funny workout partner. A native of Lake Geneva, she knew everyone in town and most of what was going on. And I had more questions I wanted to ask her about the Dentons.

I reached Mary on the third ring. "Are you up for a hike to celebrate this gorgeous day? Actually, it'll be more of a slow walk; I'm still nursing a sore ankle. And I warn you, I also want to pick your brain about someone."

"Hold on."

Through my office window, I gazed upon sun-drenched, colorful shrubs. The day was picture-perfect for anything but staying indoors. I hoped Mary would be available. She came back on the line. "Sure. I'm nursing the baby. Does that make us even? As for my brain, I hope you can find something useful in there. I'm sleep-deprived. Where shall we meet?"

"How about the lake trail between Williams Bay and Fontana?"

"Okay. Bill can babysit—he's home early. I'll meet you downtown Williams Bay in half an hour. Bill can pick us up in Fontana afterward and drive us to our cars so we don't have to hike back. Is an hour long enough?"

"Perfect."

Next I dialed Chris. "Hey, girl."

"Jennifer! Nice to hear your voice. What's up?"

"My ankle's fairly healed, and I'm going for a short hike with a friend. Want to join us?"

"Thanks for the invite. Can't. I'm in the middle of paperwork. A rotten task but it's got to be done. I hope to be on the road for home by five. Keep in touch."

"Call me if your business brings you back to Walworth County."

When I reached Williams Bay, cool breezes stole the afternoon's warmth. No matter. The exquisite Lake Geneva waters held a million beckoning sun diamonds on their surface. I parked in the visitor lakefront area and popped my trunk to pull out my gym bag and running shoes from the collection of golf clubs and tennis rackets. I liked to be ready for any sports opportunity.

Ducking inside the restroom, I donned a gold cotton sweatshirt and jeans then slathered sunscreen on my face. I folded my clothes and placed them in the car before starting down the paver brick path.

Mary appeared behind me race-walking, arms bending at the elbow and moving rhythmically. My dear friend gave up a posh public relations job to mother her third child, born three months ago. Her small mouth shaped into a smile. "All set. I didn't take time for make-up."

"I'm sure the trees won't mind, nor I." I marveled at her natural beauty.

Mary laughed. She didn't have a shred of self-focus—by-product of a super-secure childhood.

We threaded our way past the picnic benches to the start of the trail. Mature oak trees and thick woodsy bushes bordered the path. "You're glowing."

"I love being home with Emma. She's such a joy. I enrolled the other two in daycare six weeks after birth. This time I told Bill no way I'm missing out."

I stumbled over a tree root and regained my balance. "Good for you. I stayed home two years after giving birth then started back part-time. I wish I'd waited even longer. I actually had a clutter-free house when I didn't work because I had time to put away all the books and papers Nick drags out, not to mention the shoes and clothes. It's stupid to rush this down time."

"You're right. Two months back on the job, people will forget I've ever been away. I've seen it happen with other gals. Financially, Bill and I are doing without a few luxuries and squeezing by, but we don't regret our decision. " She winked at me. "So what if Goodwill is my clothier of choice."

"Hey, I'm all for bargains. Consignment shops are my Macy's substitute. I need to economize to pay for my husband's hobbies—fishing and golf. It's better than gambling or other women, he reminds me often enough."

Mary chuckled. "Bill likes having me calmer, although he jokes about living like a missionary. Come to think of it, we both laugh a lot more." She chattered on. "I know not every woman can be so lucky."

"Or brave. It takes guts to walk out of a successful career and hope to hop back in."

"I should have done this before, but I was too scared to give up my paycheck. I figure being a calm, focused mom is what God wants, and He'll provide to make it work."

"So Bill's good with your being home now?" We walked side-by-side as the path widened.

"The hardest thing was persuading him to downsize our house. Now he thinks it was his idea. Go figure. Our friends think we're crazy, but we're truly happier in a smaller nest."

Two walkers approached from the opposite direction. We exchanged greetings, edging over to give them room to pass.

"What's the latest with Lenora's situation?"

"The police completed their investigation."

"I'm out of the news loop since we're using our daily paper for the new puppy. At the speed he goes through them I won't be getting more than iPhone headlines for a year."

"Mary, who but you would get a puppy and a new baby at the same time?"

"There aren't many women this dumb."

"No, just on the unpredictable side. The police are pinning Lenora's shooting on Kirk Corsini, the ex-convict she befriended, but evidence is circumstantial at best."

"I hope Kirk didn't do it. For Lenora's sake."

"I'm counseling Lenora's clients and trying to get a line on any other potential assailant while nosing around in her world. Speaking of that, I could use help."

"Sure. How?"

"Some local info."

Mary stumbled on the steep path and began to slide down the hill toward the water.

I lunged for her, eyeing Lake Geneva fifteen feet below us. She'd already grabbed a tree branch with her other hand and secured her feet again.

We straggled over to a white wooden bench bordering the path.

Mary was panting. "That was scary. I'm happy to help if I can stay out of the lake. Shoot with the questions."

"Okay. What do you know about the Denton family apart from what you already shared about their daughter, Joann?"

"Chuck and Angela Denton?" She brushed her forefinger across her lips. "Well, she grew up here. Maiden name was Ty something. Tysen, I believe. She's older than me by three years and was a senior at Big Foot High my freshman year. I didn't know her personally. As I recall, she left the area after graduation."

"But they returned?" I propped my legs up and wrapped my arms around my knees.

"Yep. She came back years later married to Chuck Denton when he got transferred to Lake Geneva to be vice-president of the biggest bank in town."

"Nice." I pulled several thistles from the hem of my pants and tossed them into the woods.

"Not totally. Sad part is I heard after Angela's child was born she had several nervous breakdowns and deals with spells of depression. Now, why are you asking? Tell me."

"I'm simply curious because they live near Lenora, and he's a member of Lenora's board for the Second Chance Foundation."

Mary tapped her chin. "It makes sense he'd be involved with the foundation."

"What do you mean by that?" I was all ears.

"Angela's daughter said her dad came from an impoverished background. That's probably why he's empathetic with prisoners and enjoys helping underprivileged people like he was growing up."

I turned to face her. "Funny. That's not what he told me. Said he was a rich kid."

Mary shrugged. "You must be mistaken."

"No, I don't think so." I drew an imaginary line under Chuck's name in my mind. In my opinion, one lie clouded a person's character. Fudging about a minor matter, how trustworthy were you? I tried to impress the importance of complete truthfulness on my children. I filed this away to consider later. "Since returning, has Angela ever worked outside the home?"

"Not that I know of."

"Does she attend any local women's groups, volunteer, that sort of thing?"

"Not that I'm aware of. It's a mystery what she does all day long. TV, I guess, maybe cooking and cleaning. I've run into Chuck picking up carry-out meals, but then so do I." She laughed. "I doubt anyone's been past the front door of their home. I sure haven't. Rumor is Angela has no interest in clothes or decorating."

A loud, cracking noise to our right shattered the peace of the woods like a hammer hitting cement. I jumped a foot and ducked.

Mary didn't flinch. "Must be a dead tree falling. We'd better get going. It's getting late."

I rubbed my arms briskly and started back onto the trail with a quickened pace. "One last thing about Angela—I want to meet her. She may have seen someone suspicious at Lenora's property since she's always home." I grabbed hold of a nearly horizontal tree branch to support me on this downhill part of the path.

"I doubt you'll get her to speak to you. We're talking first class recluse."

We walked on in silence except for Mary occasionally naming species of trees we passed. I pondered this new information about the Dentons, tuning in to Mary again when she said, "Can you believe this lake is five thousand acres, twenty-six miles around and two miles wide?"

"Where are you pulling these numbers from?"

"When I was a teen I volunteered at the Chamber of Commerce and sometimes gave walking tours. Now it's a paid job. Want info on fishing in Geneva Lake? Pan fish, bass, walleye, lake trout and Northern in this still-clear, spring-fed lake water. Shall I go on?"

I laughed. "No. I'd prefer to hear anything else you know about the Dentons."

"Their daughter seems normal enough. Gets good grades in school. Wishes she had a sibling." She shrugged. "That's it. I don't know much."

"On the contrary, you're amazing." We formed a single file as the path narrowed.

"That's small town living for you. Lots of chitchat. How do you think we natives pass the winter?"

"Let me guess. Gossip parties?"

Mary chuckled.

The Abbey Resort in Fontana came into view. We crossed over the road, leaving the lake path behind. Mary spotted her husband, Bill, in their mini-van, and we sauntered over.

He leaned his head out to kiss Mary, then greeted me warmly.

"Been here long, hon?" Mary asked.

"Perfect timing. I just arrived."

I peeked in the van at the sleeping baby nestled in a car seat behind him.

Mary reached in and stroked her baby's cheek. "Hi sweetie, Mommy's back."

"Hop in, Jennifer, we'll drive you to your car," Bill offered.

Bill drove us both back to Williams Bay to collect our autos.

I headed for my car, savoring the vibrant peach and yellow sunset capping the lake waves. *Lord, how magnificent You are.* I stopped to take a picture with my iPhone.

My talk with Mary convinced me the sooner I met Angela Denton the better.

CHAPTER THIRTY

BEFORE GOING TO sleep that night, I recited my favorite verse from the book of James: *"If any of you lacks wisdom, let him ask the Lord who gives generously and graciously to all who ask."* I asked for a way to connect with Angela.

When I awoke the next morning, a plan occurred to me via my subconscious. Figure that.

During my mid-afternoon break, I scurried over to City Hall, a tan brick building, one block from the heart of downtown Lake Geneva. I pulled out my credit card to pay for parking and checked my watch. A meter watcher ten yards away was scheduling her stroll to dispense tickets. I played it safe when it came to parking violations.

Inside the bright interior, a clerk with hair the color of ashes and the body of a gymnast greeted me from behind a counter. She must have exercised from the day of her birth.

"How can I help you?" She stared vacantly past me.

"May I examine the plat books, please?"

Not cordial, not rude, simply an automaton in demeanor, the woman turned her back, wordlessly bent over and peered down at some low shelves. Seconds later she dragged a big book almost the size of a card table top onto the counter and helped me locate the Lawrence's Plat Section and Unit. I jotted down the size of their property and noted the ownership of the Denton acreage abutting the Lawrence's property. Pulling out a pad of blank paper, I drew a quick sketch of both.

I thanked the clerk and gathered my papers to leave, glancing up at the clerk. Wonder if she could take Nick in Indian wrestling? Certainly I'd be no match.

On my way out I checked the time on my cell phone. If I rushed, I could get to the Denton property and back before my next client.

Fortunately, traffic was light and I made every green light through town. Day of miracles.

The Denton land, secluded like Lenora's, was heavily wooded. The air, clipped and brisk, carried the scent of pine, one of my favorites. I studied the exterior of the house before exiting the car. The early Colonial architecture appeared structurally sound but lacked the painting maintenance, yard care, and flowers that spoke of a beloved home.

A chipped white overgrown trellis served as the skeleton for tentacles of grape vines. Hostas and ground cover planted perhaps by previous owners were untended. Bedraggled shrubs in the yard looked almost as sick as the nearly dead plants on the porch. Three rusty metal flowerpots on the railing contained pitiful-looking herbs. My nose burned when I caught a whiff. I'd bet they could poison soup. The landscaping would never qualify for a spread in House and Garden and didn't befit the image of a bank-vice-president's residence.

Since I was technically company, I figured I'd use the front entrance. I picked my way through lacy spider webs adorning the front walkway. The family must use the garage door. I doubted anyone had been on this path in weeks. A rake and broom leaned near the doorframe like skinny greeters.

A lone gray cat lumbered down the steps, as if to announce I've kept watch long enough, it's your turn. Two porch chairs served as catch-alls for stray objects—garden shears, a box of plastic bags, a pile of twigs. Disorder reigned everywhere. I hesitated. Did I want to pursue this?

Stop being squeamish, Jennifer. I squared my shoulders to knock but stiffened at the sound of a man's voice shouting words I couldn't make out. His tone was clearly demeaning. The harangue from inside the house lasted for what seemed minutes. Fingers shaking, I pulled the rusty horseshoe doorknocker.

Silence followed. The window curtain moved. A woman's face appeared then disappeared from the window.

Seconds later, Chuck Denton opened the door. His wide-eyed, darting expression told me he didn't get much company or welcome it.

I forgot he kept banker's hours and probably had the afternoon off. He hadn't changed from his white shirt, but his tie was loosened and shirtsleeves rolled up. Was his the voice that had been yelling? Who else could it be? The TV?

Chuck stepped onto the porch through an opening just wide enough for his thin frame. He plastered on a smile, instantly friendly.

I looked with narrowed eyes to see past him into the house, but he moved fast, blocking my view. He called over his shoulder, "Turn the TV down, Angela. It's too loud." Then he slammed the door shut behind him.

"Hello, Dr. Trevor. This is, er...unexpected." He didn't add "a pleasure" but the smiles I'd seen in Tucker's driveway reappeared.

Out of the corner of my eye I caught sight of a woman's face in a corner of the window. Chuck followed my gaze, glared, and she dropped the drape.

"What brings you here, Dr. Trevor?"

"A purely social visit."

"Social?"

"I wanted to talk with your wife. Chatting with my friend, Mary, I realized our daughter goes to school with yours. I'm planning a mother-daughter tea and wanted to invite her. May I introduce myself, since I'm here?"

"It's kind of you to come, but Angela's not feeling well today. I'm sorry you made the trip for nothing."

Denton's brush-off was smooth.

"Perhaps another time." I turned to leave.

"Dr. Trevor," Denton stepped a few feet farther out onto the porch. He lowered his voice and looked at me intently. "I don't think you understand; my wife isn't comfortable in social situations."

"Chuck, forgive me, I don't mean to be rude, but didn't she interact fine socially with Lenora?"

Chuck's eyes darkened. "What gives you that impression?"

"Lenora's calendar." An image of Angela's name crossed out sprang into my mind. Had she and Lenora ever connected? My words were pure bluff, and I was a great poker player. A tinge of guilt gripped my gut. Quickly I rationalized I hadn't lied, just implied.

Denton studied me. "My wife's on her calendar? I can't imagine why."

I didn't tell him that his wife's name, if it had been her, had been crossed out in Lenora's appointment book, and there were no counseling records.

His neck veins pulsated. Was Denton distressed, furious, or merely surprised? I couldn't tell. "Must be a mistake."

"The week Lenora was shot, in fact."

Denton's cold stare made my stomach queasy. I sensed his emotions could become ugly fast. Was Angela safe?

"I'll ask my wife about it and give you a call."

"That's kind of you. I'm hard to reach, so I'll get in touch with you." I wasn't going to leave the making contact ball in his court. I turned to leave.

"As you wish. Now if you'll excuse me." Denton disappeared into the house.

An inside door slammed. I retraced my steps down the walkway. I wished I wasn't hunting blindly not knowing for sure if the two women had met.

But if Lenora had gotten through to Angela Denton somehow, I would, too.

DRIVING PAST LENORA'S property on my way home sent shivers down my arms. A close proximity to the scene of her near death distressed me on several levels, one of which was contemplating my own demise.

If I died tomorrow, I'd leave behind a precious husband and family, a household of stuff special mostly to me, appointment calendars with people's names in hourly slots, and professional writing that I hoped signaled my life had been of use. My husband and kids would treasure my personal journals, describing the events of our shared lives, my reflections on God, people, and myself. I often shared about God openly in the movement of everyday life. There'd be few surprises in my written expressions of love for them, which they received often.

Slowing my speed through downtown Lake Geneva, I enjoyed seeing its unique retail stores with colorful shop awnings. I devoted my attention to avoiding hitting tourists meandering across the streets in small droves, not always with the light. Groups of highschoolers sauntered along the sidewalk in their uniform jeans. Intermittent benches held tired shoppers, mostly men, resting while their wives scoured the quaint shops and artsy galleries strategically dotting the main street.

This friendly tourist city seemed an unlikely environment for attempted murder. Not any longer.

Who had fired the shot that nearly killed my friend? I sensed Angela might be a key to unraveling this. How could I get through the barrier her husband had built around her?

CHAPTER THIRTY-ONE

THE NEXT MORNING, I nosed Nick's Chrysler convertible in the direction of my office. Riding with the top down gave me the illusion of a fun and carefree life. What a lovely deception.

I borrowed Nick's car every chance I got—unfortunately, seldom. What soccer mom carpooled in a convertible? A van worked best with plenty of seatbelts for all the urchins' bodies I transported with their sticky fingers and book bags and every kind of sports equipment imaginable.

On the way to work I called Kirk, intending to give a boost to his spirits. I had nothing new or substantial to offer. The call might be considered a waste of time. But, I was a born encourager.

This was the third time in two days I'd been unable to reach him. I bristled. Something wasn't right. I pulled over and looked up the number of the owner of the building where Nick had put him up temporarily, since the foundation wouldn't allow him into their quarters.

The landlord informed me that Kirk had packed up and left no forwarding address. I pounded the dash with a clenched fist. So he'd disappeared on us. So much for proving his innocence. How guilty did this make him appear? Instead of gratitude, Nick and I got this in return. I resolved to find the number of the guys who put up bail for him.

I followed up by phoning the local police chief for any new information in Lenora's case. The chief was a friend since our mutual work in community anti-drug programs at the local high school.

After a few minutes of small talk, he said, "We're putting together a solid case against Kirk." He assured me nothing had changed.

I didn't tell him about Kirk's sudden departure. "Even though he made bail and the evidence is still circumstantial?"

"Says who? He's our primary suspect. My gut says it's a clear-cut crime of passion. Very common. Prison can make an already angry man into a furious bear."

"But Lenora had helped rehabilitate him…" *Yeah, sure.*

"I know it's hard for you counselors to realize you can't play God and transform every life you touch, but this is truth, raw as it is. Some people won't change; they just pretend well. May as well accept it."

I winced. Not what I wanted to hear.

The chief continued. "Why try to make something more out of this shooting? The summer season's upon us. We're super busy. This case is straightforward. You're a counselor; what do you know about ex-convicts? With all due respect, do your job and let us do ours."

Ouch. Wait until he found out Kirk had taken off. I wasn't about to be the bearer of that news.

"Thanks for your time." I stretched the words to avoid sounding sarcastic. It was hard.

Chuck Denton reached me by phone five minutes after I walked into my office.

"Dr. Trevor, I'd like to discuss yesterday's visit with you. May I stop by this afternoon? I don't need much time. Say, about fifteen minutes?"

I skimmed my desk calendar. "I have a break at three. You're welcome to come then. I have several questions for you as well."

"Thanks. See you later."

I'm impressed, Mr. Denton. I didn't have to call you.

I speculated on the reason for his visit. Had Angela confessed to Denton that she'd met with Lenora for counseling? If she had? Had therapy taken place or a social visit? Was her name crossed out because she'd come and the appointment was over or because she'd cancelled? A casual friendly visit wasn't likely given Angela's apparent aloofness.

Or, was there another woman named Angela? I couldn't rule that out.

If Angela had met with Lenora, would Denton be upset? Some husbands, like Rob Malone, were creepy. They got scared at the prospect of having their wives become healthy. Often that meant the husbands would have to change some of their own erratic behavior. Might that be true of Denton?

The day passed uneventfully, a pleasant and rare event of late.

On the dot of three o'clock Denton sauntered in wearing a pinstripe suit, maybe the same one I'd seen the other night. "Now, about Angela." He plopped into a chair making himself at home. I braced myself. Could I trust a husband's perspective? I worked hard not to let my impressions of a person be colored by what family members said. It wasn't always easy to block.

Denton flashed his banker's smile, not too much teeth, good eye contact, showing no trace of his former testiness. This man could exude great warmth. Great demeanor for a salesman. He definitely looked trustworthy. If the logistics were right, I'd buy insurance from him. Banking was competitive nowadays, too. He probably did well. So why the rundown house? Lack of interest in personal surroundings? Financial issues? Doubtful. Or to keep people away? Strange. He dressed professionally, though.

"Jennifer, I want to apologize for appearing rude yesterday."

I bit my lip to keep from saying, "More than appearing. You were. Let's be accurate."

He turned one of my straight back chairs backwards and straddled it. My body analysis kicked in. I considered this a motion of exhibiting superiority.

He glanced behind him. Was he checking that the door was locked? "I'll get right to the point. Few people know about my wife's situation. I certainly don't intend to broadcast her past, but you seem genuinely concerned. Under the circumstances of what happened to Lenora, I'm going to confide in you."

"I appreciate your trust."

He nodded. "My wife has suffered from severe emotional problems for years."

"How far back are we talking about?"

He took a deep breath. "Since after our daughter was born. It's why we only have one child. Angela had postpartum depression and never fully recovered. She's been seen by specialists in Chicago and Milwaukee for years of cognitive therapy off and on." He paused a moment, looked at his hands, then continued in a dull monotone. "Nothing they ever did has helped except putting her on medication. Even electro-shock failed."

"How sad for her and you as well."

"No words could describe it."

I studied him. Words, no, but I'd expect some sign of emotion to match what he was saying. I made a note of his lack of affect while staying tuned in to what he was saying.

"You can't begin to imagine what it's been like. Before we married, Angela was training to be a nurse. Now she barely functions as a recluse. At least currently, she's getting out of bed. She's had spells when she won't even do that."

"This must be very difficult."

He nodded vigorously. "Walking and housecleaning are Angela's only activities. In some strange way, walking seems to soothe her. Thank God for that. I rarely hire household help because she's fearful having strangers around. Our daughter helps cook and do some chores, and I do what I can."

I nodded my understanding

"It's hard on all of us. There are times when Angela withdraws altogether. It's crazy. I never know what to expect when I walk in the door. I know I may sound insensitive. I don't mean to, but it does get wearisome struggling to keep up with my job, a home, and care for my daughter."

I squeezed my hands together and pressed them under my chin. "I understand."

"I hoped you would. That's why I'm here." He stood, turned the chair around, and sat facing me. "It helps to have someone appreciate the reality of our situation. I'm telling you this because I can't be having my wife regress."

"Surely there must be something that can be done to help her…"

"The professional consensus is that her issues are best left dormant. Whenever we try to address them, she shuts down. After the last attempt at therapy, Angela cried for days and wouldn't come out of her room except to use the bathroom. I vowed I'd never put her or us through anything like that again."

"Is she on medication now?"

"Several drugs. For acute depression and anxiety. I don't know how many prescriptions it took before the psychiatrist found an effective combination."

He gave me their names and dosage levels, which I recorded.

"My concern is that her tolerance level will increase, which has happened before. Then we're back to square one for treatment."

Denton rattled off clinical terms like a professional, and what he said made sense. But for a reason I couldn't quite identify, I found it hard to feel sympathy for this distressed husband and father.

He pulled out his handkerchief and blew his nose. "The bottom line is, we finally have a routine working fairly well. I'm not willing to have Angela go through more trauma. For her sake and ours, I want her left alone." His tone intensified. He became more emphatic with "I" and repeated himself.

I leaned forward and held his eyes with mine. "Without further intervention, Angela may remain a recluse forever and not move toward the recovery she's capable of experiencing. Surely you don't think this is wise?"

His demeanor visibly hardened. "Did you hear anything I said?"

"With all due respect, your wife deserves a chance at a normal life. You can't stop making an effort to get her help. Has she ever been in a support group? Some individuals are helped best in a group setting. It can be less threatening to hear other people talk about similar issues and can be highly therapeutic."

Denton's complexion shaded from pink to red. "You counselors are all the same. You each think you have the magic dialogue or pills to help. Don't you get it? I'd stick Angela's feet in axle grease every day if it would make her better. I tried everything psychologists suggested. Forgive me if I've lost confidence in this mind scrabble you play. Fifteen years without results is long enough. My wife won't be a guinea pig anymore."

"Prayer is also an important part of my therapy. I've seen the Holy Spirit do some pretty remarkable things. Don't let her give up hope."

Denton's face became redder by the minute. "I thought I could make you understand. You're as egotistical as every clinician. You think you can find a way when no one has."

"Sometimes clients do get worse before they get better. You may have stopped too soon. The good news is, it's never too late."

"No more psychological garbage." His eyes sparked.

A shiver climbed up my spine. "So Lenora counseled Angela privately?"

He slumped in the chair. "She had one session. I could tell immediately by her distress when she came home."

"And you wanted Lenora to stop? Did you insist Angela ask Lenora to cancel her future appointments?"

"You bet I did." He pressed his palms hard on the arms of his chair.

"When did you tell Lenora? The day she was shot? You may as well tell me. Her housekeeper says she can recognize the voice of the man who argued with Lenora that day."

"All right, I was there." He spit out the words and looked at me as if he wished he'd swallowed them instead. "I told Lenora what I'm telling you. I couldn't have her digging into Angela's pain and making her worse."

"How did Lenora respond?"

"Got huffy. We talked at length. I didn't convince her."

"Talked? According to the housekeeper, you yelled."

He rubbed the back of his neck. "I may have gotten a little hot."

Suddenly Chuck looked old and tired. "Do you have any idea what's it's like to be married to a woman for years and have her refuse to allow you to touch her?"

"I'm sure it wouldn't be easy living with a wife who doesn't function in any aspect of the role."

"Not only handling all the family responsibilities but having to forego physical intimacy?"

I put down my notepad. "My heart goes out to you."

"There's not a day I'm not tempted to leave Angela, but she's my wife. Who would take care of her?" He turned his hands over in a helpless gesture.

"What you've gone through has been terrible, I agree, but still, Angela should have a say in the decision about counseling. I simply want to let her know my services are available to Lenora's previous clients. I promise I won't try to influence her one way or the other."

Denton stood up, eyes blazing. "Let me be very clear. I'll slap a lawsuit on you if you try to treat her without my permission."

"On what grounds?" The skin on my neck tingled.

"I'll find one."

"I don't think it's wise for you to threaten me, Mr. Denton. Your wife is an adult. You have no right to keep her from seeking therapy." I used my voice of authority. Who did this man think he was? A seat on the foundation board didn't give him a license to intimidate me.

Denton swore then charged toward the door and stomped out.

So much for banker's manners.

I disliked confrontations, but sometimes they were necessary. Chuck's visit had given me an idea.

Two, actually.

CHAPTER THIRTY-TWO

THE FIRST BREAK in my schedule, I called Nick. "Hey handsome husband, got a minute?"

"For you? I might be able to arrange it. What's up?"

"You're not going to like this. Hear me out. I want to re-enact the circumstances of Lenora's attack. She was shot on a Thursday; today is Thursday. How would you like to take a hike up the hill behind her house tonight?"

"Right, I don't like the idea. What good will that do? The police have been all over the area."

"But I suspect not thoroughly."

Nick, seldom one for subtlety, blurted out, "I think it's one of your dumbest ideas ever."

I grimaced. "At least I can always count on you for total honesty. Okay, never mind. Don't give it another thought."

"Jennifer, hold on. You don't back off this easily. You'll go without me, right?"

I didn't want to answer so I hedged. "It's no problem, really."

Nick sighed. "I have to review material for a deposition tomorrow. I need to finish before I leave. I don't want you going alone. What time?"

"Around eight. We know the shooting occurred somewhere between eight and ten. I lined up a sitter and will give the kids an early dinner. We can eat later."

Nick laughed. "You've already thought through everything. Okay, I should be home by seven thirty."

AT SEVEN P.M., I dressed in jeans and polo shirt, crisscrossing the sleeves of a dark blue sweatshirt across my chest. My legs needed to be covered for traipsing through the woods. I wasn't going to let any skin-piercing, sucking insects attack my epidermis. Fashionably dark, Jennifer the Ripper was ready for her night job. Only one thing was missing. Hunting in my closet, I found two navy baseball caps and plopped one on my head, sticking the other in my back pocket for Nick. I tucked my bangs under the hatband.

When Nick pulled up the drive, I was at the outside porch table skimming the paper for news. He moaned when he saw me. "I was hoping you'd change your mind."

I rose, walked over, and kissed his cheek. He loosened his tie knot, now two inches from his Adam's apple.

"You look tired."

"I can't imagine why. I've only been up since six and had a turkey sandwich for lunch and…"

I kissed his lips. Guilt cinched my chest. "Want to change your mind?"

"No. I need some exercise. Give me a few minutes to greet the kids and change."

"Your clothes are on our bed; we'll be twins."

"A dream come true. You better not run into any clients in your get-up," he teased.

I tossed my backpack with our supplies on the back car seat, jumped in and pulled out the rough drawing I'd made of the Denton and Lawrence properties to review my penciled-in marks for Lenora's house and the ravines on the north and east sides. Approximating the size of her acreage, I'd already drawn in their neighbors on either side.

Ten minutes later, Nick returned looking like my clone several sizes bigger.

"Cute." I whistled.

He ignored me. "Okay, tell me why we're doing this." He started the car and we were off.

"I want to know how long it takes to climb the hill and return to a car parked below. The sniper could have driven up Lenora's driveway and walked around the house into the woods, but if so, Lenora would have heard the car. Chances are he or she came up the back through the woods on foot. It's likely a car parked somewhere back there would have gone unnoticed because the houses are so spread out."

When we reached the spot where I told him to stop, Nick examined the map. "What are these dots?"

"The dotted lines show the easiest area to climb up from the road below. I'm guessing the police were so sure Kirk did it that they didn't expend manpower checking details. They figured when Kirk pulled up to Lenora's the night of the shooting, he'd been there earlier and came back with a weapon to shoot her."

"And Kirk said he was an hour late for his appointment with Lenora because of a flat tire."

"Remember though, I doubt Kirk is capable of that kind of duplicity."

"The police wouldn't waste men investigating a case they see as clear-cut. Okay, let's go."

Nick put the convertible top up.

"Perfect timing. I want to start up the hill just before it's completely dark."

I pulled two flashlights from my backpack. Before we exited, I checked the back seat and flipped the door locks. I didn't want to return to a guy crouched inside. It showed how jumpy I was.

"As we ascend, keep your eye out for anything unusual, broken branches or an item that would indicate someone trekked through," I said.

"Big deal. The police roamed through here, so we'll be on their trail."

"Maybe, maybe not." I checked my watch. "Let's head up."

Halfway to the top, two paths about sixty yards apart converged into one.

I glanced at Nick. His mouth was set in a grim line. "Look happy, love."

"Sorry. Hunting for evidence of a potential killer doesn't thrill me."

"Me either." I shuddered.

CHAPTER THIRTY-THREE

THE GROUND, STREWN with wet leaves, nearly obliterated the narrow, ancient path. I let Nick lead. He parted the mass of brambles. A thorn bush snapped back, and I blocked the sure slap in the face with a quick hand in front of my face. This area hadn't seen tourist traffic ever. Forging through the brush with no designated path was far from a fun walk.

Every now and then Nick mumbled, "This was a dumb idea" to let me know how thrilled he was to be here, in case I forgot.

"Thanks for coming, sweetie. Keep your eyes open. I think the shooter came up this way."

"Why do I let you talk me into these things?" Nick's voice reeked frustration.

"I will admit, it's tougher than I expected. I'll lead for a while."

"Why couldn't we do this earlier in the day?"

"I told you. I wanted to see it at dusk."

"Some view. Even if there were evidence here, nature's quick to cover man's intrusions."

Snarled, thick vines scarfed broad oak branches. We entered an area where the terrain resembled more jungle than forest with thick foliage.

I struggled to keep a steady pace, using my flashlight to sweep the area in front of us. Not that it was totally dark, but the light helped illuminate shadowy areas, and I also hoped it would warn any critters to move out of the way.

We penetrated a chunk of particularly dense woods. I held out my arm and stopped.

"Nick, did you hear that?"

"What?"

"It sounds like a car creeping along the road beneath us."

"So?"

"Cars usually speed by here; they don't creep." I looked down the trail. Trees blocked my view of the road. No lights were visible, so if there was a car below, its headlights were off.

I grabbed Nick's arm. "I heard it again."

"Somebody probably saw our car down there and wondered what kind of crazy people were up here walking around."

"Not necessarily. They might think we ran out of gas and went for help."

"Whatever. Come on, Girl Scout. Let's get this over with."

I waited a few more minutes but heard nothing.

"C'mon. Whoever had been down there must have moved on." I whispered to Nick, as if the animals were interested in overhearing our conversation. "I had told Tucker to leave the house lights on in Lenora's study when he went back to the hospital. Hopefully he remembered."

We continued to thread our way up the trail with care. I stumbled on a fallen pine tree jutting into the trail.

"Be careful," Nick snapped.

"I'm trying." I worked to keep irritation out of my voice. "When I was a child I remember running into the woods behind our house looking for places to hide. I'd pretend the huge oaks were guards protecting me." I fell silent, reliving struggles of my childhood and the emotional quirks I'd developed for survival in an alcoholic home.

Two hundred feet from Lenora's house we came across an actual once-upon-a-time-used trail, bordered by long overgrown day lilies now struggling for existence. Rocks set about two feet apart on either side of the trail showed someone had once cared for this section of woods. The trail split into a "Y" with two forks as it approached the rear of Lenora's house. At the center of the "Y" sat an old, weathered, almost hidden, bench.

"Look, Nick. Long ago somebody dragged a bench from the house along this rugged narrow path. It's a perfect spot for seeing the house."

"But how would the sniper know the bench was here? Certainly Kirk wouldn't know these grounds unless he did yard work for Lenora."

"I asked. He didn't. Estelle said Lenora's had the same gardener for years. A gentle old fellow—very unlikely he'd have a motive to shoot her or be capable of scurrying back down this hill if he did." I lowered my body gingerly onto the bench, testing out the once-green wooden slats. Could it support my weight? It was probably strong enough to survive ten children.

Lenora's house was now visible straight ahead. We had a clear view across the rear deck into the study. "Someone waited here for the light to go on in Lenora's study." I pointed to show Nick the line of access. "They could see her exactly where she sat."

"The view is good, I agree. The police would have found this spot when they checked the trajectory of the bullet, and they should have combed the area." Nick scanned the ground with his light.

"They might not have, not with Kirk all wrapped up with a bow. Move the beam slower. The police would have looked at this spot after they had Kirk in custody and assumed he was the perpetrator."

"They still had a job to do."

"How thorough would they be?"

He shrugged.

"Let's synchronize our flashlight beams."

We scanned the ground inch by inch then raised the level of the light in one foot increments making a circular sweep within a diameter of about eight feet. It was tedious. We had to move slowly. About five feet up, I elbowed Nick in the ribs, calling his attention to the low-hanging branch I illuminated. "I think I see something. Keep your light steady right there." I walked over to where a speck of white had caught my eye in the sweep of the flashlight.

Nick edged closer. "What is it?"

"Something caught." I pulled a glove from my pocket, slipped it on and reached up pulling a tiny rectangle of cloth from under a leafy branch. It had green thorns on it that I removed one by one.

"Looks like a clothing label." Nick read, "'Members Only' A popular brand. Maybe it got plucked by this branch as the sniper ducked under, that is, if it was already loose to begin with. Otherwise the tugging would have been noticeable."

I studied the tag. "Maybe there was the sound of a tear, maybe not. You can't stop if you're rushing away from a crime scene. Lots of branches the shooter would have brushed against, maybe even got caught on. The missing label probably wouldn't be noticed afterwards."

"If it was here after the sniper attack, why didn't the police find it?" Nick helped me put it in the plastic bag I brought.

"It was blocked by all these leafy branches. During the day it'd be harder to see. The darkness accentuates the white. When the police searched the area, the white was less obvious." I put my arm around Nick's shoulder. "So it is good we came tonight. I'm lucky I happened to catch it in the flashlight beam. I doubt the shooter knew it came off."

"Wait a second, Jennifer, we're making assumptions. This could be anybody's, even from a policeman's jacket."

I frowned. "Like they wear Members Only?" I turned the slightly off-white, inch-high label over searching for a size. "Perhaps it came off an unzipped jacket or maybe he got hot and took it off and carried it."

"One point in favor of this being left the night of Lenora's shooting is it couldn't have been outside long or it'd be more battered."

"You're right. The timing is perfect." I adjusted my cap.

The soft murmur of a motor drew our attention to car lights moving slowly across the road beneath.

I froze. "The creeping car is back again. This time with lights."

Nick grabbed my hand. "Someone checking on us?"

I snapped my flashlight off. "Put out your light. We don't want anyone seeing us," I whispered. We remained still a few minutes until the car was no longer visible.

Nick nudged me. "Let's finish up. Since you picked up the label on the right side of the fork, we'll look around some more there."

We flipped our flashlights back on. The trail twined around raspberry bushes with thick green underbrush filling gaps between them. I stopped at a spot where brush had been pushed to one side.

"Nick, why do you suppose Lenora's assailant didn't get closer to the house to make sure he or she didn't miss?"

Nick shrugged. "Too much risk. Or maybe supremely confident of his or her shooting ability."

"Okay, I've seen enough. Let's head back."

The trip going down was harder because of the wet, slippery leaves.

We were halfway back to the car when a shot split the night air.

"Hit the ground," Nick yelled.

No need to give orders. I'd already plunged to the earth.

Nick dropped on top of me. Moist leaves pressed into my face. My heart beat so fast, it pulsated against the earth. I feared I'd pass out.

Another bullet ricocheted off a tree near us.

"That was too close." Nick's hot breath panted against my neck.

Then silence. We waited. I lost all sense of time.

"Are you okay?"

"I think so," I said, trembling.

Leaves crackled and branches snapped just below us as someone raced through the woods. I sprang up and took off toward the sound. Nick was right on my heels.

He yelled, "What are you doing? We're not armed. This is ridiculous. We'll never catch up."

"I want to see the car down there."

"Why didn't you say so?" Nick charged out in front of me.

I slid down the hill and fell headfirst, barely missing hitting my head on a rock. Nick returned to help me up. Leaves clung to my jeans. The gloves protected my hands from what would have been bloody scratches.

The car below turned on its motor and pulled away without turning its lights on. "Strange." I strained to see the make of the car. It was too dark and far away.

"Jennifer, this escapade is dangerous. Somebody just tried to kill us."

"Or scare us enough into quitting."

I struggled for breath and checked my pocket for the label.

"Not a chance I'm giving up now."

CHAPTER THIRTY-FOUR

NICK AND I drove in silence to the police station to report the shooting. On top of his displeasure over our evening hike, I knew he had to be starving. The aroma of burger and fries inside somebody's office made my mouth water too.

I didn't waste time going into detail about what we were doing in the woods, only spit out the main points about the shots. The sergeant, curt and efficient, was non-committal as he listened. I'm not sure why, but I chose to not mention the label and fortunately neither did Nick.

The officer handed Nick paper and a pencil. He drew a rough map, showing our location in relation to the area where the shots were fired. "You should have no trouble finding bullets in daylight."

The sergeant sighed and grumbled but filled out a report and promised to investigate. "We've had some young gang members infiltrating our area. Kids take pot shots to scare people. We'll get right on it but don't expect we'll turn up much. These kids are a smart, nasty bunch."

On our way out, I poked Nick. "Do you think they'll follow through?"

"They have to at least make a semblance, but after what he said, it may be a waste of time."

AFTER AN UNEVENTFUL work day, the next evening I returned home as Estelle was packing her cleaning rags following her monthly, deep scrubbing visit. The house smelled deliciously of bleach and furniture polish, two of my favorite scents after Red Door perfume.

"Almost done, Dr. Trevor. I'll be out of your way soon as I finish and return the vacuum cleaner and supplies to the utility room." She twisted the vacuum cord around its hooks.

"After I change I'm headed there also, to put in a load of laundry."

As I filled the washing machine, Estelle shelved her cleaning items. We chatted briefly about our children.

Out of the blue she turned to me and said, "Funny you and Mrs. Lawrence don't lock your office like Mr. Lawrence and you got all those important personal papers."

I dropped in two more towels as I responded automatically. "Estelle, we lock our counseling files in cabinets. It's the law. It's not necessary to lock doors to our home offices if our files are locked."

"Mr. Lawrence's office in the basement has got double locks. I don't go near it."

I stopped midair pouring soap into the machine. How would she know that unless she'd tried to get in? "Estelle, will you repeat what you said."

"I'm not allowed to clean the locked basement room Mr. Lawrence uses for his home office. Seems a bit peculiar. I can't help wonder why. But then, I expect his research is real private and important."

"Estelle, why are you telling me this?"

"No reason. For sure I wouldn't be questioning his doings, but there sure is a bunch of noise that comes outta that room sometimes."

I couldn't get her words out of my head after we returned to the kitchen, and I wrote out her paycheck. "Thanks. Goodnight Estelle."

My cell phone vibrated. Nick's name appeared. Estelle waved as she exited.

The voice I loved more than any other flowed through the air. "Don't hold dinner for me, sweetie."

I slumped. "What's up?"

"The deposition ran over, and we ordered in sandwiches. I'll be home around nine unless I can compress this report and finish sooner."

"No problem."

"Don't be upset."

Did my voice sound testy?

After ending the call with Nick, I tossed together a dinner of chili and brown rice with corn bread. I decided to put together a plate of food for Tucker to take over later.

The children settled into their homework at the dining room table, no TV on school nights. I was a stickler on that. I sat with them and opened my brief case. The hum of mental activity was in the air.

The atmosphere was perfect for writing client discharge paperwork, but my brain wouldn't focus. So much for using the evening for catch-up.

I stood and stretched. "I'll be gone about half an hour, kids. Tell dad, if he gets back early that I went to Tucker Lawrence's to drop off dinner for him."

It was light outside, and I'd be back by dusk. No concern. Right? Wrong.

My dinner gesture wasn't totally altruistic. On the drive over, I recalled Tucker's hovering when I was at the house. What Estelle shared about a locked room on the lower level intrigued me. This conscientious woman's curiosity had transferred to me. I recalled what it did to cats.

As university staff, Tucker would have an office on campus. So why have one at home with papers important enough to lock up? What kind of research project was he working on?

I had no reason to be suspicious of his activities. I scolded myself.

Maybe Tucker's offhand comment the other day was right. Had the sniper meant to shoot him, not Lenora?

When I arrived at Lenora's, Tucker's car wasn't in the driveway. I knocked just to be sure it wasn't in the garage.

No answer. I twisted the doorknob. It opened with no resistance. *Unlocked? So much for a man who has something to hide.* Under the circumstances, I considered it an invitation to march in and leave the dinner I'd brought.

I deposited his dinner in the nearly empty fridge then searched through the twenty plus things in my purse for my notepad and pen to inform him I'd left a meal for him.

The silence of the house was broken by a loud thud, as if something fell from a high perch. The sound came from downstairs and was loud enough to startle me. Lenora didn't have a dog or cat. Was Tucker home after all? Why hadn't I checked the garage for a car?

I called his name and waited.

No answer. Had I imagined the sound?

I pulled my tiny notepad and pen from my purse, dashed off a note, and placed it on the kitchen table.

As if on cue, the thudding echoed again from downstairs like an object dropping. I called out Tucker's name again.

I collected my courage. Maybe a door had blown open. If so, I should go down and close it. I approached the stairs off the kitchen and tiptoed down. I'd never been on the lower level. Estelle had said the office was down here. Maybe Tucker was inside and hadn't heard my calls.

When I reached the last stair, although the light was dim, I could make out several rooms: storage, laundry, and the largest, a billiard room, were open. My gaze fell upon a closed door at the other end of the large area. Could that be Tucker's office? I worked my way through baskets and pool cues and tried the door. Locked. I jiggled the handle, and a thudding noise sounded inside. I shivered.

Perhaps an outside window had a shutter banging. I struggled to get my mental bearings and visualize the external structure of the house.

Suddenly a door slammed above me. Footsteps bounded straight down the stairs.

My feet locked on the floor. Seconds later, hot air breathed onto the back of my neck, and I whirled around and stared into Tucker's wide eyes.

"Why, hello," I stammered. "I heard a noise and decided to check. I mean, I came down here looking for you." My face was hot all over. I am so completely non-cool when flustered. "I've brought you dinner."

His eyebrows lifted. He looked at my empty hands.

"It's in the refrigerator," I blurted. "I understand from Estelle you have a home office in the lower level and a loud noise seemed to come from down here..." Stupid chatter.

A weird look crossed his face. I couldn't define it. His eyes bored into me. "Let's check." He withdrew a set of keys from his pocket and unlocked the door before us.

My heart was in my throat. He grasped my wrist and said simply, "We'll look together."

Tucker reached into the room, flicked the light switch, and gently pushed me forward.

It took several seconds for my eyes to adjust to the fluorescent light and fasten on a huge snake slithering along the floor toward me. I did a double take, gasped, and jumped back. Another reptile curled up in a ball next to a carton on a table. A discarded snakeskin lay coiled in the corner of the room.

My mouth fell open, my vocal chords paralyzed. I was a lousy screamer, or I might have broken Tucker's eardrums.

"You don't like my pets?" An amused expression played around the corners of his mouth.

"It's not often I'm at a loss for words, Tucker," I whispered. "Had you prepared me, I might have handled this better. I don't appreciate your bizarre sense of humor."

"Annabelle's restless. When she's active, she often knocks things down."

"That's the sound I heard."

"She probably bumped something. She gets to eat tonight. You can watch. It's an occasion. Snakes only eat once every seven to ten days."

Tucker strode past me to the large cabinet against the wall.

I watched dumbstruck.

He picked up a snake that had stretched itself across the chair. "Here she is." Annabelle made no effort to recoil and seemed to relish the attention. Tucker advanced toward me. "Isn't she adorable? Some snakes live twenty years as pets."

"Stop!" I shouted with the gusto of a football coach now. "No closer."

"Jennifer, don't scare my sweet snakes. Annabelle won't hurt you."

If the snake slithered up my arm, I might go into apoplexy.

Pleasure was written all over Tucker's face. He appeared to be stifling a grin as he savored my revulsion.

"Won't it get out?"

"The top of this cage is weighted so the snakes can't push it open."

I gulped. "Do you buy these in a pet store?"

"Most are special order."

"Isn't owning these snakes against the law?"

"Only one of my eleven snakes is poisonous—the Diamondback rattlesnake from northern Wisconsin." Tucker pointed to a cage in the far corner. "I have a special permit from the Department of Natural Resources to keep the rattler for scientific research."

"But, is it safe to keep it in a private home?"

Tucker shook his head. "The rattlesnake is in a padlocked vivarium. If it should get out and bite, the person would have to be allergic or unable to get an immediate antidote in order to die from the venom."

"How comforting." A stone clattered off the ledge rimming the room.

"Be careful, Annabelle."

I glanced around. The cages had labels with each snake's name and classification.

"Annabelle's on the prowl for food. Usually snakes are quite complacent but get agitated when hungry."

Tucker pulled a heavy cardboard box from under a counter. I stood mesmerized as he opened the lid. Inside seven white mice scurried around helter-skelter. He turned the box on its side, removed the perforated metal mesh top of the glass cage, and shook the mice into it. "Dinnertime. Sorry, mice, time to die."

I squealed. "You're some kind of masochist."

He appeared offended. "Nature's food cycle, Jennifer."

"I know, but…"

"Watch closely or you'll miss it." He never took his eyes off the ghastly, fascinating event. With a quick, barely perceptible move, the snake strangled and ingested each mouse in one smooth swallow. All seven mice were gone within seconds.

Finally, he placed the satiated snake in a glass-sided cage on the floor.

If it hadn't been more than an hour since I'd eaten, I'm sure I'd have been sick.

"The warming brick in the cage helps Annabelle with digestion. Like that shiny skin? You'd be surprised how dull it gets when about to be shed."

Good grief. Tucker was giving me a science lesson. He continued, "Sometimes they shed every couple weeks, really depends on how fast a snake is growing."

Tucker affectionately picked up another reptile, a Florida Kingsnake, to fondle. My prior knowledge was zero, and I didn't welcome today's learning experience.

"This little guy will be about six feet. Want to hold King?"

"No thanks. Your snakes are incredible, just not my thing, sorry. Plus my children need to be tucked into bed. I can find my way out." I inched to the door careful where I stepped. "I hope you enjoy the dinner I brought, nothing fancy, but it is home-cooked."

"Great, I'm starved. Thanks for your kindness." Tucker returned the Kingsnake to its cage. "I'm sorry you don't like them." His mouth turned down, and his voice trailed off.

I waited while he shut the door to the snake room and followed me. "I prefer pets that bark or meow and have legs."

"I selected snakes because I'm away a lot, and they don't need daily care." He winked. "I don't tell our friends about my herpetology hobby. Lenora was concerned our housekeeper, Estelle, would be squeamish being here with them. She doesn't even know they're here. I keep the room locked. You wouldn't know either if you hadn't wandered downstairs."

"Never in my wildest fantasy would I picture you with an eighteen-foot Burmese snake crawling on your lap." I started up the steps. "Does Lenora interact with them?"

"It took time, but she got used to them. She rather likes them now, in fact."

"Seriously, don't you think it's dangerous? Somebody might have a heart attack just seeing them. I almost did."

"I keep them tucked away for their safety so no one steps on them accidentally. They roam the house freely only when I'm home alone."

The thought of putting my foot on one of these creatures in the dark appalled me.

Tucker added, "It's a shame the snakes weren't out the night Lenora was killed. Kirk might have thought twice."

When I reached the front door I turned. "I don't know when I've been so scared."

Tucker smiled. "You provided my first chuckle since Lenora's shooting."

I wanted to say get your laughs another way but checked my tongue to avoid being rude. I had traipsed through his house without permission.

What else did he keep downstairs? I wondered as I whisked out.

CHAPTER THIRTY-FIVE

I HURRIED HOME and immersed myself in ordinary household chores to dispel the horror of the previous hour. Folding laundry on my bed, I listened to Tara practice her speech for the next day, a persuasive on "Why We Need More Police."

When she finished her presentation, I offered a critique. "Great eye contact. You barely looked at your notes. I can tell you've practiced well, but I'm not sure your reasons are convincing enough. More police protection on the streets isn't necessarily the total answer to the crime problem as you suggest. I think you could stress the importance of strong families promoting a work ethic and responsible citizenship..."

Her eyes bored into me and her jaw set. "What are you saying? Why didn't you tell me that last week when I asked if you liked my subject?"

"I do. The topic is great. I thought you'd delve deeper, that's all. I don't disagree with your arguments. Maybe if you add that families must also teach good values so the burden isn't totally on the police..."

"Forget it. Thanks a lot for nothing!" She rolled her eyes and dashed from the room.

Where did that come from? She still had plenty of time to refine the speech. I'd praised her good points before pointing out the negative. Such a drama. Female hormones? I sighed. Being a mother and juggling other responsibilities wasn't easy.

I always put family first. The children got both quantity and quality time from Nick and.me. What was her problem?

I left the laundry and headed into the family room. Dropping down next to Nick on the pillow-backed sofa, I closed my eyes and announced, "Tara's in a mood. I pushed her buttons. Now she says she's in a time panic to change her speech, but she's got all night."

"She spoke disrespectfully again?" Nick plucked the remote off the coffee table and turned down the TV news, giving me his undivided attention.

"Why does she think being defensive and temperamental is the way to assert independence?"

"Ignore her reaction. She needs to accept your criticism and make the changes."

"I just wish she wouldn't get so bent out of shape. Our parenting style doesn't seem to be working."

Nick chuckled. "It's working, only she doesn't like it or us at times."

"Dislike I can deal with. Since when is parenting about being liked?" I smiled and went about the rest of my evening chores.

God, out of His love, created us with purpose. Tara needed to identify His plan for her and develop her interests accordingly. My great comfort regarding Lenora was knowing she loved Christ and that whatever happened to her she'd live in joy with Him forever. Still, I'd be lying if I said her brush with death didn't scare me.

This shooting happened to Lenora, but it could be my body stretched flat on a hard cot, lingering in a valley of total vulnerability, connected by pronged, electrical outlets to the mechanical, artificial breath sustaining life. All life is brief. I had to make sure I taught my children well before I was gone.

God, please let me live to see my kids grown. And please take away any fear my humanness feels. I believe there's an appointed hour when I shall leave earth. Nothing I do will speed or delay the time. But I want to complete your purposes first and share what I've learned with my children. I trust you now and forever.

Around eleven, Nick and I embraced in bed after a breathless time of closeness.

"Have I ever told you I love you tons?"

Nick laughed. "Never enough."

"When I think of you and the kids, I get all choked up. God has been so good to us. We have health and each other. I'd like everyone to have the happiness we do."

He stroked my head. "Me, too, sweetheart."

"Tomorrow, I hope to connect with Angela Denton. I think she's part of this mystery surrounding Lenora's shooting at Wooded Hill. Only, I haven't figured out how yet."

Nick prayed, "Lord, give my wife wisdom and keep her safe."

A distinct chill raced down my spine. "Amen."

CHAPTER THIRTY-SIX

I BIT INTO a cinnamon bagel slathered with cream cheese, breakfasting at my kitchen table while watching a male cardinal enjoy his breakfast at our cedar bird feeder. Two yellow finches flitted close by, intimidated by the larger bird. When the cardinal darted off, the tiny birds flew over and confidently perched on the ledge and ate heartily while a simple, sweet idea popped into my head.

I snapped my fingers and spoke aloud to the empty room. "I know a possible way to connect with Angela."

Denton had said walking was her only activity. She had been outdoors the day I drove back from Lenora's. Often people had routines. If Angela walked during heavy rain, I'd bet nothing interrupted her daily regime. Perhaps I could meet her out in her natural terrain during Denton's workday. Very logical. Very "iffy."

I put aside my *God Calling* devotional book and stood up to pace across the wood floor. What time had I seen Angela? After I visited with Estelle the other day it must have been around twelve thirty or twelve forty-five. What was I doing today around that time? I stepped over to the counter, reached into my purse and pulled out my phone. I didn't take switching clients lightly; fortunately, I wouldn't have to. My calendar showed a follow-up session with a newly discharged client ending at noon. Assuming I went a few minutes over, I could get away without a problem.

I sent a text for Ellen to block out the hour in my schedule. Catching Angela on a walk was a long shot, but maybe I'd be lucky.

I downed my tea, still standing and packed my phone into my purse.

Lord, for Your honor and glory, may I be a blessing and be blessed this day.

That little daily prayer readied me for a day of surprises. My hours as a counselor were often full of them, a few too many lately. Yet, I was privileged to deal with people's fascinating lives and see God at work guiding, sometimes admonishing, and gently healing the hurts either the world or poor choices had dealt them. I left for work with a light heart.

The morning zipped by. I devoured a PB & J sandwich after I finished with my clients, then climbed into my van and whipped over to the Denton's property. This time, I parked on the road, not far from where Nick and I had left our car the other night.

I opened the trunk, pulled out my sports bag, took off my heels, and slipped into gym shoes. Carefully laying the jacket of my pants suit in the back seat, I pulled a gray sweat shirt over my wash and wear hair. I stuck the bag in my trunk and locked the car.

After walking a few yards, I stopped to survey the area.

A field of soybeans cut the black earth into neat rows. Cows mooed in the distance. Skirting around the field, I entered a row of trees along the west side and took a path adjacent to Lenora's property near where I'd seen Angela.

About thirty minutes later, I scanned the horizon and caught sight of a woman moving toward me. She turned north at the fringe of the woods without noticing me. I studied the figure to determine if it was Angela.

When she was fifty yards ahead of me, I called Angela's name. The woman sped up and glanced back several times. She had to know I'd seen her. Suddenly, she disappeared into deep woods. I yelled again and quickened my steps. She re-emerged and to my surprise stopped, apparently waiting for me.

I ran up to her breathless, fearing she'd take off any minute.

Angela was dressed in a long sleeve, shirtwaist dress with cotton pants beneath. Her gaunt figure made me think of an anorexic who hadn't recovered. The fragility of her bone structure was similar to a reed that might break if bent too far. Shoulder-length, perfectly straight hair framed a doll's porcelain face. Only when she blinked did she seem real.

"Hi. I'm Jennifer Trevor."

Angela's arms hung loosely at her sides. Her face remained expressionless. Glassy glaring eyes stared straight through me as if she didn't care one way or another what I was saying. I was within a few feet now.

"I'm a friend of Lenora's," I said slowly. Would the name bring light to her eyes?

Angela's hands tightened into tiny fists. "You knew her?" Her lower lip trembled, and she bit it still.

"Yes, very well."

Angela mumbled, "It's awful what happened." She wheeled about abruptly.

"Wait, don't leave." I touched her shoulder lightly. "I made an effort to visit you at your home, but your husband wouldn't let me to talk to you. I must confess, I came here today hoping to find you out walking."

She flinched. "I must get back."

"I'm a counselor, like Lenora. I want to invite you to come to a small group counseling session. Lenora's husband asked me to take over her clients so they wouldn't be left unaided. Were you her client, too?"

Angela focused on the ground, saying nothing.

"Lenora had your name on her list. I'm guessing you were and hoping I'm right."

She didn't deny it but fidgeted with the buttons on her dress with shaky hands. She seemed to be struggling. Her cheeks paled, and a deep furrow embedded her brow. My heart went out to this wounded woman. Whatever had happened to her must have been traumatic.

I kept talking. "As I said, I'm handling Lenora's counseling clients until she's…better." I tried to make my voice sound hopeful. "Would you like to come to my office tomorrow at two p.m.? We're having a group session with a few women."

"Maybe. I'll think about it." Angela's voice shook.

I gave her directions to my office. She listened then turned on her heel and bounded off to get away.

Angela faded out of sight over the hill, head thrust down like the first time I'd seen her in the rain.

Scripture teaches, "You have not because you ask not." I asked, but what answer did I get? None.

Just maybe she would show up.

CHAPTER THIRTY-SEVEN

SANDY AND CARRIE glanced through women's magazines in my conference room. The wingback chair overwhelmed Carrie's slight frame. In case Angela was coming, I intended to wait until five past the hour to begin.

The kind of counseling I had in mind was a small, personal growth group. I'd facilitated many with positive results. I hoped that would be true today.

One of my first goals was to break the isolation each woman experienced in her life that contributed to keeping her locked in dysfunction. It's hard for women going through trauma or depression to reach out and make connections with other women. They were consumed by self-centered thoughts. Therapeutic friendships in a group setting could become lifelong or at least be a model for future relationships.

The minutes ticked by.

By seeing all three women at once, I could fit them into my schedule and still find time to work with Kirk. Three was a small number. Five was ideal, according to research data, although up to eight worked okay. By limiting the group to only three, I could be highly sensitive to individual issues.

I didn't want to begin without Angela but finally gave up hope and began the introductions.

A minute later Ellen tapped on my door, opened it. Angela's bowed head appeared behind her. Ellen led her in.

I blinked back tears. The air in the room stilled. *God, only You know what's about to transpire. Guide me.*

Angela's face shone. Was it eagerness? More likely sweat? She must have walked.

A subtle change had occurred in this dear woman from the day before. She was a tad less stiff, like she'd removed her shield and hung it on a hook near the door. Or, was I only hoping she'd let herself become vulnerable?

I greeted Angela and made introductions, first names only. "Before we start, I have an update on Lenora." I gave them the details I had.

Carrie clapped.

Sandy said, "That's good news. Thinking of her in that coma made me creepy crawly."

Angela remained silent, but relief showed on her face.

"Typically we begin with discussing individual and group goals. Here are my primary goals as your facilitator. To help you know yourselves better; create a safe place for discussing feelings; and work to free each of you from any emotional pain you may be dealing with like guilt, bitterness, unhealthy interactions with others, depression. It may take time, but together we can begin to move forward. Do you have any questions?"

The gals stared at me silently.

"Okay, then does everyone agree with these treatment goals? Would you like to add others, discuss, or modify them?"

"Works for me," Sandy said.

Carrie agreed. "I like them. I want to get more confident and not be afraid to make decisions. I always worry I'm choosing wrong even about simple stuff like what to wear. I spent twenty minutes changing from one thing to another before coming today."

Sandy looked at Carrie's black slacks and beige blouse. "Good choices. I like your outfit."

"Thanks." Carrie blushed and beamed.

"Carrie, maybe you don't know what you like because you haven't had many chances to make choices and develop decision-making skills," I said.

"Could be. Rob makes all the decisions and never asks my ideas about nothing," Carrie said wistfully.

"Rarely being able to choose even little things in your life can cause loss of normal feelings of self-control. That in turn can create emotional confusion and feelings of worthlessness."

"Got that right," Sandy interrupted.

I shot her a smile and continued. "When you're allowed to make decisions, it helps you feel worthwhile. As parents we train our children to become ever more independent of others while remaining dependent on God."

"Don't put up with anybody bossing you," Sandy insisted in a brash voice. "Talking about emotional pain, I've got a pile of past hurts myself I'd like to be free of."

"Freedom is a good goal. Getting locked up with bitterness only hurts you." I swiveled my chair toward Sandy. "Would you like to describe some specific ways you've felt hurt?"

"No, but I can. I was a pawn in my parents' fights. My dad insisted I clean the entire house and do the laundry because my mother refused to do housework. He was a slave driver, pushing me 'cause he knew Mom did nothing."

"How did your mom react?"

Sandy tossed her head back. "She hated me for doing the chores she was neglecting to do to get back at my dad. And I ended up caught in the middle."

"You've described passive aggressive behavior to a tee, common when a strong spouse dominates, and the weaker one finds ways for payback." I maintained eye contact with Sandy. "Have you ever heard that term?"

"Yes," she answered, "but I had no idea what it was."

Angela leaned forward, remaining quiet but attending to every word.

"Repeated childhood experiences like you've described can make you passive-aggressive as well," I inserted. "This means being compliant on the outside while inside holding onto growing hatred and sometimes fear, too. Then you might try to get even in subtle, negative ways that create tension and dysfunction."

"Been there, done it," Sandy said. "People think I'm fine on the outside but inside I'm not. Eventually it comes out."

Angela spoke for the first time. "I know what you mean. I feel like a fake because I see ugly things about myself I can't let anyone else know."

Everyone's eyes turned to her. I was surprised and pleased with her openness.

Sandy's honesty may have made her feel safer.

"At least you can admit it now." Sandy reached for a Kleenex. "It's taken me years."

Angela's eyes darkened. "Have you ever abused yourself by doing what other people want because you feel guilty or simply want to avoid hassle?"

"Can't say I have, but people say I seem so sure of myself. I'm really not." Sandy turned her face away.

"I can't imagine hurting myself," Carrie said.

I stepped in. "It can happen from stifling real feelings and needs."

Angela continued. "I've become good at playing a part."

"Oh, I get that." Carrie jumped in, "I'm not as phony as I used to be. Counseling has helped me know my feelings and work to get my needs met."

"Without being mean to others," I added. "Sometimes women who have neglected their own needs too long go overboard with selfish focus on themselves."

Angela pulled up her sleeves. "I'd like to be able to say that." Angela held her arms out so the undersides were visible. "I cut myself sometimes."

Everyone stared. Angela's wrists and arms had a series of scars an inch to two inches long. One had a trickle of dried, dark-red blood—recent.

Carrie gasped. She got up, knelt in front of Angela, and placed her hands tenderly over each arm. "Why?"

"Not because I want to die, but because I hate myself." Angela's face was expressionless.

Sandy's eyebrows shot up, but she didn't speak. Angela pulled down her blouse sleeves.

"Angela." My jaw tightened. I worked to control my concern. "Women cut themselves when they experience extreme psychological distress. Would you like to talk about yours?"

"I think it best not to say more."

My chest tightened. "All right, Angela, but I need to ask, have you ever contemplated suicide?"

"I'd never leave my daughter. I cut because I'm numb. My feelings are dead." Her eyes darted around the room, stopping on nothing in particular. "Cutting gives me a sense of being alive. In some weird way, it sort of releases stuff locked in me. A voice inside tells me I deserve to suffer. I have no idea where it comes from."

"No one deserves to suffer. Jesus died to set each person free from guilt and shame." It would take more than my words to change these powerful beliefs. *Holy Spirit, this is your territory.*

Sandy spoke barely above a whisper. "Angela, when we get our secrets out, they can't control us anymore."

Angela lowered her head.

Sandy continued. "People think hiding pain is a solution, but I found it's not."

Carrie chimed in. "It kills self-esteem and rots our bones. Lenora said that."

I remained silent, knowing the value of group members counseling one another could be huge.

Angela waved their words away with a sideways motion of her hand. Despite the scars, her arms moved gracefully like a ballet dancer in unhurried, mesmerizing movements. The control she exerted over her body was extraordinary. She looked my way. "I'm sorry. I took up too much time. I'm done now."

"No, go on," I urged.

Carrie and Sandy agreed and leaned in closer.

"Last night I woke up sweating. I had the bad dream again." Angela started to shake. Specters of fear marched across her wide eyes.

"Can you tell us about it," I encouraged gently.

She rubbed her arms.

"Honey, you can trust us," Sandy said with more compassion than I'd ever heard from her.

"Please go on," Carrie urged, her chin lifted.

"When I dream, it always becomes the same nightmare. I'm falling off a cliff and my husband watches but can't catch me." Angela dragged the words as if they came from the depths of her soul, slowly, shyly. "I dread falling asleep."

"It's good to get this out." Hope for her washed through me.

"Have you ever told your dream to anyone else?" Carrie's eyes widened.

"One person, then she got hurt."

"Lenora?" I asked quietly.

Angela nodded. Tears formed in her eyes. "Chuck says counseling with her made me worse. He said to stay away."

My blood boiled. "That's not true. Counseling can help."

Sandy interrupted. "You're cutting your body, and your man doesn't want you getting treatment. What's with him?"

Angela started to cry softly. "He'll be wondering where I am." Tears dripped across the bridge of her nose.

I checked my watch. "Our time has flown by. We'll continue Tuesday." I rose. "Angela, can you stay behind? Please. Just for a few minutes."

I sensed her hesitation.

Her face reddened. "Only a minute. I need to get back." Carrie and Sandy left without another word.

My heart ached for Angela. I longed to teach her to value herself as God did and stop desecrating herself.

Her eyes begged me not to press.

"Promise, if you feel the urge to inflict any cuts or other hurt on yourself, you'll contact me first?"

She ran the edge of her thumb along the zipper on her jacket. I waited, acid in my throat. Would fear close her up again?

Finally, she nodded yes, and I released my breath.

"Now I must go."

A nagging fluttered in my belly. I hated her leaving in this condition. She might regret that she got involved in the group experience and shared her feelings.

The three women walked out together.

I wrote up my notes, capturing Angela's words in ink. My fear relaxed a bit. I believed that her feelings for her daughter would be a deterrent to suicide.

Angela had begun to open herself. My fingers whitened around my pen. How would her husband respond if he knew she came today?

Did Chuck know about Angela's counseling and harm Lenora?

If so, would I be the next victim on his list?

CHAPTER THIRTY-EIGHT

NICK, THE CHILDREN, and I ate dinner quickly that evening. He took the kids to my sister's, following a tearful farewell on Jenny's part, not our teens.

I began packing for his two-day conference and my meeting with Thomas Hartford. I laid outfits on the bed, choosing black and white garments, simple and interchangeable.

We drove to Mitchell Airport and self-parked in an outlying lot. The driver of our shuttle whisked us to the departure terminal along with eight other travelers of mixed ages.

At security I whipped out my plastic bag of cosmetics and slipped out of my shoes, a reminder our country changed in inconvenient and ugly ways forever on 9/11. We boarded ten minutes ahead of schedule. A minor miracle for air travel these days.

Nick and I sat side by side. Our comical crew was talented enough for Saturday Night Live. The flight attendant demonstrating the oxygen masks suggested picking the child you liked best to put the mask on first.

I stiffened at the increasingly loud hum of the engines, then grinned when the pilot's voice came across the sound system saying, "Whoa Nellie." Nick sensed my tension and reached for my hand. Takeoff and landing were the most dangerous parts of flying. I researched it. How comforting to hold the hand of the man I love and toss up a silent Our Father in case I was en route to eternity.

When the seat belt sign went off, Nick unsnapped his and opened his book. I put a pillow behind my head, IPOD buds into my ears, playing Chuck Girard's "Voice of the Wind," and I slept most of the way to Virginia.

The landing was uneventful, my favorite kind.

At Norfolk Airport we picked up the white Lincoln Town car the school had arranged for us to rent.

"I could get used to this, Nick. Compared to the mini-van I drive strewn with school papers and an occasional tennis ball rolling on the floor mats, it's like I'm in a princess's carriage."

Nick grinned. "You are. So what does that make me, a mouse-turned-driver for Cinderella?"

I slapped his shoulder. "Time to listen." I dictated Mapquest directions to the Conference Center at Virginia Beach.

In no time, we pulled up to the Boston style, red brick Founder's Inn at Salem University. While waiting for the reception clerk to help the middle-aged couple ahead of us, I gestured toward the deceased gentlemen portraits on the wall. John Adams and Ben Franklin looked out with steely eyes and a stiff demeanor. "Intimidating poses."

"Right," Nick whispered. "Each guy looks like he's got a toothache."

"Remember, photographers didn't want people to smile back then."

"What a shame. I love your smile. Have I mentioned that lately?"

I hooked my arm through Nick's. "That does it. I'm spending the night with you."

A bellboy escorted us to our room. Nick tipped him generously, drawing an enthusiastic "Thank you."

I walked into our suite and clapped my hands together. "It's perfect. Refined, historic, and comfortable." I pulled a Sprite from the mini-refrigerator stocked with soft drinks and snacks, then examined the bathroom. "Nick, look at this. A flat screen TV next to the bathtub."

Nick wrapped his arms around me. "How luxurious. I want this to be a respite for you. I wish I could burrow you somewhere absolutely safe. I hate having you leave to see Hartford without me."

"Purely a timing issue. Now this may sound corny, but you know I mean it—God's with me. I'm never alone."

"Still, be careful." Nick put his face against my hair and brushed his lips across my neck.

I pushed him back lightly. "Don't you tease. You have to review your speech, and only have an hour, right?"

"Two. Time enough..." Nick pulled me down on the bed.

Much later my sweet husband held me close and murmured, "Let's extend our visit by a day. When the conference is over, I'll go with you then to see Thomas Hartford."

"Sweetheart, you know I can't take another day off, and changing our plane reservations could be a nightmare. Stop worrying. Hartford is an electronics executive with a reputation to protect. That's why he agreed for me to come by his home rather than meet in public at his business. He has way too much to lose to jeopardize himself. I won't be alone anyway. Remember, he has a huge house party going on."

"So he says."

"I've no reason to doubt him."

Half an hour later, I sat in the audience and proudly listened to my husband project his voice with authority based on his education and experience. His sincerity and solid arguments about Christianity and the moral law as a basis for American government were convincing.

After his speech, a swarm of law students surrounded him. Sidling up as close as I could get, I gave him a thumbs up and a little wave. He signaled back, and by arrangement, I left Nick to give his private presentation to the faculty and attend his reception while I drove to my meeting with Hartford.

Thanks to Mapquest, my reliable travel companion, I had no trouble locating Hartford's estate, although I suspected it took me by the longest route possible.

A gray cedar sign, Hartford Woods, etched in six-inch letters, hung from a black iron double gate.

I stopped my car, buzzed down the window, and spoke into a microphone cradled in a metal cubbyhole on the brick gate pillar on the left. The instant I spoke, a formal, male voice asked my business. I glanced around. Was there also an observation camera somewhere?

"Dr. Jennifer Trevor. I have an appointment with Mr. Hartford."

"Come in."

The heavy gate swung open as if by magic.

Why the tight, protective cocoon, Mr. Hartford? I'd dislike the self-imposed isolation some ultra-rich people created around themselves.

I parked in the circle drive area marked GUESTS. Three lannon stone buildings differed only in width and height and sprang from the earth like giant towers. Residence, guesthouse, and office?

I gravitated toward the stone and cedar porch extending from the largest building, judging it to be the residence, and pushed the doorbell.

Moments later a woman clad in a gray full-skirted uniform pulled open one of the two massive oak doors. Soft music floated from inside. Her thin face, accentuated by a pointy upturned nose, greeted me with indifferent but polite courtesy. I was about to introduce myself when she said, "Follow me, please, Mrs. Trevor."

I complied, glad that my arrival was anticipated. I'd feared Hartford would do a convenient Freudian forget.

I followed her down the marble-tiled foyer past an archway leading to a living room full of smiling guests chatting and holding drinks in their hands. The maid glided quickly past the group through glass French doors to a rear wing.

A powder room to the right attracted my attention, and I stopped, asking permission to use it.

She clucked, "I'll be waiting here."

Inside the spacious room I admired the ceiling papered in maroon fleur-de-lis. Mirrored, angled walls gave the feeling of being in a large octagon and turned me into eight people. It had been almost worth the visit just to see this room.

When I emerged, the maid stood stiffly outside the door. Hartford may have instructed her not to let me roam. She escorted me to a large olive green study. Beneath the crown molding, an artist had painted a border depicting classical books. Mahogany bookcases lined two sides of the room. Heavy paisley drapes framed tall narrow windows.

"Mr. Hartford will be with you shortly." She turned and left, closing me in like I carried the E Coli virus, and she had to protect other guests from exposure.

I browsed through the books to get a feel for the topics. After a few minutes perusing a person's books, I could usually summarize their interests and know a bit about their personality. I took pride in that.

Hartford's taste flowed toward history and psychology, a little fiction, no financial or how-to.

The door creaked open, and Thomas Hartford strode in. I appreciated his promptness.

He shut the door brusquely, walked behind his desk, and lifted a candy dish in my direction. "Care for one?"

I declined and studied him as he selected a piece of red and white striped peppermint. He had gray-black hair, thick eyebrows, and a classic nose with a strong jaw that made him handsome despite facial scarring probably from teenage acne.

Slipping the wrapper off, he stuck the candy in his mouth, flashing a gold watchband studded with diamonds. It went well with his half-inch thick gold neck chain. I noted his thick fingers and couldn't help wonder if one had squeezed a trigger.

Mr. Hartford neglected to invite me to sit. Obviously he didn't intend for me to stay.

"Mrs. Trevor, allow me to clarify. Because this misfortune happened to Mrs. Lawrence, I decided to oblige you with this visit and answer your questions. Not because you have a right to know anything but because I have nothing to hide."

"I appreciate that."

"All right, Mrs. Trevor, get to the point of your visit."

No time wasted on formalities. Fine by me.

"First, Mr. Hartford, when did you last see Lenora Turner?"

Using measured words he responded, "In Lake Geneva a week ago." Stoic self-control. This was why I'd come: to study the effect of my words and read the body language of this man before me.

"Prior to this visit, when had you last seen her?"

"Not since graduate school."

"I understand you held her responsible for having you removed from the graduate program?"

He lifted his chin. "Absolutely."

"Which resulted in your threatening her at the time?"

He stiffened. "Who told you that?"

"Her husband." No harm naming Tucker, I figured.

"How would he know? Lenora wasn't married at the time. Regardless, that's an exaggeration." His veins became more pronounced in his neck. "Why are you bringing up ancient history?"

I met his gaze. "I think it may be pertinent."

"Graduate school isn't a time of my life that I like to recall. Not because I wasn't doing well. In fact, I had a 3.5 average. My classroom work was impeccable. I simply didn't meet Lenora's definition of the perfect mental health counselor. The woman claimed I wasn't compassionate, not enough of a people-person, however she defined the term. She claimed I had the ability but not the temperament. Back in those years, an advisor could make or break a student."

Today, it would be unthinkable to give a professor that much power. I couldn't hide my surprise. "Her opinion was based on an assessment of your personality and clinical work?"

"Yes, a completely subjective evaluation." He picked up a carved ivory letter opener on his desk and drummed it into his hand. "Basically, Lenora criticized my directive style with clients. I'm a problem-solver. I favored William Glasser's pro-active Reality Therapy, very solution-oriented."

"Sounds logical to me."

"Not to her. Lenora was a devotee of Carl Rogers's non-directive method. Rogers, before he died, admitted his theory was ineffective and rejected it."

I shifted my weight from one foot to the other and wished we were having this discussion sitting. "Theories come and go. You're saying Lenora used a difference of professional approaches to discriminate against you?"

"You bet she did. Only on paper were students free to determine their counseling style; professors pushed pet theories. I knew this caused her rejection of me. Frankly, I don't think she cared much for my conservative politics on campus either."

I tried to conceal my frown. This sounded unjust and unlike Lenora. "So you fought her decision?"

"Naturally. To say I was miffed is putting it mildly. I complained to her to no avail. Then I appealed to the administration, protesting I hadn't been given a fair evaluation."

"Then you stalked her..."

He shrugged. "No. She objected to giving me another hearing. I wanted to talk her into an independent review."

"And she still refused?" Despite Hartford's lack of invitation, I lowered myself into an arm chair.

"Absolutely. I was furious." He followed suit.

"Filled with rage?"

"Yes, I admit it. Back then."

"What happened next?" My eyes probed his.

"Another professor encouraged me to give up on it. Said I'd get nowhere. I slid into clinical depression for six months. The experience was hard on my marriage, naturally distressing to my young wife. We'd only been married a short time. I was unable to work."

"What came out of the appeal to the school?"

"It went nowhere. Lenora's decision, despite being subjective, carried weight. She triumphed, and I was out on my rear. It was humiliating. I didn't want my friends to know. Only my wife knew what really happened."

I shook my head slowly left to right. "I'm sorry."

He smiled. "Years later I could admit Lenora was right."

"Why keep it secret if you benefited?"

"Shame. The Master's program is the only thing I've ever failed at in my life."

"You've done well since." My glance roved over the ostentatious surroundings.

"Quite." Satisfaction rang from his voice but no haughtiness. He pressed his palms together. "Eventually I sought help for my depression, received counseling, and in time, pursued my hobby of computers."

"Back to your recent visit. You went specifically to see Lenora?"

"No. I was attending a computer programmer conference at Grand Geneva, a resort in the area. But why are you asking? You know I saw Lenora then or you wouldn't be here."

"That's true. But I don't know why."

"Why I took the trouble to look her up?" He sighed. "I've asked myself, too. It's hard to explain. A journey into the past where I lacked closure, I suppose. Perhaps, simply pride. I wanted her to know what I'd achieved as a result of what she did to me."

Hartford gestured around the room at his trophy-laden bookcases and awards peppering every bit of available wall space.

"Unjust as it was, I believe everything turned out well. We had a brief visit, satisfying to me all the same."

I pictured his hands working a computer keyboard, then imagined him holding a rifle. "Your being there the day Lenora was shot is an amazing coincidence."

He bristled. "I suppose one could call it that. So?"

"Quite a shift of focus to computers."

"Yes, and it turned out I had a natural affinity. I started manufacturing and selling hardware, then software. My timing for entering the field couldn't have been better. In a perverse way, I owe everything I've achieved to Lenora. The outcome but not the circumstances of my dismissal brought me a great deal of happiness. Hardly a reason to shoot someone." A shadow crossed his face. "Except..."

"Except what?"

"My wife Sheila's dilemma..." His eyes darted toward the door. "But that's a separate issue."

"What do you mean?"

He sighed. "At the time of my expulsion from the counseling program, Sheila was three months pregnant. She'd started spotting. The doctor wanted her to stay off her feet. With me clinically depressed and unable to work, Sheila had become our breadwinner. I took out a loan, but it wasn't enough. She insisted on keeping her job."

"Despite the strain?"

"Financial debt was a source of fear for her."

A tap on the door interrupted us. We turned as a lithe, five-foot, obviously athletic woman strolled in. A whiff of gardenias flooded the room.

She gave Hartford a peck on his cheek. "So this is where you're hiding. Our guests are asking for you, darling." She turned to me. "And you are?"

Hartford straightened as he introduced her. "Sheila, this is Ms. Trevor."

Her hand stayed at her side so I didn't extend mine. How could her eyes reflect ice while the tone of her "Hello" was so sweet? I shivered.

Her thin lips enlarged by dark orange lipstick curved into a slight smile. Her deeply tanned skin contrasted starkly with her blonde hair. Had he told her previously about my coming?

"Dr. Trevor was in the area and stopped by to discuss our recent trip to Lake Geneva. We have a mutual acquaintance there."

Can facial features become concrete in seconds? It seemed hers did as her eyes became daggers. She eyed me up and down like a slab of beef.

I sucked in air, pulled my shoulders back, and gave Sheila my best smile, envying her tight tummy. She probably did forty abdominal crunches a day. "Did you enjoy your visit to Lake Geneva?"

"Loved the resort. We didn't see much of the town." Her words dripped out like a politician's.

A memory of my senior year popped into my brain—the clicky cute cheerleaders.

"Excuse me, I must get back to our guests. Hurry please, darling." Sheila stretched out the last word reminiscent of Ava Gabor. "May I say you're coming any minute?"

He nodded. "Absolutely dear."

Sheila swirled out, but her gardenia trail remained.

The way Hartford gazed after her spoke of his affection.

I let out a deep breath. "You were elaborating about Lenora's decision to dismiss you from the graduate program being hard on your wife as well?"

"Sadly, soon afterward she miscarried."

"I'm sorry."

Anguish was visible in his eyes. "We thought there'd be other kids, but she was never able to conceive again. It was rough at first. Eventually, Sheila had to have a hysterectomy. She still blames Lenora for her childlessness. I wanted to adopt, but Sheila wanted children of our own. It's harder than ever for her as she approaches menopause."

And she saw a chance for her to get even, but I didn't say it aloud.

"Sheila pours herself into our animals. Treats them as if they're children." He cocked his head to one side. "I'm not sure I'd have been a good dad." He diverted his eyes and swallowed hard.

I looked away.

Hartford composed himself and resumed. "Dr. Trevor, my subsequent success eliminates any motive to shoot Lenora, although I will admit in an earlier timeframe, I'd have liked to kill her, if I were the killing type, mind you. I wasn't then, and I'm not now. Do you believe that?"

"Frankly, I don't know what to think."

"Well then, that's your problem. It's regrettable the timing of Lenora's accident, but it's unrelated. I used my trip as an opportunity to apologize to Lenora in person. She was fine the day I left and appreciated that I'd come."

"Lenora's cleaning lady heard you yelling. What was it that you argued about?" I was begging the question, but it might get me more information.

"She mistook me with someone else." Hartford drummed his fingers on the desktop. "We didn't have a cross word. I expressed my gratitude."

I wanted to test his anger potential. "Your wife's distress gave you a motive for revenge. Sheila, too. Might this have festered into a motive for revenge in your wife? I'm not saying she pulled the trigger, but she could have hired someone. Your visit might have stirred up her pain again."

Hartford glared at me. "Don't go there! Sheila didn't shoot anyone nor did I." His face turned deep red. "It's time for you to leave, Dr. Trevor. You've overextended your welcome. The maid will show you to the door." Hartford marched out and summoned his maid.

So much for ruling him or his wife out as a suspect.

CHAPTER THIRTY-NINE

NICK AND I arrived home after midnight. I slept well until seven a.m. when I hugged my children who greeted me happily jumping on our bed. They warmed my spirit as much as the emerging sunshine beaming through the skylights.

Jenny flopped next to Nick while Tara and Collin sat on the edge and chattered.

"I don't like it when you go away," Jenny announced. "But I like having Aunt Joy and Uncle Dave play Monopoly with me and Scrabble with Collin. Aunt Joy always wins."

"I'm glad you had fun, but I missed you, precious kiddos. Get dressed now. On the way to school I want to hear more."

I savored the children's reports and regretted having to drop them at school.

My first client called, saying she'd be late. Fine by me. I could use some quiet time.

I opened my purse Bible to Hebrews, Chapter 11 for a nugget of spiritual nourishment. "Faith is the assurance of things unseen."

Good memory verse I noted. I repeated it several times as I awaited a call from Tucker.

A decision had been made to try to wean Lenora from the ventilator. The doctors wanted to see if she could sustain her own breathing. Today would be the test. *Lord, You are still a healing God. Fervently, I beg you to heal Lenora.* As I prayed, my eyes noticed a spot on my office wall where the paint had gobbed.

Ellen flitted in. "Your husband's on line one." Soundlessly, her rubber-bottomed shoes turned back to the waiting room as I reached for the phone.

"Hi, sweetheart. I got some info on Lenora's group of ex-cons from our PI. He found every recently released ex-convict she aided except one gal they couldn't track down. All the others have a solid alibi for the night Lenora was shot, and there's no apparent motives to link any of them with Lenora's shooting."

"Who's the one he can't find?"

"Name's Sarah Nichols."

I made a note on my iPhone. "Thank him for me. He's been a huge help. You, too, by the way. Maybe my friend, Inspector Jarston from the Dells, can find something on this gal."

I strolled out to Ellen's desk and rattled off her explicit TO DO list. I took a deep re-focusing breath and returned to my office to review notes on my next client.

Tucker buzzed an hour later. "Good news.' He sighed. "Lenora's off the ventilator."

"Great! Hey, you sound exhausted."

"It's been stressful, that's all. Her lungs are maintaining a steady oxygen level. There's no guarantee she can sustain her own breathing, but the doctors are hopeful." I detected a tremor in his voice.

"I'll stop by the hospital on my way home."

"The nurse said it takes about twenty-four hours for the effects of the drugs to wear off. She may not even remember the shooting because of being in a coma. Don't expect much."

"I'd still like to see her as soon as possible."

"She won't be herself for a while. Promise you won't upset her by mentioning the shooting."

I agreed.

He hung up.

I bowed my head and whispered aloud, "God, thank You. If not today, hopefully the questions surrounding the attack upon Lenora can be answered soon."

My thoughts returned to Nick's phone call. Who was this ex-convict, Sarah Nichols, who had completely disappeared into society so that none of her family or former acquaintances knew where to contact her? And why? Had she returned to a life of crime? Was she involved in Lenora's shooting?

I punched in Detective Jarston's number and waded through two screeners to him. It helped to have friends in high places—sort of a friend, sort of a high place, anyway. I'd met him when he was a detective in the Wisconsin Dells area, and we worked together to solve Albert Windemere's murder. He now handled special assignments in semi-retirement, not that he was old, probably mid-sixties.

His gravelly voice barked, "To what do I owe this surprise?"

"I notice you didn't say pleasure," I bantered.

"Implied, of course, but I need to know the nature of this contact before I become ebullient."

I laughed. "I haven't heard that word in a while." Jarston loved the English language, the longer the word the better. Why a five-letter-word when he could come up with an eight or ten-letter one? And the quicker the repartee, the better.

"Let me guess. You're involved in another murder?"

"An attempted one." I told him about Lenora's shooting.

"You seem to have a flair for attracting intrigue. I hope you're limiting your involvement to paperwork and phone calls. You know how I feel about women in police work. There's no reason for…"

I interrupted. "Chivalry lives as long as your blood flows. I'd simply like to tap your information network for a female ex-convict we can't trace. Sarah Nichols is her prison name. It appears she's gone to some pains to conceal her identity."

"Why?"

"That's what I want to know. A hunch is all I've got."

Jarston harrumphed. "Hunches are usually a waste of time. How long ago was she released?"

"Three months ago."

"We'll do what we can." Jarston used the plural pronoun like royalty. "It may take a while."

"This is urgent. Can you speed? Like twenty-four hours?"

"I can't promise, but I'll try."

"You're a dear."

"Maybe a buffalo, never a deer."

CHAPTER FORTY

WHEN I STEPPED off the hospital elevator on the fifth floor, memories slammed into my brain. I'd spent enough time in hospitals while our son was treated for leukemia to despise the hubbub of medical machinery, the somber hushed voices of family members, and the scurrying of staff that never stopped. It simply changed pace from daytime rush to nighttime slow and names and faces of people were new.

I worked my way through these emotions as I strolled down the hall, wishing I were in my back yard or any safe, familiar place.

Did everyone feel as if they ought to tiptoe when they entered intensive care? I did. A male nurse glided past me on noiseless rubber soles, a reminder for me to quiet my walk on high heels.

Despite Tucker's tentative good news, it took courage to stick my head into Lenora's cubicle. Could she sustain breath, or would death take her from us?

The intrusive, tubal ventilator invasion remained in the room although the connection had been removed. Lenora lay on her back, eyes closed, looking surprisingly composed within her frame of metal bars. Clumps of hair matted close to her face, which was the color of putty.

Tucker dozed in a chair at Lenora's right side but awoke when I entered. He greeted me with a frown. No wonder, I'd disturbed his nap.

I slipped over to Lenora's left side and gently covered her hand with mine as my words tumbled out. "Hi, my dear friend. You had us scared."

Lenora's eyes fluttered open. "Jennifer?" Her words, soft as light rain, were delivered with a weak smile.

I patted her hand and exhaled in relief. "You recognized me. You've made my day." *Thank You, Jesus.*

She lifted a finger in response.

"This is no way to take a vacation," I said gently.

Tucker gestured me aside. "Don't strain her. She's still disoriented. The doctor expects her memory of recent events to come back gradually, if at all. She has no recollection thus far and must stay very quiet," he warned. "I'll leave you alone a few minutes." He sauntered out.

I returned to Lenora's side. For the first time, I glanced at the hospital décor. The walls were a pretty shade of robin's egg blue. Everything seemed more cheerful now.

I pulled a chair close, longing to ask if she had any idea who shot her or why. Those answers would wait until she was stronger and could think clearly.

"You're looking amazingly well for having been through such an ordeal." I squeezed her hand.

"Thanks for all you've done. I owe you big time. Tucker told me you've been a saint." She pressed my hand ever so slightly.

"Nothing you wouldn't have done for me. Just get better now, okay?"

She sighed. "Jennifer, I can't remember anything about the night of the shooting. It's so frustrating." She started to cough.

So much for not bringing the subject up. "It'll come back in time." I stroked Lenora's arm.

A nurse, middle-aged and hefty, charged in, and leaned across Lenora's bed to check the IV. She input data into the computer using the bed tray as a desk and then addressed me. "You may have a brief visit but don't tire her. She's very weak."

When the nurse left, Lenora motioned me closer. "Tucker thinks Kirk did this, but he couldn't have. I'm sure."

I smiled wryly. "After meeting him, I agree it seems unlikely." I wanted to ask about her relationship with Tucker but couldn't risk something potentially upsetting.

"How I wish I knew who was responsible." She spoke so faintly I put my ear next to her lips. A shadow of distress crossed her already pale face. She twisted her head on the pillow. "Everything's so hazy. Do you suppose it could have been a hunter, a chance thing? Why would anyone want to shoot me?"

I recalled my visit with Thomas Hartford. *Some people have reasons.* "You're getting better; that's the important thing now. When will your doctor let you go home?"

"They won't give me a date yet. How's Kirk dealing with all this? I'm concerned for him. I never for a moment believe he'd hurt me."

"Kirk's been through the wringer but hanging in there. He'll be thrilled to hear you're getting better. He asks about you whenever I see him." I smoothed back the strand of black hair that had fallen across Lenora's forehead.

"He's very sweet."

Tucker returned and settled in his chair. He opened his newspaper and began reading.

Suddenly Lenora shuddered. "I had a strange dream. It was so real. I remember it vividly like a vision. I want to tell you about it."

"Yes?" I leaned in.

"People talk about near death experiences, seeing a powerful light, smelling beautiful flowers. Do you believe in them, Jennifer?"

"I've read such stories. And I believe some are true."

Her voice trailed off. "Well, my experience wasn't pleasant but seemed quite real. Jesus took me to hell, not to stay, but to see what was going on."

Tucker interrupted, "Lenora, please don't talk if this distresses you."

"No, I want to tell Jennifer. The sight broke my heart. Fortunately, Jesus never left my side. I remember a gray mist, an odor of burning flesh, and thousands of people trying to dodge flames. As I watched, worms ate through an incredibly beautiful woman's flesh, leaving a blackened skeleton. And it happened over and over; time was frozen. The woman cried piteously, 'Help me.' It was horrid."

Tucker closed his newspaper. "Lenora, are you sure you want to continue with this?"

She nodded. "I begged Jesus to get the people out. He looked at them lovingly and said in the saddest voice I ever heard, 'I gave them every chance, but they refused me.' A handsome young man engulfed in flames stood next to this woman. He said, 'I thought my intellect and prosperity made me superior. How foolish.'" Lenora shivered. "Jennifer, I must confess, I've felt that way at times." Her voice grew softer.

Tucker fidgeted in his chair. "Lenora, let's talk about this when you're stronger."

Her eyes flitted in his direction. "You simply don't like to hear about anything supernatural, Tucker."

I sat speechless and entranced. Had she really seen hell? The mind played strange tricks. But Scripture said that people do see visions. John, the beloved apostle of Jesus, wrote about his in the book of Revelation. I inclined toward believing Lenora.

"I intend to tell everyone I meet about the reality of hell." Lenora continued. "I pray I'll recover my strength and be able to influence even more lives."

Tucker stood. "You've already done your share."

"Nonsense. There's more to do."

"And you will help," I patted Lenora's arm, "but right now you need to sleep."

Lenora murmured. "I am tired." She leaned back and closed her eyes. I arranged her pillows, swept a few strands of hair back from her forehead, and pulled up the cotton bed cover.

"You're such a dear friend, Jennifer. Thanks for coming,"

"I'll be back soon now that you can have visitors." Her breathing was already deepening as I reached the door.

For a moment I felt infused with joy. Lenora was still in physical and emotional distress, but the healing miracle had happened. She was breathing independently. I'd witnessed her restoration for myself.

Then the dark thought returned, the one that haunted my waking hours.

Until we found out who shot Lenora, she'd never be truly safe again.

CHAPTER FORTY-ONE

I RELEASED STRESS two ways, by vacuuming or exercising. I chose exercise when I returned from Lenora's — a walk though, rather than a run since I was still in recovery from my fall.

I peeked into the family room. The kids were engrossed in the football movie, *Facing the Giants*. "Hi guys, anybody want to go for a walk with me?"

Blanks stares glanced my way, then back to the screen. I pulled Collin aside a minute. "Dad's at a meeting. I'll be right back. You're in charge of your sisters, son."

I changed into my tan nylon jogging suit. With an athletic bandage supporting my ankle, I could handle a short walk. A glance in the mirror showed the thin scar still on my forehead.

At the end of the driveway, I pulled on neon orange wristbands and let the peacefulness of the woods filter through me. An eyebrow of a moon accented the spectrum of stars above. Steady, serene wind kept the oak leaves in a perpetual waltz.

The sense of being alone with God was delicious.

I walked for about a mile. When I reached the main blacktop road, a car illuminated by the streetlight approached. The driver rolled down the window and called my name.

A wave of surprise overcame me. Chris? What's she doing here?

She parked on the shoulder of the road.

I trudged over. "Hey girl, I'm just heading out for a walk."

"I know. I stopped by the house and the kids told me. I'll leave my car here and join you, if I may?"

"Sure if you don't mind my setting the pace. I'm taking it easy on my ankle."

"Wise girl. I came to say goodbye. I'm leaving tomorrow."

We fell into a comfortable stride. "I've been so busy. I'd hoped to have you over for dinner before you left, but it's been crazy."

"Hey, you have a lot going on. Thanks for the thought anyway."

We'd gone another half-mile when Chris slowed. "I wanted to have a private conversation with you before taking off. This is hard." She hesitated. "I have a confession to make. Is this a good place to stop for a minute?"

"It's a dark stretch here, up ahead the road makes a sharp turn north. There'll be a bench and more light."

We reached the iron bench and sat. I turned to her with undisguised curiosity. "What's up?"

"Something I must tell you..." She paused, apparently hunting for words. "It's important you know…" A car pealed around the corner and halted a few feet from us. Chris was stopped mid-sentence.

I recognized Nick's vehicle. He hopped out, my second surprise of the night. "I thought you had a meeting."

"I got a text message about your friend here and came back." Nick stared steadily at Chris as he spoke. She looked as if she might bolt any second.

Nick directed his next words to me. "Inspector Jarston called with Sarah Nichols' physical description. Tall, angular build, short dark hair. According to the prison summary, she's intelligent, capable of carefully executed, well-thought out con jobs and may be armed." He faced Chris. "I checked with the company you're supposed to work for. They never heard of you. You lied. Why?"

Chris turned away and became antsy. "You have no idea what I'm trying to do."

"I know you're a former convict with parole violations, and you've given false information to my wife."

"I did my time, and I'm only trying to help." Chris clenched her teeth.

Nick put his arm around me. "Chris knew Lenora."

My eyes danced back and forth between Nick and Chris.

"I met her a year ago."

A police car screeched up. A young officer sprang out of the driver's door and a gray-haired female police officer with kindly blue eyes from the passenger's side. She frisked Chris and took a small revolver from Chris's waistband, then rattled off her Miranda rights. "We'll check your permit for this gun and talk at the station."

The hair bristled on the back of my head. "Chris...Sarah." My voice broke. "Were you involved in Lenora's shooting? But why...?" I couldn't finish.

She looked me in the eye. "Of course not. I've done nothing wrong." Chris squirmed, trying to shake herself free as the officer handcuffed her.

Chris, that is, Sarah, directed a desperate glance my way. "Jennifer, please believe me. I wasn't anywhere near Lake Geneva when Lenora was shot. She was my benefactor. I wanted to help. Don't let them take me to jail. Do something."

I stood with my jaw hanging, staring at Chris. This was TV crime show material, not my life.

"What about the night Jennifer fell?" Nick yelled accusingly. "You showed up because you were stalking her? When she fell, you drove back pretending an offer to help. Right?"

"No!" Chris's voice held an edge of panic. "Jennifer, the night of your accident I was driving by to find out where you lived to keep an eye on you and protect you. I knew you were friends with Lenora and feared you were the next target. I also followed you the day you met with Russell."

So I had seen her that day. How could I believe in her innocence? Hadn't she deceived me with lies? *Was this how you felt, Jesus, when your friends betrayed you?*

Her eyes pleaded. "Somebody was following you the night you fell, Jennifer. How could I protect you and Lenora without a gun? I'm not supposed to have a weapon. It's the only thing I did wrong. I'd never hurt you; I only intended to help."

I heard my voice as if coming from a cavern. "The shot in the woods?"

"Wasn't me." She groaned and twisted her body toward me. "Lenora helped me get my life together. Guarding you, investigating her shooting, snooping around on my own to find her shooter was the least I could do."

The police officer tugged on Sarah's handcuffs. "Let's go. We'll check her story, Ms. Trevor."

Mesmerized by the scene, I was speechless. *Lord, can I believe her? Should I?* "Chris…Sarah, I'll see what I can do."

Her frantic final glance was one of the most pitiless sights I'd seen.

When the police car pulled away, I fell into Nick's arms. "How did you know where I was?"

"Collin said you went for a walk and that Chris came by. Chris, that is, Sarah may have been watching our house and waited for when you went outside. She seems to excel at that." Nick spoke in soft and soothing tones. "We have our sniper."

I climbed into our car, numb all over. "I'm not so sure. Something doesn't fit."

CHAPTER FORTY-TWO

WHO SHOT LENORA? If not Chris or Kirk, who? I sat in my office writing the three words over and over on my yellow legal pad. The gold ball hanging in the sky outside my window reminded me of the amazing God who alone could bring good from this huge mess in Chris and Kirk's lives.

I'd blocked out two hours in my office to prepare for a workshop later in the day, but Lenora's situation disrupted my concentration.

Lenora would be home soon. I wanted her to have twenty-four hour police protection, but that wasn't going to happen because her husband and the police believed the case was sewn up against Kirk, although to their credit the police were combing through Sarah's recent activities.

Raucous drilling from a jackhammer destroying the cracked sidewalk outside my building made it even harder to concentrate. I went to the window and closed it to deaden the noise and block the dust drifting in.

Jagged-edged concrete chunks soon would become archaeological history in some landfill project. Dear Lord, we'll all be history, too, one day. May it be Your perfect plan, Your way, and Your time. Please keep Lenora alive to complete her normal life span, okay? And me, Nick and our precious family, too, please.

Returning to my desk, I picked up my pen to write another question on my pad, a pressing and mysterious query that had never been answered. Who called the hospital pretending to be Lenora's brother checking on her condition? I never believed it to be a mix-up in names or rooms. Way too coincidental for me. Besides, the nurse had said the caller clearly wanted to know Lenora's condition. Undoubtedly checking if she were capable of revealing information about her assailant yet.

Had it been Denton? I'd had bad vibrations the first time I met him, an uncanny sense he was involved in some kind of deception.

Ellen knocked and entered my office.

I blinked. She was dressed in a bright lime green short-sleeve knit shirt and 1970's beige and green jacquard slacks. Nothing neutral about my office assistant. "Nice outfit."

"Thanks. I bought it in a consignment store and spent the money I saved on more mystery books. At least those I can solve in my head," she added with a twinkle in her eye.

I ignored her comment and smiled as she consulted her message pad.

"Carrie called. Rob is furious about her joining the group. She wants to come anyway but is letting you know in case he succeeds in stopping her."

"Okay, thanks." *Lord, don't let this man take his anger out on his poor wife.*

I loved my job but it definitely wasn't easy. When I became a psychotherapist, I didn't know it would lead to tough situations like this. I'm privileged that clients work on personal issues with me. The depth of their pain continued to surprise and distress me.

For Rob to be m-a-d seemed appropriate. The acronym in military circles stood for mutually armed destruction. Wasn't this exactly what some marriage partners engaged in? Would Rob shoot Lenora to keep her away from his wife? I wrote his name down as a possibility.

My cell phone began to play Marimba, my musical tone of the moment. I checked caller identity and tapped the screen. "Hello, wonderful husband."

"I've got news you're going to like. Chris, it turns out, has an airtight alibi putting her two states away the night Lenora was shot. Her only crime was carrying. I'll try to get leniency for that since she was protecting you and hunting for Lenora's shooter."

"That's a relief. I'm eager to talk to her."

"She has an aunt posting bond for her and will be released this afternoon. Now to my next important item. What's for dinner?"

We chatted about choices.

Nick offered to stop by the store and pick up vegetables and French bread to serve with the homemade spaghetti sauce I froze in quantity.

"You're a sweetheart."

"I'll show you how sweet I am later. Hurry home."

I returned to my notepad. Back to the top of my page, I underlined "Who shot Lenora?" There still seemed to be something, someone I was missing.

Hartford and his wife, Sheila, needed to be added to my list. What was he capable of doing for the sweet satisfaction of retaliation?

Next I wrote the name Angela Denton. Was she capable of an aggressive act? Did she regret sharing her secret with Lenora and want to silence her? Buyers had remorse, sometimes counselees did too. I'd see her again next week if she returned to the group.

Could Angela handle a gun? People under duress often performed amazing feats of strength, and some multiple personalities developed extraordinary acting ability.

It was time to pay another visit to the Denton homestead. I picked up the phone. To my surprise, Angela answered. I didn't give her a chance to object. "I'll be there in twenty minutes." I mentally finished my workshop planning during the car ride.

Half an hour later, I picked my way through vines seemingly even thicker than my last visit and rapped on the paint-chipped door.

Angela's slim, white hand pulled the picture window drapes back, then dropped them. Moments later she drew the door back. Her terrified eyes reminded me of a little girl's who had been spun in circles too many times. I pressed past her into the living room before she could retreat in fright or shut the door on me.

In a corner of the living room I saw a bucket of soapy water and some rags. She must have been scrubbing the tile floor on her hands and knees. Everything looked spotless. So that was what she did all day. The home, a remodeled cottage, had a very simple design — country décor, stark motif, and a few knick-knacks.

I shaped my lips into a smile while my mind whizzed in several directions. Concise and direct, I reminded myself. Why not try a bold approach? "Angela, I know," I said with conviction.

She froze in place and remained motionless, feet planted on the floor. Her coloring, pale pink at first, turned gray.

"You may as well tell me the truth." I spoke in the tone I'd use with a child who misbehaved.

Angela shook her head as if to lose sight of an ugly picture. She began to babble. "He's always sorry afterward. He doesn't mean to do it."

Professional ethics loomed before me. "Angela," I said gently. "I can't offer confidentiality for what you say if I believe you or anyone is in danger, but I will help you in every way I can." I feared these words would silence her, but I had to do the right thing.

She talked like a wound-up doll. "To protect our daughter and our home, Chuck said I needed to keep quiet. He can make me agree to anything. I always did." Angela shuddered. "I stay home so nobody can see the marks."

What she said didn't shock me. At some level perhaps, I suspected all along.

I fought the sudden urge to throw up. "Why not tell the police?"

I asked but knew the answer. In our first apartment I'd wake during the night and hear our neighbor beating his wife. The next day she'd smear make-up all over her face and deny it.

"Chuck said the police would believe I made it up because he's such a respectable citizen. Said it would support the mental illness story he told about me. He laughed at the idea of my telling."

"Did you ever try calling them?"

She shook her head. "You don't understand." Angela's eyes blazed. "Chuck can persuade people. He's powerful with words. He talks 'till you think yellow is black and lies are the truth. Everybody trusts him. Nobody would believe me."

"But there'd be physical evidence."

"He'd say I appeared beat up because I fell and was hallucinating because I was demented. He'd lie his way out. I know." Angela pled with her eyes for me to understand.

"Did you ever consider escaping to a shelter for battered women?"

"He'd find me. I wanted to run away lots of times, but where would I be safe? And, what about our daughter? He would take her away from me. I've quit caring about myself. As long as I stay drugged up enough, I can manage."

"Exposing him and getting free would be hard but not impossible. I'll help. I promise. You and your daughter don't have to live like this."

"Nothing will ever change." Angela's eyes darted toward the door with a worried look. "I shouldn't be talking with you."

"Did you really go to several psychologists as Chuck asserts?"

"Only once for meds before my visit with Lenora. He stayed with me all the while. Said I was afraid and I had fits if I was out of his sight. He's such a liar."

"Your daughter?"

"Chuck threatened that he'd hurt her if I ever let on and she told anyone. I cover the bruises as best I can, but sometimes she sees me beat up. He tells her its part of my illness. I keep falling down."

I sensed my fists clench. I had to keep my rage toward him under control.

"The beatings happen usually late at night. In the beginning, he'd stuff my mouth with a handkerchief, but it's gotten so I can't cry out anyway. I just go numb all over."

"Angela." I spoke with infinite tenderness. "You can't go on this way."

"I want to die but can't because that would mean leaving my daughter with him. He swore he'd put me in an asylum and take away my freedom if I ever talked about what he does. I finally told Lenora—more like she guessed it just like you did. And look what happened to her. I should never have shared this with anyone." Her eyes widened.

I'd seen this before. The exhausting release that follows truth-telling, coupled with concern for what will happen next.

I helped her to a chair at the kitchen table. She dropped her head in her hands and sobbed. "Now I've put you in danger, too."

I patted Angela's back soothingly. "I'll be okay. And think of revealing the truth as giving Chuck a chance to get help, not an act of betrayal. Maybe it's not too late for him. Some men respond well to treatment for spousal abuse."

"There's something else you don't know." Her sobbing intensified. "My husband killed his first wife in a fit of rage one night after he'd been binge drinking."

I wasn't surprised. Without an intervention, the behavior would continue. "Want to tell me details?"

"One night he said she threatened to leave him and report him. He caught her, dragged her back, knocked her out, and set fire to the house they were renting rather than face being exposed. He made it look like an accident and was never caught. Life's all about image for Chuck. He'll say anything, do anything. You see?"

"You could accuse him of murder."

Angela bowed her head. "I know he's afraid if I go for treatment there may be questions leading to re-investigation of his first wife's death. I think he wishes he'd never told me. He did it to scare me into keeping quiet about the beatings."

"This isn't the kind of life God wants for you, to be continually depressed, fearful and abused. God wants you free."

She shook her head. "I walk in the woods and fields almost every day. Things are free there. I feel close to God when I'm outside. It lifts me a little. When the weather is bad, I walk to punish myself for the bad decisions I made ruining my life."

A thud reverberated from outside. Angela rushed to the door and clicked the lock while I peered out the window. I reassured her. "No one's there."

My mind moved 100 mph. Had Lenora confronted Chuck Denton in her office and threatened to turn him in? Was that when Estelle heard a man's raised voice?

"Chuck's due home soon. Now that you've come, I'm afraid for you. He'll guess I told you, too. He mustn't find you here. I need you to leave."

"I'll go, but first tell me exactly when did Lenora learn about your husband's treatment of you?"

"The week she was shot."

"Did Chuck know you told her about the beatings and about his first wife's death?"

"I told him Lenora was going to help me with my depression. I don't know what he believed." She broke down sobbing. "Leave! I won't press charges against him. I'll never repeat what I told you. He'll..."

"But if you inform the authorities, he'll go to jail, and you'll be safe."

"No one can guarantee that." Angela's eyes darted toward the window before answering. "He'll get out of it somehow."

"My husband is a lawyer. He and I will help you."

"You can't. I know you mean well. I didn't want to talk to you. I'm just worn down." Angela crossed her arms across her chest and rubbed her forearms vigorously.

How I hurt for this poor woman.

"Lenora made me feel something I'd lost—a sliver of hope. I sensed life inside me again. I don't want to go back to feeling nothing, but I don't want anyone else hurt. I saw what he did to her."

"We can't be sure he shot her. That has to be investigated. But, you don't have to endure his treatment any longer." I used every argument I could think of to persuade her to turn Chuck in and come for counseling.

Nothing worked.

She stared at me like I was a crazy person for even suggesting it and dropped onto the small tweed sofa near the door. She sat silent for several minutes before lifting her head and stiffening her shoulders. "I know you're right and mean well, but we'd get hurt real bad."

Outside, a car spit gravel as it came up the driveway. We stared at each other.

Angela froze.

Denton had to be confronted but not here, not when we were alone with him.

"Angela, let's leave by the back door, both of us. Now."

"I can't. My daughter's due home soon. If I make him angry, she won't be safe."

"We'll get help and come back for her."

Footsteps grew louder.

"No, he'll be crazy. He has to know where I am every minute."

"All right, then when he comes in, let me do all the talking. I'll greet Chuck, then leave and get help. He mustn't know you've told me."

I moved back toward the entry area as if I'd just come.

Seconds later Chuck barged in, his face tight with fury, his teeth set in a grim line. "What are you doing here?" he demanded of me. His coal black eyes gazed menacingly at Angela.

I rifled through my purse with shivering fingers. "Hi, Chuck." My voice was a decibel high, but I tried to make it sound casual.

"I'm delighted to see you. I was just hunting in my purse for pen and paper to leave you a message."

"Why not just tell Angela since you were here?"

"Good question." I motioned him aside. *God help me; let him believe me.* "Angela won't speak to me," I whispered. "She's petrified." No lie there. "I told her but wasn't sure she'd give you my message."

"Angela, why don't you go and lie down? I'll handle this." Chuck turned back to me. "What's the message?"

"An emergency foundation board meeting's been called tomorrow morning at Lenora's home office, nine a.m. It's important everyone be there. Tucker wants to discuss safety precautions. Lenora's going to be released, and he wants the board to come up with a press statement about her work continuing." I'd suggested this plan to Tucker so it wasn't a lie. He just hadn't come up with a time.

"Is there a problem with sending a message or using the telephone?" Denton's voice reeked with sarcasm.

"I didn't want to disturb you at the bank with foundation business, and I was heading over to Lenora's just down the road. Sorry, I didn't realize how difficult my stopping by would be for your poor wife. I see how challenging your situation is."

"Well, now you know." His icy tone chilled me. No wonder Angela was afraid of him. Chuck's facial expression softened slightly. "It's kind of you to be so, so thoughtful." Sweet-talk again. How can a man devoid of morals speak sensitive words but never feel them?

"Okay, I'm off. See you tomorrow, Chuck." I took a deep breath and turned the door knob. I felt his eyes on my back as I walked to my car. The need to get this poor woman and her daughter help fast stilled my trembling. I hated leaving Angela alone with Chuck, knowing he'd interrogate her. She wouldn't go without her daughter. I had no choice.

I slipped behind the wheel. *Angela, don't reveal what you told me.*

CHAPTER FORTY-THREE

INSIDE THE CAR I reached for my iPhone. No signal. How could the battery be dead? I forgot to charge it. I berated myself and sped to Lenora's house down the road to make my call.

Torrential rain pounded my car as I ascended the long driveway. Would there ever be a day of solid sunshine again?

Relief flowed over me at the sight of Estelle's truck and Lenora's van in the circle drive. Somebody was here at least to let me in. I jumped out and sloshed up the front walk through inch-deep puddles.

Estelle opened the front door, eyes glistening.

I froze. "What happened?"

"How did you know? They've only just arrived a bit ago."

"Know what?"

"Why, that Mr. Tucker brought Mrs. Lawrence home in the van. She's still weak and exhausted but home. Praise God. Isn't it wonderful?"

I stared at her, taking her words in.

"What's wrong?" Estelle's big eyes bulged.

"Of course it's fantastic. I'm glad…surprised, that's all. Tucker didn't tell me. He distinctly said last night it would be at least another two days, his exact words." The edge of anger rang out in my voice, and I bristled inside. I was among the first to know the bad news after Lenora was shot, but good news, he held back. Why? I regained my composure. Perhaps he hadn't known ahead of time. He'd probably been too busy to call. Maybe it was a last minute discharge.

"Don't know 'bout none of that. I'm just glad she's here."

"Me, too. I can't wait to see her. Where's Tucker?"

"He went to the pharmacy to fill her prescriptions. I'm staying until he returns. Mrs. Lenora is napping now in her room."

"I need to use their phone to make a call. Excuse me." I entered the study and shut door behind me.

When the sergeant came on the line, I introduced myself, rattled off my counseling credentials, and explained about Denton's treatment of Angela and my fear that he'd shot Lenora. Stressing that his wife was in imminent danger, I gave him Denton's address.

"I don't need the location. I know it. Are you aware, Dr. Trevor, that Mr. Denton is a respected member of this community? He's informed us of his wife's problems. She reported him for abuse several years ago and again once last year. When we got there, she denied it, and we saw no evidence. Both times."

"Did you require her to have a physical exam?"

The Sergeant ignored my question. "Mr. Denton explained her confusion is an issue of her psychosis. We didn't want to pester. She claimed she was fine."

The response both shocked and unsettled me. "But did you order a complete physical examination of his wife? Please answer the question."

"The woman's a pathological liar. We've seen psychiatrist's reports on her."

"So the answer is no." I wanted to slam down the phone.

"That's correct, mam."

Chuck Denton could be quite convincing. I was trusting my intuition that Angela had told me the truth. My pulse throbbed in my temples. "My name is Dr. Jennifer Trevor. As I said, I'm making this report as a licensed professional counselor. I'll hold you responsible if anything happens to this woman because of your negligence. Get out there. This could be a matter of life or death. Once abuse is reported you are required to respond, need I inform you?"

"Okay. You can deal with the consequences, Dr. Trevor."

"She's alone with him. How soon can you get there?"

"I'll leave right away."

"I intend to have my husband meet you. He's a lawyer."

I called Nick and gave him a quick summary of the events of this crazy day. "Angela's going to need legal counsel. Can you head over?"

"I'm on my way. Where will you be?"

I inhaled a deep breath. "Since Tucker's gone, I'll stay here with Lenora in case Denton heads this way."

"Okay. Stay in touch."

I sat in the chair and pondered my next move. Was Lenora safe at home? Hopefully Denton wouldn't come after Lenora because he wouldn't know she was back. Then again, maybe he'd been in contact with Tucker today. I rubbed my forehead. Who knew what was in Denton's head? I made another call.

I emerged from the study and bumped into Estelle outside the door. "Sorry if I sounded snappy earlier. Nothing personal toward you, Estelle. I like to be kept in the loop through Tucker about Lenora because I care so much."

Undoubtedly Estelle was trying to overhear my phone conversation through the closed door. I didn't doubt her affection for Lenora.

"Dr. Trevor, believe me, I get it." Estelle hugged me briefly against her apron. Vanilla wafted from her.

I pulled back and gazed at her. "It's thrilling she's home. I'll stay until Tucker returns. Maybe she'll wake up."

"While you wait I'll make you a cup of tea."

"That would be wonderful."

"With honey?"

"Yes, please."

"No trouble. I'll just make one cup." Estelle microwaved a single mug of water.

When it beeped, she pulled out a green tea with mint bag from the tea basket and placed the steaming cup on the Corian counter. I picked it up and hugged the ceramic in my hands.

The tea bag floated on the boiling water until it was waterlogged. Poor Angela, sinking more each day, with no hope for her future. Not if I had anything to do about it, I resolved. Living with a two-faced man must have been a hellish life. Hell. That reminded me of Lenora's vision and the forces of good and evil. *God, I long for Your kingdom to come upon earth.*

When the tea had cooled, I sipped the warm liquid and chatted with Estelle as she bustled about in her usual diligent fashion, emptying the dishwasher, opening and closing cupboards to put each dish and pot in its proper place.

I checked on Lenora several times. She hadn't awakened. Twenty minutes passed, then thirty.

The house phone rang.

Estelle answered, "Lawrence residence," then handed me the portable kitchen receiver, whispering, "It's Mr. Trevor."

I snatched it from her hand. "Hi, darling. Is Angela okay?"

"Fine. The police squad came over. Denton had already left. They're hunting for him as we speak. He probably suspected something was up from your visit."

"Or maybe he knows Lenora was released and is heading this way. I hope not." I shuddered and looked out the window.

"Be careful just in case. As soon as you see Tucker tell him to be on guard."

"His car is pulling in now. One more thing. I've arranged for Angela and her daughter to stay with Ellen a few days in case Denton comes back. Ellen's on her way to pick them up. I'll head home from here. Gotta go."

I smiled a greeting to Tucker as he hurried in with an apology to Estelle for being gone so long and an annoyed glance in my direction. "What are you here for?"

His voice, harsh and loud, startled me. I'd have preferred a cordial hello. My smile disappeared.

Estelle turned pink, glanced at each of us, then reached for her sweater and keys. "I'll be on my way as long as you're back," she said. "My husband will be wanting supper."

"Don't bother to come tomorrow. I'll be staying home with Lenora."

"As you wish. Dinner's in the oven on warm—fried chicken, corn and peas and mashed potatoes. Mrs. Lenora's sleeping comfortably. Dr. Trevor just checked her."

Tucker paid her in cash at the door and threw his wet jacket over a chair at the table next to where I sat. Then he stomped over to the coffeepot and poured himself a cup. In a more polite tone he asked, "What brings you over?"

"I'll get to that in a minute. First, why didn't you tell me Lenora was coming home today?" I thrust my hands on my hips.

"I thought it best she have a quiet homecoming." He sipped his coffee still standing. "I didn't want a houseful of people bothering her until she regained her strength."

"Her close friend is hardly a houseful."

"She needs time before being barraged with visitors. Plus, for security reasons, it's best not too many people know."

"You couldn't trust me to be discreet?" Rain came down in rivulets outside the window, matching the outpour of my emotions.

"I planned to call you tomorrow, but total peace and quiet is what she needs at the moment."

I still bristled but forced myself to accept his concern. "And she needs protection more than you realize." I set down my teacup. "Tucker, I have distressing news." I explained Lenora's intervention with Angela. "It's likely Chuck tried to silence Lenora and missed. He may be on his way here as we speak."

"Denton? Do you have proof?"

"I'm hoping now that Denton knows he's backed against a wall, he'll confess. The police will have him in custody soon. In the meantime, keep everything locked. He's a sick and violent man."

Tucker went to the table and slouched in a chair. "I must admit, he certainly had me fooled. I'm sorry I was so short with you a moment ago, Jennifer."

"I understand. It's an emotional time, Tucker. When the police interrogate Denton, all the pieces will fit."

"I'm truly impressed with the way you've investigated this. Lenora will be forever grateful." Tucker rubbed his hands together. "You've not only identified the person who shot her but saved the foundation's reputation by clearing Kirk. And now Lenora is home safe. I couldn't wish for a better outcome." He beamed at me. "Now, if you'll excuse me." He stood up abruptly.

"All right. I'll leave you to your dinner." I should have been happy, but the sudden switch of Tucker's emotions made me uncomfortable.

THAT NIGHT AS Nick and I undressed for bed, the home phone's shrill ringing pierced the air. Nick reached it first and relayed the message to me. "The police picked up Chuck Denton. They've questioned him at length. He admits the abuse but denies shooting Lenora."

"I'd hoped he'd confess immediately to make it easier on everyone."

"He's smart enough to know there's no proof he shot her so he won't incriminate himself without further evidence. Hopefully, the police will get the truth out of him. Otherwise, they can't hold him long."

I pulled on my velour robe and tied it loosely, snuggling in its warmth. I followed Nick into the bathroom. "This is weird. I should feel great. But something seems not quite right."

"You're worried Denton will get off?" Nick squeezed toothpaste onto his brush.

"He better not. Angela's petrified of him." I swallowed my bedtime calcium and magnesium supplements with water.

Nick began brushing. "Has she really been to all those doctors?"

"Denton made that up. By claiming out of town specialists, he could get away with it. Nobody would have a reason to check."

I returned to our bedroom, pulled back the top sheet, and slid into bed. Nick joined me moments later. "Something doesn't fit, but

I'm too tired to think. All the cross-motives and web of secrets has fried my brain."

"You're exhausted. We both are. Let's call it a night." Nick snapped off the light.

I pounded my pillow into a comfy shape and savored the cool cotton beneath my head. My mind wouldn't shut off. I tossed and turned, unable to reach a deep repose. Sleep finally came after a long time, and when it did, it was fitful. I repeatedly recited the words from Psalm 16, "Even at night my heart instructs me." Why wouldn't my subconscious let me totally relax?

A little after two, my body switched from restless to totally alert. I bolted straight up in bed, squeezed Nick's shoulder, and began to rub it briskly. "Wake up. Throw some clothes on."

"What are you talking about?" Nick grabbed the portable alarm clock. "Jennifer, it's two a.m." He groaned and rolled over.

I pulled his arm and leapt out of bed. "Nick. We've got to go to Lenora's. I'll explain on the way."

I sprinted to our walk-in closet. Groping in the dark, I snatched the first sweatshirt I found and slipped it on, followed by sweat pants over my nightgown. Grabbing my gym shoes, I headed into Collin's room. He was harder to awaken. I shook him several times between putting on my shoes. When I was sure he was alert enough to comprehend me, I said, "Collin, it's the middle of the night. Dad and I have to go to Lenora's. I want you to go sleep on the sofa in case your sisters wake up. Keep your cell phone next to you."

He lifted his head groggily but caught the urgency in my voice. "Okay, Mom, got it." He headed unsteadily for the living room, dragging his pillow and comforter behind him.

I yelled for Nick.

He came out of the bathroom dressed. "Jennifer, what's going on?"

"There's no time. Please, just come."

He muttered but kept moving and bounded down the stairs behind me. "This better be good."

I tossed him a jacket off the coat tree and grabbed my leather one. "Only a matter of life or death. I'll drive."

CHAPTER FORTY-FOUR

THE COOL NIGHT air blasted my hot cheeks. I jumped behind the steering wheel and started the van.

"Okay, talk," Nick demanded, settling into the passenger seat.

I pressed hard on the accelerator and peeled out of our driveway while explaining what awakened me. If a police car saw me speeding and followed us, all the better.

When I finished Nick sucked in his breath. "Then Lenora's in mortal danger."

"Call the police and tell them to meet us at Lenora's house. Lord, don't let us be too late."

When we arrived at Lenora's, the darkness of Wooded Hill engulfed us. Our van broke the silence of the forest as it crunched across the gravel.

I pulled within fifty yards of the top of the driveway. "I'm dimming the lights for the final approach. We can find the way and creep up from here. Stay left or the sensor light on the drive will come on."

Nick opened the glove compartment and pulled out a penlight. I turned on my I-phone flashlight. We climbed out, staying close to the ground until we reached the walk, slippery with wet leaves.

I tried the front door. "Locked," I whispered. "Let's try the side porch entrance."

We crept over. I turned the door handle. So much for being sealed up tight. We slipped inside.

It took several seconds for my eyes to adjust to the darkness. I grabbed the door frame and gasped. Tucker stood in the great room entrance not ten feet from us. In his right hand he held a revolver.

I stammered. "Why are you pointing that at us?" My insides chilled. I knew perfectly well why he held the gun.

"You two would never make it as burglars."

"That's right, Tucker, we wouldn't. You're the expert on stealth aren't you?" Nick said.

"You shouldn't be here." A bitter expression formed as his lips pressed into a hard line.

"I don't suppose you're holding that because you're planning to commit suicide," I said in a shaky voice, too aware of the answer.

"Your arrival is inconvenient, but it will be easy to dispose of you." Tucker sneered and pointed the gun at my heart. "You're breaking into my house in the middle of the night. Because of what happened to Lenora I can't take any chances with intruders. I'm going to shoot you. Perfectly logical."

"We only came to make sure Lenora's okay. Don't be stupid." Nick started forward.

"Stand still. Sure you came to check on her," Tucker said sarcastically. "In the middle of the night? Forgive me if I wonder why that doesn't make sense. She's in my capable hands now. You know that, or you wouldn't have come." He laughed sardonically.

"Where is she?" Panic smashed into my chest. "You better not have harmed her." Had he already killed her? I glanced toward the hall.

"Don't move, Jennifer. Before I shoot you, I have a question. My pride wants to know how you figured out I shot her. I thought I had you thoroughly convinced of my innocence."

"Pride and arrogance. That would be typical of you." I made myself focus on his eyes despite wanting to turn away from their blackness. "I'm delighted to tell you. When you threw your jacket on the chair this afternoon, I saw the brand name, Members Only logo, on the breast. Coincidental, I thought. I noticed the frayed white edge inside the collar, but it didn't register at the moment. I was caught up in the Chuck Denton event. My subconscious worked during the night and fit it together."

"You played the concerned husband well, slimeball," Nick interjected.

Go, Nick. Keep Tucker talking. I scanned the room for a weapon. Could I grab the floor lamp and hit him? No, it was plugged in. There were two of us and one of Tucker. His gun counted as a thousand. *Jennifer, you must disarm him before he pulls the trigger.* Could we rush him and topple him before he got a shot off? Where were the police?

"I've answered you. Now answer a question for me." My voice shook, but I tried to sound in control. "I must admit, I'm having trouble figuring out why you tried to kill your wife? Why not simply file for divorce?"

"For as many divorcees that Lenora counseled, she didn't believe in divorce. Even though we've led separate lives for some time. Except for my involvement with the foundation and occasional dinners on the weekend, we rarely spent time together.

Plus I had another relationship, my hobbies, let's say, and she had hers."

Nick took a step closer. Tucker's eyes locked on him. "Freeze."

"Most men insist on divorce, not murder, Tucker."

I scanned the softly lit room. If only it wasn't so dark. I tried to remember the items in the room.

"I had my reasons."

"How did you expect to get away with it?" I asked. Perhaps showing off would play to his pride again. If he intended to kill us, he could speak safely about his plan and reveal his motive.

Tucker sneered. "I'm not a tenured professor. I married Lenora for financial security. She had a substantial bank account and a portfolio of mutual funds. All that dwindled when she got religion and began pouring money into her various charities and the foundation."

"For a worthy cause," I added.

"In her opinion, not mine. Lenora had lost interest in money. In fact, she had the gall to say she'd be happy to die poor. I needed to stop her before she gave away everything except the house. I began moving funds into my private account. I have no intention of becoming a pauper. My retirement plans don't involve a modest lifestyle."

"You'd kill her for money?" I couldn't conceal my disgust.

"For love and money. It so happens, I met a woman at the university who shares my interests. Tricia's a young, pleasant research assistant with my values. She enjoys traveling and has an appreciation of the finer things life offers."

"Did Lenora find out?" Nick asked. His eyes darted back and forth between Tucker and I, searching I was sure as I was, for a way to disarm him.

"In the beginning she was too busy tending to her ex-con counselee. She started paying more attention to me and may have sensed something was going on. I heard her setting up a meeting with her lawyer next week. I couldn't let that happen."

"In my counseling experience, I've found women almost always know if their husband is having an affair, at least on some level, whether they say it aloud or not."

"You fooled everyone by speaking fondly of your wife." Nick and I were on the same page. Keep him talking to stall until the police arrived.

"I was good, wasn't I? A bit of amateur theatrics in college. One never loses the talent." He flicked the gun at me. "I know how to shoot, too. Learned that during my hunting days. I'm not bad at fencing either. A shame you won't be able to appreciate seeing me demonstrate."

The rain beat the roof like a clock ticking off seconds of our lives. Out of the corner of my eye, I made out a candlestick on the table beside me. I inched closer, praying Tucker wouldn't notice.

"One thing doesn't make sense," Nick interjected. "Why let Jennifer counsel Lenora's clients and get involved?" Nick edged toward the table.

"I knew Jennifer would offer anyway." His dark eyes riveted on me. "I'd hoped counseling Lenora's clients would keep you too busy to do any investigating. I'd heard about your solving the murder of Albert Windemere. Efficient little witch, aren't you?"

"Using your husbandly concern, Tucker, to throw me off was total genius. Why would I doubt you?"

"Not with suspects like Kirk and Thomas Hartford," Nick added. "Brilliant."

Tucker snapped, "Keep your hands where I can see them. Start walking toward the porch."

"Why shoot her now?" My lungs ached for more air. I was on the verge of hyperventilating.

"When Kirk started his position, I knew she'd examine the books again and turn over some bookkeeping to him. She'd already started asking questions. I had to move quicker than I planned. But that's of no consequence now. We've talked long enough."

"Supposedly your alibi was airtight. You were in Illinois the night Lenora was shot? Quite clever." Why weren't the police here? We were running out of time.

Nick picked up my thread. "Right, how did that work? I'm curious how you managed it."

"Having an analytical mind helps. I knew nobody would figure it out. I left my car at the train station in the morning, took the train halfway downtown, and got off. I'd had my girl friend rent a car under her name. Then later I drove back, hiked up the hill through the woods, and shot Lenora. I had time to drive the rental back, take a cab to the train station, catch my usual late evening train, and pretend as if I just got get back from downtown when it pulled in."

"Clever," I interjected.

"The police did inquire at school, but the secretary never pays attention to research professors coming and going. She actually told the police she thought she'd seen me."

I turned until I stood in front of Tucker. "You were the one who called the hospital pretending to be Lenora's brother?"

He grinned sadistically. "Naturally, I disguised my voice. I planned to pull the plug on the ventilator in the hospital and blame it on a phantom brother, but nurses kept popping in. It never seemed safe. Your deaths will be easy in comparison. I'm glad you came tonight to join Lenora in her heavenly fantasy. She's dying as we speak."

I groaned. "What have you done to her?"

A siren blared in the distance. Nick bent over and head butted Tucker in one smooth motion.

Reacting swiftly, Tucker grasped my arm and pulled me in front of him, pressing the gun into my temple. I swallowed hard and held my breath. "Move again and she dies, Trevor."

"How will you explain both our deaths?" Nick said through clenched teeth.

"Very logical. I went to bed and was awakened by you in the dark and shot in defense of Lenora." Tucker turned me abruptly with his free arm toward him and cocked the gun.

I lowered my head. "I think I'm going to be sick." At the same moment I kicked my leg up backward hard and fast, knocking the gun out of Tucker's hand. *Thanks God for my kick-boxing class at the Y.* When Tucker bent to retrieve the gun, Nick rushed forward and tackled him.

They scuffled on the Oriental carpet. A lamp fell to the floor and shattered. Nick cut his head as he rolled onto the shards.

Nick grabbed Tucker by the neck and began squeezing. Tucker leveraged his arms against Nick until Nick was forced to loosen his grip. I struggled to reach the gun pinned underneath them. The two men kept jabbing and rolling.

The sirens were coming closer, but the police might be too late.

First Nick was on top, then Tucker. Nick's head bled, splattering the carpet. I spotted a brass candlestick in the adjoining room. I ran for it and waited for their next roll. When Tucker was squarely on top, I smacked his head with all my might.

The blow stunned him a few seconds. He rolled off Nick. Tucker shot up and lunged at me. He missed me as Nick made a dive for his huge legs, toppling them both. Nick, nowhere near as big as Tucker, had the advantage of fewer years and a well-coordinated body. I struggled to grab the gun on the floor before Tucker could.

"Got it." I gasped. I raised the weapon and pointed it at Tucker and screamed, "Don't think I won't use this."

"You wouldn't," Tucker said.

"Try me. Don't move."

Nick scrambled up, breathing heavily. "I need some rope. I'll tie him up."

I scanned the room. "Get the cords on the blinds at the windows, Nick."

I forced Tucker at gunpoint onto the desk chair. "Where is she?" I demanded.

He responded with a shake of his head.

Nick ripped off the cord and whipped it around Tucker's wrists and arms, tying them behind his back to the chair.

With external calm that could only be grace, I punched in 911 on my cell phone and gave Lenora's address. "Send an ambulance." I was already moving toward the bedroom wing.

"I'll check the lower level," Nick called out.

We left Tucker secured to the chair and raced through the house, switching on lights, searching for my beloved friend.

My skin turned to ice outside her bedroom door when I saw the boa coiled up against it. Every snake scared me. I could never identify which were poisonous. Was this one? I held my breath, petrified it would wrap itself around me. How much time would it take to choke out life?

The bedroom door was slightly open. I inhaled deeply, slid past the snake, and barged in. My eyes adjusted slowly to the dim light. Crumpled blue sheets stuck out from a purple comforter halfway off Lenora's empty bed. She must be in another room. I was about to leave when I heard a scraping coming from below on the other side of the bed. I walked around and gasped.

Lenora lay on the floor, stretched out on her back. A diamond-back rattler slithered less than four feet from her. Instantly, I was drenched with sweat. My mind raced. How to awaken her so she didn't panic?

My voice spoke with a poise I didn't feel. "Lenora, it's Jennifer. Listen to me. Wake up and roll to your left. Don't ask why, just do it." She didn't move. "To your left." I swallowed my scream. "Move slowly." Still she didn't move.

Even in my terror, the perfectly spaced diamond markings of this reptile from hell registered in my brain. In the distance, another siren came closer.

I edged near the bed. Lenora's right forearm was swollen. God help her. She'd been bitten. An antidote might be too late. The snake had already done its damage.

The snake started to slither toward me. I willed my body to move. Its head, now inches from my foot, mesmerized me. Someone from behind yelled, "Drop onto the bed. Now."

I did as told.

A crack filled the air. I lifted my head and saw the snake wriggle its last.

Minutes later, ambulance attendants entered the room and began to work on Lenora. A vial of pills on the night table caught my eye. I picked them up—sleeping tablets. Tucker must have drugged her to sleep, then positioned the snake so it would bite her. I was sure he had total confidence in his diamond-back.

I turned as I fought faintness trying to envelope me. "Where's Nick?"

"Right here, sweetie. I found the empty cages in the basement and grabbed this policeman to run upstairs with me." Suddenly his arms enfolded me.

Sounds of commotion came from the living room and we headed downstairs. A handcuffed Tucker was led out. The officer who'd shot the snake came over and introduced himself. I thanked him profusely and offered the pills as evidence.

"I doubt Mr. Lawrence will be a problem any longer. Nothing to be afraid of now." The police officer tried to be reassuring, but I couldn't stop shaking.

Everything happened so fast, my head spun. "Nick, will you go home and get the children off to school? I need to be sure Lenora's okay and make sure they test her blood for an overdose of sleeping pills. I'll follow the ambulance to the hospital."

Hours later, Lenora's internist, followed by a resident, strode into her intensive care room. I jumped up from the chair at the side of her bed. The doctor flipped through her chart before turning to me. "She was heavily sedated, but it'll be wearing off soon. We got the antidote in her just in time. It's a good thing you arrived when you did. She should recover completely."

I resumed my post in the chair beside her bed. When she awoke, I wanted to be there, needed to be. Her physical agony would be nothing compared to the emotional shock of Tucker's betrayal.

Lenora stirred, focused her eyes, saw me, and smiled. Her lovely wide lips held a smile until she looked around the room. She struggled to sit up as a light of recognition darkened her eyes. "How did I get back into the hospital?" She started to cough.

"Would you like some water?"

"Please."

I held a plastic cup with a straw to her lips. Then, taking her hand in mine, I spoke in the same tone that I used when Jenny awoke from a nightmare. "I have some good news and some very bad news. Do you think you're up to hearing it now, or would you like me to wait awhile?"

"Tell me, Jennifer."

"First, the good news is you're going to be fine. And you can leave here soon." I smoothed my palm over her hand. "I don't know of an easy way to break this. I'm so sorry, dear friend. Tucker's confessed to being unfaithful to you. He's been having an affair with a woman from the university and also embezzled money from the foundation."

Lenora gasped and fell back. "No. It can't be true."

I leaned over and wrapped my arms around her. "Sadly it is."

"It's like being slammed against a wall."

"I can only imagine how hard this is. I wish with all my heart it wasn't true. There's more."

"What else?"

"You're here because he used one of his snakes and almost killed you last night. Tucker's responsible for shooting you in his earlier attempt to kill you."

Lenora sat back up. "No!" Her eyes bulged, and her mouth fell open. She seemed to age in front of my eyes.

"He's been cunning with his affair. My heart breaks for you."

"But the poisonous snakes are locked up. Tucker never lets them out. Are you certain you're not mistaken?"

I'd expected she'd be in denial at first. I knew she'd need a few details to convince her. "Last night he released them all." I gave her only as much information as necessary to support the truth. "He put the snake in your bedroom after giving you an overdose of sleeping pills. No way could you have called 911 for help. Tucker meant for you to die."

"How did you find out?"

"It's a long story. We got there in time to get you to the hospital where you could receive the antidote to the venom." I bit my lip. I'd give her a full account another time.

Lenora rubbed the back of her hand across her forehead. "I remember feeling weak and groggy before falling asleep." She stared into space.

I waited as she tried to make sense of the horrid pain of total betrayal. Was there any agony worse for a woman?

When she spoke again, her voice was a whisper. "I thought Tucker loved me. He seemed to care for me and be sincerely interested in my work. He helped me start the foundation." Her eyes pleaded with me to agree.

"Tucker wanted your non-profit protected. He saw it as the source of his future income in perpetuity. As President of the Board he could give himself a huge salary and no one would object."

Lenora crossed her arms across her chest. "How was this girlfriend involved?"

"Are you sure you want to know?"

"Yes."

"The police interrogated her. She claims to have known nothing about his plot to harm you. Tucker had told her he was deeply unhappy in his marriage and in the process of divorce. She claims he spoke of extensive travel plans for their future. He recently took a leave of absence from the university."

"No way!" Lenora pulled herself to a more upright position. "Last night's coming back to me. Tucker gave me three sleeping pills. I asked him if that wasn't too many. He claimed they were super mild." She turned her head away and reached for a Kleenex.

"What you're saying is beginning to make sense. I mean, I knew he was unhappy about my large charitable donations, especially to the foundation. This week I'd intended to see our lawyer and accountant to check on a few financial discrepancies I'd noticed. I'd asked Tucker about them, but he couldn't explain. I never dreamt he would be unfaithful and dishonest." She shook her head again. "Talk about stupidity."

I patted her arm. "Tucker's deceived me, too. The man is smooth and cunning."

"If I died at home, wouldn't Tucker be the first suspect?"

"I doubt it. He'd spilled a glass of water on the floor to make it look as if you'd gotten up for a drink then fell." I shook my head. "He said he went to bed, assuming you were fine, claimed the snakes got out, and he never suspected one was in your room."

Tears flowed now from her stricken eyes and trickled down her cheeks. "Everyone would believe him based on all the concern he's shown."

"Exactly."

"I can hardly comprehend all this. One thing's not a surprise. Tucker's very materialistic. It didn't matter when I married him because I was too." She snatched another Kleenex.

"Praise God for saving your life. He's still got work for you."

Her eyes widened. "The snake could have killed you, too."

"But didn't. I'm okay and so are you. We'll focus on that. And on the One who will never betray you or leave us for a moment."

Lenora sighed. "He said he was a Christian. He even went to church with me."

"Only God knows the heart."

Lenora interrupted. "I know going to church doesn't mean you're intimate with our Lord. Being in a garden doesn't make you a flower. I've said as much to clients."

"If he was genuine, he'd live by different values. No way did he ever surrender to the Lordship of Jesus Christ."

"My poor protégé, Kirk. How can we make it up to him for all he's been through?"

"You can start by putting him back to work at your foundation. I'm sure he'd like that. You need to rest now and get home. I'll be back later tonight."

I went home and slept for hours.

It would be a long while before Lenora recovered emotionally from her husband's betrayal. This was not how the world should be. I'd coached lots of strong women through similar devastation. In time, she'd be okay. Christ, the Lover of her soul, would restore her.

EPILOGUE

SIX WEEKS AFTER we survived possible annihilation, Nick and I drove to downtown Chicago for a three-day museum holiday. We stayed at the Marriot on the nineteenth floor. The second morning there I savored my morning prayer with room service coffee and oatmeal.

Waiting for Nick to awaken, I reviewed what I'd written in my journal open before me: Lord, Kirk's a living symbol of Your miracle-working power. He apologized for running away, and Lenora reinstated him to his position of administrative support liaison with the prisoners. The foundation hired Sarah Nichols to handle paperwork. Sarah and Kirk recently started dating. How cool is that?

When I confronted Chuck Denton shortly after he was taken into custody, he admitted he'd developed the bad habit of unleashing personal frustration on his defenseless wife. To avoid jail time, he was willing to accept help for anger management.

Fortunately, it turned out Chuck hadn't set fire to the house with his first wife in it after all. The police investigation came up with proof positive. He'd been at a banking seminar in another state when she died in the fire started by lightning. Chuck used the fabricated story as a threat to keep Angela submissive.

Like anyone who fell into sin, Chuck had woven such a web of lies he hardly knew truth himself. I made a counseling referral for him.

In the meantime, I've been working with Angela and hoping for the best for their future. Nothing thrills a marriage and family counselor more than a healthy restored marriage.

Lenora invited Thomas Hartford to sit on the Prison Board. He refused because of present business commitments but seemed sincerely flattered and said maybe in the future. I hooked him up with a charity involved in medical mission trips for children at orphanages in Honduras. He and his wife will travel there next month.

Carrie enrolled in a college program for returning women students to study counseling. Her personal experiences will make her a gifted healer. Rob amazed me. Within a few sessions, he learned how to be an encourager. His motivation level upped when pressed against the emotional wall of losing his wife. He even watches the kids without complaining while Carrie studies. Another miracle.

Rob arranged a date for Sandy with a buddy from work. I wouldn't say there's romantic interest necessarily, but they enjoyed each other's company. That's a mile of progress for Sandy.

As for Tucker, he hired a crackerjack lawyer who accomplished nothing except draining Tucker's savings. Truth has a way of ringing loud when the facts are revealed. Tucker will probably be in jail the rest of his life. I'm devoid of sympathy.

I closed the journal.

From my point of view, the pieces of Lenora's tragedy had come together in a perfect manner except one item. Lenora kept all Tucker's snakes, except the rattler. She reported she had grown fond of them. Ugghh! I could love all God's creatures with legs, fins, wings, or tails. The slinky ones, I excluded.

As for me, I'm back to my unpredictable normal. A delightful blend of God and family plus work. I've developed a reputation, to my amazement, as a local crime solver. If my services are needed, I'll give it my best shot, but I'm not going out of my way to look for trouble. But I did get a call yesterday that sounded intriguing…

AUTHOR BIO

Judith Rolfs minored in English and creative writing at college but her major focus became psychology and ultimately marriage and family counseling. Her first article was published in Fresh Ink magazine while a student at Marquette University.

At her first writer's conference her novel proposal won the Best New Novel Award. Mystery writing is her first love, although she has ten non-fiction books published on various family issues.

Twenty-five years listening to marriage and family clients further validated Rolfs' awareness that words are the messengers of the heart. She learned to listen for the meaning behind words and tries to convey emotional depth in her characters.

Writing *Bullet in the Night* from the perspective of her own and her heroine's counseling profession lets her share insights with readers who may never enter a professional counselor's office. Rolfs says, "I value the opportunity to contribute a word or two of wisdom: life is hard, people can be evil, but God is amazing all the time."

Judith shares life with her husband and best friend, Wayne, and their chocolate lab, Alex. They enjoy biking, golfing, and spending time with four adult children and seven grandchildren from home bases in Wisconsin and Florida.

Find her on Facebook https://www.facebook.com/judith.rolfs and twitter @judithrolfs. Judith loves to hear from readers. Email her at: jwrolfs@gmail.com

Her website is www.judithrolfs.com. Read her blog Thoughts on Fun, Faith & Family at www.judithrolfs.blogspot.com.

Thank you for your Prism Book Group purchase!
Visit our website to enjoy free reads, great deals,
and entertaining, wholesome fiction!

http://www.prismbookgroup.com

Made in the USA
San Bernardino, CA
30 August 2014